"WARREN WRITES WITH COMPASSION AND WARMTH . . . SHE HAS AN UNCANNY ABILITY IN PROBING THE MALE PSYCHE, AND HER EVOCATIVE DESCRIPTIONS OF THE BIG SKY COUNTRY ARE SUPERB."
—*Best Sellers*

"AN IMPORTANT, SENSITIVE CONTRIBUTION . . . WARREN'S CHARACTERS ARE WARM AND REAL . . . THEIR POSITIVE IMPACT COMES PRECISELY BECAUSE THEY ARE NOT SIMPLY GENITAL MACHINES BUT HUMAN LOVERS."
—*Dignity*

PATRICIA NELL WARREN is the author of *The Front Runner,* also available in a Plume Fiction edition. Her most recent novel is *One Is the Sun.*

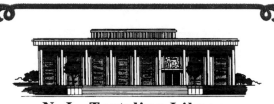

The Fancy Dancer

by

Patricia Nell Warren

A PLUME BOOK

PLUME
Published by the Penguin Group
Penguin Books USA Inc., 375 Hudson Street, New York, New York 10014, U.S.A.
Penguin Books Ltd, 27 Wrights Lane, London W8 5TZ, England
Penguin Books Australia Ltd, Ringwood, Victoria, Australia
Penguin Books Canada Ltd, 10 Alcorn Avenue, Toronto, Ontario, Canada M4V 3B2
Penguin Books (N.Z.) Ltd, 182-190 Wairau Road, Auckland 10, New Zealand

Penguin Books Ltd, Registered Offices: Harmondsworth, Middlesex, England

Published by Plume, an imprint of New American Library, a division of Penguin Books USA Inc.

PUBLISHER'S NOTE
This book is a work of fiction. Names, characters, places, and incidents either are the product of the author's imagination or are used fictitiously, and any resemblance to actual persons, living or dead, events, or locales is entirely coincidental.

BOOKS ARE AVAILABLE AT QUANTITY DISCOUNTS
WHEN USED TO PROMOTE PRODUCTS OR SERVICES.
FOR INFORMATION PLEASE WRITE TO PREMIUM
MARKETING DIVISION, PENGUIN BOOKS USA INC.,
375 HUDSON STREET, NEW YORK, NEW YORK 10014.

This is an authorized reprint of a hardcover edition published by William Morrow and Company.

 REGISTERED TRADEMARK—MARCA REGISTRADA

Library of Congress Cataloging-in-Publication Data

Warren, Patricia Nell
  The fancy dancer / by Patricia Nell Warren.
    p.   cm.
  ISBN 0-452-26320-4
  I. Title.
[PS3573.A776F3 1988]
813'.54—dc19
                                                    87-30016
                                                        CIP

OCLC
17258370

First Plume Printing, March 1988
3 4 5 6 7 8 9 10
PRINTED IN THE UNITED STATES OF AMERICA

To Sidney Walker
and to Paul R. Reynolds, Inc.
to whom I owe so much

1

I had a few spare moments before confessions that Saturday evening, so I headed for the church loft to play the organ a little. The days were so busy that there wasn't much time to play it anymore, and this was one of those evenings when I felt like I was going to bust with frustration.

As I hurried through the dim old sacristy, Father Vance stopped me.

"Oh, Tom?" he said.

"Yes, Father?" I said, trying to smother my irritation at losing even one minute of music.

Father Vance had just finished his own confessions. They consisted mostly of old ladies in town who felt that the young whippersnapper (me) didn't know anything about souls. Now he was on his slow arthritic way back to the rectory for an hour of meditation before supper.

"Did you see Mrs. Pawling?" he asked me.

"I wasted an hour and a half with her," I said. "She says no."

Father Vance shook his head in amazement. "And all the money she has . . ." With one gnarled hand, he made a mute scrawl of frustration in the air. "I'm surprised you couldn't convince her. She even goes to confession to you."

"Well, she was real nice about it, and all," I said. "But she says she's doing enough for St. Mary's by giving money to the town. As if those trees she's planting are going to raise the GNP of Cottonwood . . ."

"Mrs. Pawling, of all people, talking like a modernist," growled Father Vance.

We both looked sadly up at the ceiling. Right in the sacristy, there were old and new rain stains along several big cracks. The church needed a new roof badly, especially since the earthquake, and we had no idea where to get the money.

Father Vance just raised his bristly silver eyebrows and tightened his lips above his bulldog chin, which always seemed to sprout a silver stubble no matter how often he shaved. He walked creakily out of the sacristy. In the doorway, he turned and shook at me a finger as knotted as an old pine branch. His rheumy blue eyes were hard.

"None of that modernist music, you hear?" he said. "Some nice old hymns, or Palestrina. You disturb the old people with that modernist stuff."

Father Vance knew that playing the organ before confessions was a venial weakness of mine. I had been a priest for two years now, but Father Vance assumed that I still got butterflies in my stomach when Saturday evening rolled around. He was kind enough to tell me that I'd get over it, and that not many priests really liked hearing confessions anyway. The fact was, I liked confessions. Dealing directly with people was the chief joy of the priesthood, and the music always calmed me for the hard work of the next hour.

Jamie Ogilvie, one of the altar boys, stood by the vestment racks listening to this conversation. Jamie was seventeen, and he was one of the few really devout high-school boys in town. In fact, he was so devout that he was a pest—always underfoot. "Father Tom, would you like me to take the dirty altar linens to Mrs. Bircher?" "Father Tom, should I sweep out the sacristy?"

I was irritated that he'd overheard Father Vance scolding me, even though it wasn't the first time.

As I turned away from the sacristy door, my eyes and Jamie's met.

"Father, I put the vestment racks back in order," he said.

"That's good, Jamie. Thanks. You run along now."

"Father?" said Jamie. It was me he hung around the most. Any day now he probably was going to tell me he had a vocation.

"What?" I said, every cell in my body yearning to get up to the organ.

"I shouldn't say anything, but Father Vance is awful mean to you."

"When we're old, Jamie, we'll have to hope that people will put up with us," I said, a little shortly, and headed out of the sacristy into the church.

I stomped up to the organ loft, trying to start working off my lousy mood. The old oak stairs creaked ominously under my 170 pounds. Switching on the light, I flicked a glance through the nave below.

The usual regulars were kneeling or sitting in the pews, examining their consciences and waiting for me. There were about fifteen of them, mostly women over forty. One of them was Mrs. Shaw, who was among my favorite parish ladies. A few more would straggle in before the hour was out. Father Vance was always saying he could remember when the church had been half-packed on Saturday nights. Now it was mostly the young people who were missing, partly because there were so few jobs to keep educated kids in Cottonwood, partly because the Church had lost so much credibility with them.

That was why I noticed the dark-haired young man right away. He was kneeling alone in a pew far away from the others. I didn't recognize him from that far away—his head was bent. I wondered who he was.

The Gothic brick church was as stately and as creaky as its old pastor. It had been built in 1889, the year that Montana became a state. Many of the bricklayers had been devout half-blood Métis who built the little settlement on the river that became Cottonwood. Later on, some of them left Cottonwood to rejoin that lost tribe with neither American nor Canadian citizenship. They left behind the church, a monument to their confused identity, their faith and their loving workmanship.

In the last years of the nineteenth century, white man's livestock money and gold-mining wealth had put in the church's magnificent stained-glass windows, and its altar of imported Italian marble, and its carved pews of good Victorian yellow oak. A little-known Montana painter, Frederick Sommer, had painted murals on the nave walls. The murals picked up on the Indian half of the building's schizophrenic identity, and depicted scenes from the lives of Father de Smet and his Jesuits as they converted the Flathead Indians.

Now the Métis, the mine owners and the livestock men lay in the little cemetery on the west side of town, and the murals were faded and draped with cobwebs. The church had been damaged in the earthquake seven years ago, though not as badly as the old parochial school building. Now several big cracks ran up through the white walls on the north side of the nave. One crack cut in half the scene where Father Point was boating down the Missouri and making his famous drawings of Indian life on the banks. In fact, the crack went right between Father Point's eyes, shifting one eye upward and giving him a kind of crazy look.

The church was half-dark—we were trying to hold down our electricity bill. In front of the side altar of Mary, the few votive candles that flickered in their red glass vials were throwing strange wavering shadows on the mural, making the Indians' robes and feathers move as if alive.

I wondered who the strange young man was.

We didn't often see somebody new appear in this church. It was more usual to see them disappear—to another state where there were better jobs, or to the cemetery.

I flicked on the switch, and the old organ started to pulsate deep in its wind-chests. Now the whole building felt alive.

The organ was supposed to be the finest in the state, finer even than the one in the Helena cathedral, which I'd also played. It had been imported from Germany as a gift to the church by the very Pawling family, silver-mine owners, whose descendant I'd argued with all afternoon. Its curlicued gold pipes and its banks of painted cherubs seemed more fit for an eighteenth-century German baroque church. Ever since the quake, the organ hadn't been quite the same either—the vox humana and a few other stops were knocked out. I had lobbied in vain to have Father Vance get a doctor of infirm pipe organs to examine it. The church hadn't even had a regular organist since old Mrs. Seckle took to her bed two years ago. So now the parishioners heard it only when I played it— which was during Father Vance's high mass on Sunday and before my confessions. They told me they liked my playing—except when I did those awful modern things.

I sat down and pulled out the stops for one of the few Bach fugues that I remembered. Then I glanced up into the flyspecked mirror over the console.

The mirror gave the organist a clear view to the front, so he didn't have to twist around like a pretzel to keep track of what the priest was doing at the altar. The strange young guy was right there in the mirror. He was

11

sitting slumped over, playing nervously with his hat. I wondered if he was feeling poorly, or was crushed by some despair that I'd hear about shortly.

It was one confession that I was looking forward to. Something in me rushed out to embrace him, and to say, "I'm here. I can help."

My hands came down on the yellowed ivory keys, for the opening voice of the fugue. Behind the dusty painted cherubs, the old pipes opened their throats and split the silence like a lovely earthquake. In the mirror, I could see the kneeling people turn and look up at me, wreathed in smiles. The young man turned and looked up too. When the others had turned back, he stayed twisted around, still looking up at me. I was glad he was listening.

As the fugue grew and boiled in the church, I had a sudden rush of exhausted feeling.

Ever since my own 7:30 mass that morning, I had been running around like a crazy man. With Father Vance so arthritic, I was the only priest within a fifty-mile radius of Cottonwood. I made half a dozen visits to parishioners' homes. I worked with the boys' football team, for which I doubled as chaplain and coach. I hassled with Mrs. Pawling about the money. I drove up the valley to the tiny community of Hernville, to give the last sacraments to a dying sheepherder, and drove down the valley to Whalen to visit a sick old lady. I went over the bills, and had an argument with Father Vance about the size of my phone bill. There was no time to eat any lunch.

Now the day came over me like a cloud shadow over a wheatfield, and I thought the buttons on the front of my cassock would fly right off. It was a pretty funny kind of exhaustion, because I was only twenty-eight, and built like a halfback, and I had no business being tired.

The ambitious thought entered my head (it wasn't the first time) that I wasn't doing the right thing by wanting to serve God in a small town, through everyday folks. The right thing was to try to climb the diocesan ladder, to try for monsignor, maybe even for bishop. That way I would have more power to deal with the Father Vances of this world, and to help all the confused young people who were leaving the church or hesitating at the door.

I put these thoughts down as venial sins of pride. I had already confessed these little sins to my confessor when he heard my monthly confession. I saved them up for my once-a-month trip to Helena to see my parents—my old confessor and spiritual director was there, teaching Thomist theology now at Carroll College.

I kept looking at the young man in the mirror. He looked familiar—had I seen him before? I wondered what he was going to tell me. Was he truly sorry he'd balled his girl friend? Had he been guilty of disrespect to his mother and called her a bitch?

I broke off the fugue. I was not in the mood for Bach.

Furiously I pulled out some different stops, and crashed into a Gabriel Fauré piece that I'd always loved. The bedridden old organ was just about going to have a coronary. Its aged wind-chests and its thirty-foot bourdons were rattling with the thunder in them. The bizarre chords made the stained-glass windows buzz. In the mirror, I could see the parishioners all turned around to look at me again. This time they looked startled and pissed off.

The young man turned around too, and grinned. That was when I remembered who he was. He was no stranger in Cottonwood at all. Now and then I had passed him on the street, but we'd never talked. He was one of the more colorful, mysterious and disreputable people in town. His name was Vidal Stump.

I played the Fauré all the way through, whaling away at the four keyboards and the foot pedals like a maniac. I must have looked like the Phantom of the Opera bending over his underground organ, except that I wasn't a masked monster—just a blond young priest in a dusty cassock.

When I finished, a sweat had broken out all over me. Silence flooded the church again, and I could hear a few discreet coughs from the parishioners. It had been as relaxing as jogging for a mile, and I felt a little better.

I looked at my watch—it was 8:05. I was five minutes late. Shutting off the organ, I rushed down the stairs. In the sacristy, I grabbed my stole off its peg in the incense-scented closet, kissed it hurriedly and slipped it over my head. It, like all the rest of the vestments, had been made by two old parish ladies, Missy Oldenberg and Clare Faux, and it was embroidered with crosses and some less liturgical bitterroot flowers.

Moments after I'd sat down in my side of the confessional, the musty red velvet curtain on the other side made its muffled noise, and someone kneeled down noisily on the other side of the lattice. I slid it open. A kitchen smell came through to me—dishwater and cooking grease. This was a housewife who had hurried away after dinner.

A woman's halting contralto voice began, "Bless me, Father, for I have sinned . . ."

The baring of souls began, for the week of June 12 through 19, 1976, in Cottonwood, Montana, Zip Code 59701.

═══

The sins of a small Western town today are pretty predictable—or at least I thought so when I started that night.

There were two old ladies suffering from the scruples that old ladies have always had (did I or did I not repent such and such a sin?). There were three teen-agers with spiritual acne. There was a rancher who was heartily

14

sorry he'd wanted to shoot so-and-so for stealing two inches of his water out of the main irrigation ditch. And a young wife who'd driven over to the State university town, Missoula, to see *Deep Throat* because, she said, that kind of movie never came to Cottonwood.

I was well into my second year in my first parish. I was finally learning how to get along with Father Vance, who resented the Bishop's sending him a no-good greenhorn assistant. Father Vance was born on a ranch near Livingston, he was sixty-seven now, and he really couldn't manage alone anymore, but he called me a "pilgrim"—the old ranchers' word for a useless outsider. Father Vance took out his resentments on me by making me do most of the hard legwork in the parish.

Father's biggest resentment came from the fact that he'd unthinkingly run the parish deep into debt. The reason was his rigidity about old ways and his conviction that St. Mary's should be run with as much pomp as St. Peter's. But Bishop Carney had decided that it was humiliating to have one of Montana's most historic parishes about to be snapped up by the bank. So he bluntly ordered both of us to get St. Mary's back in the black, or else.

Father Vance had no choice but to sit down with me and do some drastic cost-slashing. First to go was the decrepit academy, which the earthquake had made unsafe anyway. The children were hustled off to the Cottonwood public schools, and the $53,000 that Father Vance had cached in the Union Bank in Helena toward building a shiny new parochial school went to pay off part of the mortgage.

Next was the utility bill—the church was now a little chillier on winter days and lit less lavishly. We stopped buying flowers from Fulton's Greenhouse and made do with potted plants—they lasted longer. We slashed our own salaries. We lived leanly at the rectory, with several

15

meatless days a week by necessity, not devotion. Our best parishioners contributed many good ideas for saving money. Housewives with too many tomatoes in their gardens would drop a basket of them by our kitchen door. Or a rancher who'd shot an elk would give us a quarter to throw in our freezer.

We scrounged, haggled over pennies, bought on sale. Now we were living more or less within St. Mary's low income, and we were making regular payments on the rest of the mortgage. But it was all very hard on Father Vance's ego.

Father Vance had no use for what he called "pilgrim morals." While college students over in Missoula lived in co-ed dormitories, and even the Bishop was liberal about young priests' life-styles, he still insisted I had to be in the rectory by ten every night. I had to have his permission to stay away overnight, and I had to tell him whom I stayed with, even if it was my parents. He even made me wear a cassock around the church, though I usually managed to shuck the thing when off the premises. To keep the peace, I gave in on these things, to have freedom in other areas.

Curiously, he could be a kind man when he took a notion to. He was a real old whang-leather pioneer priest, upright as a man on horseback. He had the undying admiration of his older parishioners. He was as faithful to his traditionalist view of the Church as the hayfield that comes up green every spring.

I didn't like him much, but I respected him. It had to be hoped that I could be as true to my view of the Faith as he was to his.

═══

The hour of confessions wore on, and I began to wonder when the colorful, mysterious and disreputable Vidal Stump would show up. So far I had known all the voices that had come through the lattice, and none had been his. There had been the manure smell and boozy breath of a ranch hand who had a drinking problem. There had been the musky perfume of one of the town's teen-age queens, and a recital of her misbehavior at a pot party in her parents' home while the parents were in Butte for a K of C convention. There had been Clare Faux, who lived with Missy Oldenberg on the other side of town. Usually the two old ladies walked to church, each carrying a big old-fashioned black umbrella, rain or shine. But Missy hadn't come today, for the first time since I'd been assigned to St. Mary's, and I wondered if she was sick.

I peered at my watch. It was just about nine o'clock. My stomach was rumbling, and I started to think worldly thoughts of the supper that the housekeeper would be getting ready. On Saturday night she always made a dish that we now regarded as a luxury: fried chicken.

The watch hand said nine sharp, then five after. Vidal Stump must have chickened out. I felt pretty sad. Maybe he would come next week.

I was just about to push out through my own musty red velvet curtain when I heard a man's footsteps approaching the confessional. They were stumbling, shaky footsteps. I had already learned to read footsteps. These were a drunk's.

The other curtain swished, and the man kneeled heavily. His head pressed against the wooden lattice that separated us—I could see the dark wavy hair pushing through the openings. His breath nearly knocked me out—booze, garlic and pot. Pot has a funny hayfield smell—I know, because I had worked on a little drug program in Helena High School, and I had also toked on a few joints myself, long long ago. He must have had supper at Trina's Cafe, a little Chicano place on the bar side of Main Street, and gotten himself high enough to face me.

He had one hand against the grille, and the fingers curled tensely through the openings—dark young fingers with broken nails and smudges of black motor grease.

"Father," he said in a thick voice. Then he stopped.

This had to be Vidal Stump.

Vidal must be a Catholic, or he wouldn't have called me Father. But he couldn't have been to church for ages, or he would have rattled off the "Bless me Father" right away. If I had been Father Vance, I would have made him go back and say the formula.

Instead, I said, "Yes, I'm still here."

My mind was picking through the little I knew about him. He was in his late twenties. He was born and raised up in Browning. Although he looked Irish or a little Spanish, he was one quarter Blackfeet Indian. He had spent two years in the state penitentiary for petty theft and learned a mechanic's trade there. He was off parole now, and married, and had a little kid. He worked in Snow's Garage downtown, and was supposed to be a good mechanic. When he wasn't working, he was roaring around the county on his big Japanese motorcycle, or getting into monumental brawls in the bars. The police were tolerant, because he kept their squad cars on a racer's edge.

People in town said he was a loner. At the garage, he worked hard and didn't say much. When he showed up at the bars to get drunk and play poker in the back room, he was always alone, and he always left alone. People said, however, that he seemed very devoted to his young wife. Few had seen her because she stayed in the house all the time, but she was said to be mentally retarded. Vidal was so good-looking that a number of "fast" Cottonwood girls had tried to get friendly with him. But he avoided them and went home to his wife. The joke around town was that maybe his wife was missing something up here, but she sure must have it down there.

I knew all this from Father Vance, who knew it from the Cottonwood police chief, John Winter. The chief was Catholic and a good friend of Father's. He loved to gossip when he dropped by the rectory for an off-duty cup of coffee. Father Vance was always saying that Vidal was the biggest lost sheep in town.

"Father—" Vidal said again. His fingers clenched hard on the lattice, and the wood groaned.

The recent encyclical *Ordo penitentae* gave priests a new kind of flexibility when counseling, and I took it literally. Among other things, I tailored my language to the age and viewpoint of the penitent.

"Relax," I said. "Take your time. I'm not going anywhere. I'm ready when you are."

"Father, man . . . the thing is, I've had a few drinks."

"I can see that," I said. "You smoked a little weed too."

"Hell," he said, "I forgot to eat a mint. I've seen you around town, and I figured I could talk to you. A guy can't talk to old whoozis, he's too goddam old and prissy."

I couldn't criticize him for that, since I was glad I could take my sins to Father Matt over in Helena.

"Well, just relax," I said. "I'm not here to be shocked or pass judgment on you. Just think of how God is ready to help you."

"I don't think God will help me," Vidal said hollowly. "I'm outside for good."

"Jesus can forgive any sin. *Any* sin. It's hard for us to understand that. I mean, there are some sins that really gross us out. For instance . . ." My mind rummaged around for a good example. ". . . Somebody who did war crimes and killed a lot of women and children. Now if he was really sorry, God would forgive him, even though *we* might not be able to forgive him."

"I'll bet you my bottom dollar I'm the first guy ever walked in here and told you about *my* sin."

"Listen," I said, "if you've invented a new sin, the

19

world is gonna beat a path to your door. But I can't help you if you don't tell me what it is."

"Uh, Father," he said, "the thing is, I don't know if I'm ready to confess tonight. I need to do some more thinking. But I wanted to make a start. You know? Maybe just talking to you a couple of times will help. Maybe you can counsel me a little."

"I'll be glad to talk to you," I said.

Vidal was silent for a minute.

Then he said, "Come sit outside here and talk to me." He rapped on the lattice with his knuckles. "This goddam thing reminds me of the visitor's screen in jail."

When I stepped out of the confessional, he was already standing beside the nearest pew, clutching his hat.

In the flickering red half-light from the votive candles, he was a strange sight.

He was wearing faded, tattered Lee Riders with a wide tarnished silver belt cinched around his narrow hips. His old walking boots were spattered with mud. His shirt was bright red satin, also worn and stained. His wavy black hair came down to his collar. Around his neck he had a couple of tarnished silver necklaces. The men in town had learned the hard way not to make fun of his necklaces.

He wore this outrageous rig nicely, because he was six feet two inches tall, just my height, and he was built slender and hard as a bronc rider. The hat he twisted in his hands was a black high-crowned thing, very Indian-looking, with a band of silver conchos around the crown.

Pushing aside the black leather motorcycle jacket in the pew, he sat down slowly and made room for me. I sat down by him.

He kept looking straight into my eyes with a hard, earnest look. It puzzled and disturbed me.

His face was the most arresting thing about him. It was handsome, but it was marred by the clash of races. His skin was so fair that it showed his beard, but it had a faint, patchy look—a pigmentation fault common in mixed

20

bloods. His eyes were alert, hard, expressive, set off by long sooty lashes—but only after a minute did you notice that one eye was blue and the other was green. His features were so fine-cut and Caucasian that he didn't look Indian at all.

Yet these flaws gave his face great character, like the pockmarks on Richard Burton's face. It was the face of someone who had done a lifetime's living before thirty.

He leaned forward tensely, one hand gripping the edge of the pew. He smiled a little.

"How do you stand it in that lousy little box?" he said.

"It's funny," I said. "We've passed on the street a lot."

"You remember that?" He said it almost shyly.

"What do you want to do? Come see me once and maybe tell me more about what's troubling you? Then, if you want to go on, we can take it from there."

He looked a little suspicious. "Do we have to talk here in the church? It's always crawling with people."

"No. We do counseling at the rectory. I have my own office, so it'll be completely private. And don't worry—I don't discuss anything with Father Vance."

At this, he seemed to relax.

"That sounds okay," he said. "How about tomorrow?"

I shook my head. "I have to play for Father's high mass at nine, and then I'm driving to Helena to see my family. It's my mother's birthday. Could you come Monday at seven-thirty?"

He seemed crushed that he had to wait two days. Now that he had made up his mind to act, the pressure inside him must have been unbearable.

"Okay," he said. He clapped his hat on his head.

We stood up. "I'll see you Monday."

He pulled on his black motorcycle jacket. "Good-bye, Father," he said, with that funny shyness again.

I didn't have the heart to tell him to take off his hat in church.

As he turned to walk away, I saw the back of his jacket.

21

There, where bikers usually have the name of their gang or club, or a death's head, was printed the word ME in large silver studs.

He walked away down the aisle with a graceful cat-like swagger. I had seen that walk before, in militant young Indians on the state's campuses. They had borrowed it from *Super Fly*.

As he opened the door, I saw a patch of glowing turquoise evening sky above the mountains. Then the door banged shut. A minute later, his bike coughed into life outside.

I couldn't help smiling. His unconfessed sin wasn't funny, of course. But he had left me with the poignant impression of a strong personality: harshness and wildness mixed with humanity and warmth.

I couldn't remember the last time I'd smiled.

Father Vance would be mad at me—I was now fifteen minutes late for supper. I hurried to turn out the lights and lock up.

It was a cool summer night in the Rockies. You'd know it was June even without a calendar—the lilacs were in bloom, and their perfume was a blessing after the staleness of the confessional. Masses of the old shrubs grew around the church and the rectory, where they had been planted a century ago. They were now nearly fifteen feet high, tangled and woody, and the children had made paths and tunnels through their jungle.

I walked slowly along the sidewalk to the rectory, feeling a strange savage joy. God had sent Vidal to me.

===

The rectory was built in the same year as the church, of the same dark red brick. It looked like a regular one-story Victorian house of the period, with tall windows and a wide pillared porch. The lilac bushes had grown up in front of the windows, and Father Vance refused to have them pruned down. "When you're doing the Lord's work," he said, "you don't need a view out the window."

As per our pennypinching policy, the only lights burning in the rectory were in the kitchen and the dining room. I went up the steps and into the side door.

"I've put your chicken on the back of the stove," said Mrs. Bircher kindly. "Sit down, and I'll bring it right in."

"Thanks," I said. "Sorry I'm late."

The old dining room was paneled with yellow oak. On the walls were large framed old photographs of the two forbidding gentlemen who had preceded Father Vance as rector. The brass chandelier had been converted from gas to electricity. In its mellow light, Father Vance sat reading the Cottonwood *Post*. His plate was covered with chicken bones clean enough for an anatomy lesson.

"You're late," he said, in his gruffest voice.

"I'm sorry," I said. "Just at nine, someone wanted to confess."

"I understand the famous Vidal Stump was there tonight. Mrs. Bircher saw him when she went to fetch me something from the sacristy."

"Yeah. In fact, that was him that came at nine."

"Amazing," said Father Vance. "If God's grace can reach him, it can reach anybody."

23

2

After high mass the next day, I shucked the cassock, and put on black trousers, a black turtleneck sweater and a sport jacket. Then I jumped into my red Triumph and started for Helena fifty miles away.

The Triumph had been an ordination present from my parents. Their motive was part generous, part selfish. They knew I'd need it for my parish work, but they also wanted to make sure I could visit them. The car was a dream, and I drove it too fast. With its thirty-two miles a gallon and its cockpit interior, it was perfect for a young guy who was counting pennies and had no temptations to start a family. But it made Father Vance grumble about pilgrim assistants who helled around in their own sports cars.

I drove out of town past the fairgrounds. The grandstand had been freshly painted green for the Bicentennial celebration that fall, and the big letters along it were updated. COTTONWOOD RODEO AND COUNTY FAIR, SEPTEMBER 1, 2, & 3, 1976, it read. And in

25

smaller letters, DON'T MISS THE HELENA–COTTONWOOD EN-
DURANCE HORSE RACE, SEPT. 3.

I was in a giddy mood. As I turned up the ramp onto
the Interstate, it was hard to remember the curate blues
that I'd had on Saturday.

All around the Cottonwood basin, the mountains were
shedding the last of their snow. The rolling foothills with
their glacier moraines had that pale green of June that
would soon be scorched away by the sun of July. The
wildflowers would be in bloom everywhere out there—
wild roses, bitterroot, phlox, prickly pear. It would be nice
to walk over the hills and look at them but there wasn't
time. I turned the radio way up—station KGLM in Butte
was playing my favorite mix of country music and soft
rock.

Up on the last foothills above the basin, I could look in
my rearview mirror and catch glimpses of the world I was
leaving behind. The great valley, seventy miles wide,
ringed by mountains, was seen in the glass whitely, as the
dust billowed up from the side of the road.

My parish was that rarity in America today, an area
whose economy was still based on agriculture. Cottonwood did have a sawmill, and a chemical refining plant.
But the income these industries brought into the county
was a drop in the bucket. Wheat, hay and cattle were still
king here, though they were trapped kings fighting off
inflation. Sheep had been king too, but imports had
nearly killed off the local woolgrowers.

Cottonwood's ranchers and farmers were not glittering
tycoons of agribusiness who flew around in planes. Theirs
were mostly family operations, held together by bank
loans, grit and old-fashioned love of the land. Even the
town folks of Cottonwood, though they might not know
one end of a horse from the other, had much the same
mentality as the rural folks out in the hills, or in the little

outlying communities like Ellis, Whalen, Garnet, Hernville, Skillet Creek. Out there, all the little old Catholic parishes were now boarded up, and the people had to drive clear in to Cottonwood, the county seat, if they wanted to go to mass.

It was a world whose scenery had hardly changed since the first French trappers came through in the eighteen-forties, if you could ignore the main power line that marched down the valley, and the curving scar of the new Interstate 10, and the green patches that meant irrigated hay and dry-land wheat. Yet it was as painfully intimate with the pressures of modern life as if it had been a suburb of Chicago or Los Angeles. Unemployment was high, and the county welfare rolls were lengthening, though the traditional mentality looked down on welfare. Cottonwood even had a housing problem—many pre-1900 homes were not fit to live in anymore, and few new homes were being built. A little band of local blue-noses fought to keep pornography out of the county, and recently they'd had the Cottonwood bookseller arrested for selling "obscene" authors like J. D. Salinger and James Baldwin (the judge had thrown the case out of court, saying the Supreme Court didn't have *The Catcher in the Rye* in mind when they ruled on dirty books). The town had its share of teen-age drunks, young divorcees, old people who ate cat food on their pensions, liberated women, bitter Vietnam vets, shoplifters.

The ranchers' year was just now starting to roll. Though they'd been calving since February, and asking for bank loans and fertilizing fields since April, the ninety-five-day growing season was just starting now—June 5 to September 15. The stores in town would live or die depending on how the cattle market would be, come fall, and what the price of baled hay would be.

I knew all this as filtered through the lattice of my

27

confessional every Saturday night, and in the regular counseling sessions in my office, and in my sacerdotal cruisings around the valley.

But right now, I was glad to see it fade off into the dust behind me—for a while, anyway.

A good feeling of being on the road and going somewhere important came over me. I had spent my teen-age years crisscrossing the Northwest, to retreats, Catholic or youth conventions, organ concerts, or just to go backpacking.

And I was haunted by the thought of Vidal. I hadn't run into a genuine down-and-out type in my year-plus of counseling. Besides, after a year-plus of talking to old ladies and children and Father Vance, it had been real nice to talk to a guy my own age.

Stepping harder on the gas pedal, I happily watched the needle creep up to eighty. The wind whipped me through the open window.

≡

The capital of Montana nestles on the eastern slope of the Continental Divide.

The dome of the Capitol building, the great pines and spruces of its city park, and the twin spires of its nineteenth-century Gothic cathedral all rise against the steep slopes of Mt. Helena. The downtown area has a bombed-out look because of a big urban renewal project. But many magnificent old homes still line the hilly streets of the elegant West Side.

As I turned off on Hauser Avenue, the main drive through the West Side, I noted—as always—how beautifully many of the homes are kept up, though they're not owned by the pioneer families anymore.

It saddened me, however, to see that a few of the West

Side houses were run down, or turned into apartment buildings.

In its day, Helena was the *haut monde* of the Northwest. It had Lily Langtry and Edwin Booth on its gaslit stages, and French on its hotel menus, and fresh oysters shipped on ice from "back East." Outside town, the mile on mile of lonely placer-mine dumps bear witness to the mineral wealth and the fever that built this city. Whenever I came back to my home city, I felt—even more than in Cottonwood—the weight of a history that was young, but heavy as precious metal. It was the weight of a society that was built on macho enterprise and daring.

My family, and my religion, had been intimate in that building. My great-grandfather, Jacob Meeker, had been the first president of the First Metals Bank in Helena. Catholicism had spread from De Smet's tiny mission up on Flathead Lake to be the major faith in the state. Mary, who allegedly appeared to a little Indian girl, was the reason that St. Mary's Lakes and St. Mary's parishes were now sprinkled over Montana's eight-hundred-mile sweep.

But as I drove into Helena that day, I felt a kind of depression. There was no denying that the state, and the Church, were in a crisis. Agriculture was still the biggest industry in the state, but the ranchers and farmers were being crushed to death between a depressed market and rising costs. The great copper mines are playing out or too costly to operate. The railroads are going broke, and fewer airlines fly into the state. The school system is tightening its belt—they'd just closed the state vocational college in Bozeman. People with college degrees leave the state to find work. Even the wilderness scenery that is such a joy to the tourists is suddenly threatened by rampant vacation development. And the Church's crisis needs no itemizing.

So Helena seemed to me, that day, like a lovely fossil—though it was still alive and well. Its population was actually growing, its old Montana Club was still open for businessmen's lunch (my father ate there every day), and the "flats" around it, once cattle range, were now peppering themselves with new suburban homes.

On Stuart Street, I parked the Triumph in the brick driveway of my parents' house.

They had talked a lot about leaving the West Side, and moving to a smaller modern house down on the flats. Their idea was that they'd do the apartment number with this towered Victorian brick thing. But they still clung to it. Dad's salary as First Metals vice president allowed them to keep the place up pretty nice.

As I got out of the car, I could see that the white trim on the house had had a new coat of paint. In the wide lawn, the beds of Talisman roses planted by my great-grandmother were coming into bloom. Dad had even cleaned some junk out of the gazebo by the huge weeping birch, and set a couple of lawn chairs in it. The same old lace curtains were at the windows. Of all the things I knew in a changing state, my parents' house had probably changed the least.

For a moment, thinking of the difference between Vidal's background and mine, I felt a little ashamed. To me, the confessional grille was a doorway to the world; to him, it was jail bars.

I cut across the lawn to sniff the copper-pink roses. Then I ran up to the porch.

The big coffered yellow-oak door opened before I could ring. My mother was standing there, flushed and glowing and out of breath. Anna Meeker was tiny and girlish in a blue sweater dress, her baby-fine white curls fluffed out with excitement.

"Tom." She hugged me and kissed me.

In the wide front hall, that fragrance of a century-old house hit my nostrils. The sameness was eerie—the mirrored umbrella stand, the Oriental rug that I tripped on so badly when I was seven and skinned my knee, the wide stairway with its twisted walnut posts. I used to pretend it was Jacob's ladder.

My father was coming out of the parlor, his pale blue eyes lit with their fey smile behind his bifocals. He didn't seem like a banker at all—with his gentle ways and his impish sense of humor, you might have thought he made his living writing children's books. He was stooped in his baggy gray suit and his favorite tie clasp with a tiny old gold nugget hanging from it. He was carrying his half-read *Wall Street Journal* (which the post office always brought to him several days stale).

"You're fifteen minutes late," said my mother. "We were worried."

"I stopped at the drugstore to have your present wrapped," I said. "You know I can't tie a fancy bow."

I put the little box in her hands. She gave a little scream of excitement, as if birthdays came just once in a lifetime.

"When you were little," said my father, "we couldn't teach you to tie your shoelaces either."

"I *still* don't tie them right," I said. "But I survived, didn't I?"

At exactly one o'clock, we sat down to dinner in the dining room. Ever since I could remember, Sunday dinner had always been at one sharp.

The table was set with a worn but fine old damask cloth, and Mother's Medici sterling and Rosenthal china. In the center was a rock-crystal bowl of Talisman roses. Mother pressed the bell in the floor with her foot, a signal for Rosie to bring out the soup. In a day and age when one can hardly hire a domestic in the length and breadth of Montana, Mother had managed to keep Rosie for twenty years.

"Oh, it's our boy," cried Rosie as she came in, managing to keep the tureen steady. She was sixty-six, tinier

31

even than Mother. I got up, and she presented me with her sweet steamy old cheek to kiss.

When Rosie had ladled the hot beef broth and rice into the wide antique plates and disappeared into the kitchen again, Mother said:

"Rosie told me the other day that she's going to retire in three months. She's going to live with her married daughter in Big Sandy."

"She's lucky," I said. "A lot of people her age aren't wanted in the homes of married daughters."

"I just don't know what I'll do when Rosie goes."

"That'll be the time to get out of this white elephant of a house," said my father.

"But you know you'll miss this place," said my mother.

The heavy sterling spoons clinked in the soup plates.

Rosie brought in the main course, a standing rib roast with pan-browned potatoes and carrots, and creamed onions on the side. My mouth watered. I ate this well only once a month. I reproached myself for caring so much about food.

My dad carved the roast with the heavy initialed sterling knife and fork, and handed our plates to us.

"How are things at St. Mary's?" my mother asked me.

Her voice always carried a tinny note of strain when she asked me this question. My parents hadn't been wild about my being a priest. As far as they were concerned, the priesthood was a fine thing, but it should happen to other families' sons. My father had been set on my working in the bank. My mother wanted me to be a musician. Both of them wanted me to have a family of my own. I was their only child, and they wanted a bunch of grandchildren. My dad had always been good about making time to be with me, and he wanted to jump out from behind his green velvet wing chair in the parlor and say "Boo" to grandchildren the way he had with me.

All through high school they had watched with uneasy

32

indulgence the faithful way I went to church, and my yawning carelessness about dating nice Helena girls. In college, the exotic atmosphere of the sixties got to me a little, and I dated some, and actually got engaged to a very nice girl named Jean Moser, and smoked a little pot. I dropped out of Montana U. for a semester, and traveled around the West working on various social programs because I was hungry to know people and places. I wound up in VISTA in California for another year, working with Chicanos.

That year was when it hit me that I wanted to be a priest. My mission was back home, at the grass roots. When my year was up, I caught a plane right back to Helena, and went straight to register for the seminary.

"Well, I'm not surprised," my mother had said sadly when I told her. "You were always very interested in people."

My dad had just said, "Well, do what you feel you should do. We're behind you one hundred percent even if we don't agree."

When I was ordained, my parents had apparently expected to see me turn overnight into a wind-up eunuch. Maybe they gave me the sports car to keep me from getting that way. Sometimes I wondered if they secretly hoped I'd do a *Wine and the Music* number and fall in love with a girl and leave the ministry. If I ever did, I certainly wouldn't have as hard a time finding a job as the priest in that novel did. My dad would give me a job in the bank right away.

"Things at St. Mary's are just about the same," I said. "They're crazy."

They laughed at some stories of my latest hassles with Father Vance. Two flushed spots came out on my mother's cheekbones, and my dad had to cough into his fine old damask napkin.

Now that we were more relaxed, we talked family talk.

But I wasn't really paying much attention. That hot white light of exhilaration still burned inside of me, brighter than ever. I could see myself dealing masterfully with Vidal's problem, whatever it was. My hands reached out and touched his. When God and I got done with him, he would be happy, sober, confident, disciplined. Nobody in Cottonwood would put him down anymore.

Vidal. The name was uncommon for whites, but it was common among Montana Indians. The French had scattered the name through the tribes when they intermarried in the early days. The name had a leap of life to it. In fact, its root was the Latin *vita,* "life."

". . . And so Mrs. MacPherson said that the Historical Society . . . Tom, you aren't listening," said my father.

"I'm sorry," I said. "What did you say?"

"Tom, you seem *miles* away today," said my mother.

"Do I?" I said. "I was thinking about a parishioner I'm counseling. A very tough case."

To stop this line of conversation, I got up and helped Rosie clear away the plates.

Then Rosie marched in with the cake. It was a real homemade "white mountain" cake, with fondant icing. Rosie had decorated it with pink and silver roses, and ten silver candles which, multiplied by five, gave away my mother's age.

My dad lit the candles and he, I and Rosie sang "Happy birthday." Mother gave one of her little screams and managed to puff out five candles. I did the honors on the rest.

We made Rosie sit down with us to have some cake, and I got her a chair and a plate.

Rosie's present to Mother was a lavender mohair shawl she'd crocheted herself. My father's present was a second three-carat diamond for a necklace he'd started for her long ago. I gawked at it—it looked almost as big as one of the headlights on the Triumph. I suspect that he regarded it as gift and investment both. He'd given her the first stone on her twenty-fifth birthday.

"And I'll give you the third one on your seventy-fifth birthday," he said, grinning slyly, "if the economy hasn't gone down the drain by then."

"And if we're both still around," said Mother. She blew him a kiss.

Her fingers were now busy with the super-professional bow that the druggist's helper in Cottonwood had built on my little package. Inside, between two layers of cotton, her girlish fingers found a Roman coin for her collection. She had just about every old silver and gold dollar minted in the United States, but her weakness was Greek and Roman coins. I had found this right at the little stamp-and-coin shop in Cottonwood a couple of weeks ago, and would be paying for it for the next six months.

The lovely old bronze thing lay in her palm—as old as the religion I served, as the traditions that bound us all.

"How sweet of you, Tom," she said. "It's one I don't have."

"Are you sure?" I said. "The guy at the store said I could exchange it if you've already got one."

"I'm sure," said my mother. "It's a *very* nice Antinoüs. . . ."

"Who was Antinoüs?" asked my father.

"He was a close friend of the Emperor Hadrian," said my mother primly without looking at me.

I had to hold back a smile. I had read enough Roman history in the seminary to know that the young Antinoüs was more than just a friend of Hadrian. My father either saw through the explanation and didn't let on that he did, or he was satisfied with it, for he just said, "Oh."

I was remembering the little velvet tray of coins on the counter in the Cottonwood coin shop. My finger had sorted through the heavy coins—faces of empresses and goddesses, faces of stern and jowly emperors—and it came to rest on this coin with its profile of a good-looking young man with curly hair. I had no idea who he was until the store owner told me he was some second-century A.D. weirdo. But I liked it anyway, and I bought it.

My mother had her hand pressed to her chest as if to stop her heart from fluttering.

"It's been quite a birthday," she said. "I feel like I'm *really* ten years old."

She sat there glowing with her air of girlish wisdom. You had the feeling that my mother had never really grown up, but that she knew an awful lot for her age.

═══

After dinner, we sat in the parlor awhile.

My father and I had a little Drambuie in his favorite old rock-crystal brandy glasses. The big color TV, which stood by the vitrine full of old bric-a-brac, stayed turned off. My mother sat with her coin books, finding the right place to slip Antinoüs in. My father and I talked about the economy—St. Mary's troubles finding money and the bank's troubles with ranchers going broke. On the mantel, the china clock ticked between the two French bisque figurines, shepherd and shepherdess, that had stood there as long as I could remember.

I sat there sipping Drambuie and looking at my parents. They were both a breath of the virile past, two living fossils shut away from the dust, like the rare seashells in the vitrine. They were so much a match for each other that they might have been poured from the same batch of white clay at the same factory, like those two figurines. They wanted me to marry and have children for old reasons, not modern ones.

36

Later, I left them for a little while to keep my monthly appointment with Father Matt.

≡

I drove across town and parked the Triumph near the cathedral. Walking into the shadow of those great spires, and under the sculptured portal, I went in.

Except for a nun in a short modern habit who was arranging flowers on a side altar, the cathedral was empty. I kneeled down in front of the altar where the Blessed Sacrament was kept, and tried to collect my thoughts. I'd learned the hard way that I had to be very still inside for these talks with Father Matt.

But I couldn't. I kept having this heady feeling that I'd just won some sort of heavenly sweepstakes. Rushes of memory kept going over me. Playing against Missoula in the state football championship, and losing. Kissing Jean for the first time, very gently, and later breaking the engagement, also very gently. Hitchhiking to Butte to hear E. Power Biggs play the pipe organ in concert, and feeling very daring because hitchhiking is illegal in Montana.

Moments of recollection were so rare now. Priests were supposed to have a spiritual life. I wanted to have one, but I didn't, and it was my fault. What I had was a sort of hyperactive hysteria that passed for loving God, and possibly for loving people too. But hadn't I always loved people?

I left the cathedral and walked over to the Carroll College campus.

Father Matt was just coming down the corridor toward his office. He stood six foot six, and walked with long springing strides that made his cassock flare out. He looked like a Jesuit Ichabod Crane. His salt-and-pepper hair was shaved close to a magnificent skull and high-bridged nose that would have done credit to one of Mother's Roman coins. Ordinarily Jesuits scared me to death, but Father Matt was a Jesuit with some horse sense.

"Hello, my boy," he said. "You look happy today."

"Oh, it's my mother's birthday," I said. "She's fifty, and she likes it."

Right away I asked myself why I had lied. A little white lie, of course. Later I would look back at it, and know that it was the first and the whitest of a lot of lies.

We sat in his office. He put his huge dusty feet up on his desk, displaying the frayed cuffs of his black trousers, and lighted his clunky briar pipe. Father Matt smoked a very sweet mixture that smelled like the prune whip Rosie sometimes baked.

Just the sight of Father Matt made me feel more comfortable about things. I put my feelings about Cottonwood in front of him. He smoked and smiled out the window.

Finally he said, "Every young curate has that moment. He suddenly realizes that the Church is a sinking ship, and that he is the chosen rat who's got to stay aboard and save it, instead of leaving it."

I had to laugh. Father Matt was famous for being a specialist in deflating first-year delusions of grandeur.

"Seriously," I said, "I like it in Cottonwood. I don't believe I had any illusions about being in a small-town parish. If I stay there, Father Vance will kick the bucket one of these days, and I'll take over. But sometimes I feel . . ."

"You would like to come back here and put your feet on the yellow brick road that leads to monsignor."

"Something like that."

Father Matt had his lanky ankles crossed, and was

bouncing one mammoth foot rhythmically, listening.

"Sometimes I feel like I'm going to burst out of that little parish. I've got so much energy it's driving me crazy. We've got the budget back in the black. Collections have gone up—a little. People are responding to the Friday-night adult education course—a little. There's less emphasis on bingo. I run around like a maniac all day long. And then there comes a minute that I start feeling like I'm choking."

Father Matt knocked the ashes out of his pipe.

"The funny thing is that all the busy work doesn't distract me from the *people*. I get very involved with their problems. Too involved. I lie awake, worrying. Did Janie have the abortion anyway? Did Mr. Hoover really hear me when I asked him if he wanted to confess, or had he already lost too much blood . . . ?"

"Pray," said Father Matt.

I felt a little crushed. Surely he'd have a more ingenious answer than that.

"You have very little inward life," he said. "So you have no defense against all the stresses. I've told you before. You've made very little progress."

"I know," I said miserably.

"Make the effort to start building the habit of mental prayer. A moment here, a moment there. Surely you can find moments. While you're driving to a sick call, even while you're eating. Build on those moments. It's the only way. The Bishop will ask you about the mortgage, but Our Lord will ask you about your heart."

"To be honest with you," I said, "I feel very close to my parishioners, but I feel very far from Our Lord."

Father Matt shook his head in disbelief, and looked out the window for a few minutes.

"You're one of the casualties of the new spirituality," he said. "Actually, I'm not sure it *is* a spirituality. Back in

39

the sixties, in the name of reform and revival, we threw a lot of the old forms overboard. Litanies, novenas, rosaries . . . do you say the rosary?"

"No," I said. "I'm lucky if there's time to say the Office every day."

"When you were down and out," said Father Matt, "the rosary was better than nothing. It was a start, a place to focus your thoughts. We haven't found anything to replace that old-fashioned spirituality . . ."

After we talked a little more about the deficiencies of my spiritual life, Father Matt filled his pipe again and said:

"Actually, your notion about moving to the diocesan office isn't all that unrealistic."

"How come?" I said.

"Well, maybe I shouldn't get your hopes up. But Bishop Carney is going to need a new secretary this fall, and he's looking around for a replacement. He wants a young priest, and you're one of the men being considered."

The gloom lifted off me with the speed of light.

"He has a special regard for Father Vance, and he's not one hundred percent sure that he wants to take you out of Cottonwood. So don't get your hopes up. Just . . ."

". . . Pray," I said, grinning.

Father Matt smiled. "Sometimes our fantasies and God's will coincide."

As I left, I wondered why I'd stuck with this one spiritual director so slavishly since the seminary days. Habit was one of my curses. On the other hand, Father Matt could make me uneasy or frighten me worse than any other priest I knew. Maybe this ambivalence about him was what was holding me back.

When I got to the city limits of Cottonwood, the clock in my dashboard said just past nine-thirty P.M.

As I drove along the darkened fairgrounds and saw the bright neon signs and the two traffic lights of Main Street up ahead, I relaxed a little and thought, Father'll be pleased, I'm home a little early. The lighted clock in the tower of the dark City Hall said nine thirty-five. The only life on Main Street was hidden in the bars, and even that wasn't as lively as on Fridays and Saturdays.

But as I stopped at the first red light, by the City Hall with its severe Doric columns, a Saturday-type disturbance caught my eye.

On the corner of Main and Placer Streets stood the City Hall. Right across from City Hall, on Placer, was the gloomy old brick Rainbow Hotel, where the Greyhound bus depot was. (That bus, or a small plane from the airstrip, or a car, or your own two feet, were the only ways you could get out of Cottonwood anymore.) Between the Rainbow Hotel and the boarded-up old building that had once been the livery stable, there was an alley.

In that alley, a fistfight was going on. I rolled down the car window and sat there in the car watching it. Even over the idling engine, the crash of hotel garbage cans, the oofs and grunts and the thud of fists were clear. I was mildly curious. Anybody who could get up enough energy for a fight on Sunday night sure must have something eating at him.

Two of the men were rolling over and over at the mouth of the alley. I recognized a black leather jacket with silver lettering on the back. One of the men was Vidal.

My insides clenched. I looked up Main Street to see if Winter's squad car was on its way, but the street was empty. Either nobody had seen the fight yet and called the cops, or somebody was just now doing it and Winter would be along in a few minutes.

41

The men got up and started punching each other, and disappeared into the alley again.

I didn't want to see Vidal arrested. Maybe I could break up the fight. It was my duty anyway, no matter who it was.

A second before the light changed, I gunned the engine and wheeled the car off into Placer Street. Parking just past the hotel entrance, I jumped out. As I ran toward the alley, the scufflings, grunts and smack of fists got louder and louder. The garbage cans crashed again, and a woman yelled from a window above the alley, "Hey, cut it out down there!"

I charged into the alley and got a good look now. The smell of dank earth, old brick and garbage hit my nostrils.

Vidal was fighting with two well-known roughnecks from the little ranch community of Whalen, fifteen miles up the valley. They were the Smith brothers, one a blacksmith, the other a truckdriver. They were both over six feet, and both would drive a hundred miles to find one good fight. Vidal, however, was holding his own with them pretty well. He was over six feet too, and if the Smith brothers were brawn, he was quicker, faster and brainier—a case of a panther fighting two jaguars.

For a moment I stood frozen at the alley entrance. I had read about violence, seen it, been emotionally affected by it, preached against it. But I had never felt so uncomfortably close to it as now. The sheer savagery of Vidal's fight was overwhelming. I hardly recognized him. The saddened, disturbed drunk with the silver necklaces who had slumped down in my confessional last night was now a "roaring and ravening lion."

Why? I asked myself.

The three men weren't doing any fancy Kung Fu stuff. They weren't even fighting like James Bond in the movies. They were just kicking the shit out of each other in the good old American way, the kind of gutter slugging that's as much a part of the Bicentennial as Betsy Ross.

Vidal took a punch in the gut and reeled back against the dank old brick wall. As one of the Smiths rushed to pin him against the wall, Vidal recovered and doubled him up with a chop of his own into the gut. Then he kneed the Smith neatly in the groin, making him yell hoarsely, and shattered him with a right to the jaw. The Smith crashed down among the already dented and spilled garbage cans, and his head came to rest between a gallon milk carton saying Meadowbrook Dairy and a pile of greasy potato peelings.

The other Smith was thrown off balance by his brother falling against him, but he recovered and tried to rush Vidal too. Vidal slammed him with a right, then a left, then a right, chopping him pitilessly to pieces like an Indian Muhammad Ali and the other Smith went crashing down in the garbage too, across some clattering soda bottles.

"I'm calling the police," the woman shrieked from above. She must be one of the few guests in the Rainbow Hotel—her window was the only one lit in the whole dank wall.

Vidal leaned panting and gasping with pain against the cold blackened bricks. His nose and mouth were bleeding and he rubbed them with his hand.

"Vidal," I said, going toward him.

He looked up dully, panting like a wounded animal. After a moment, his eyes softened just a little with recognition.

"Get the hell out of here before Winter comes," I said.

Moving stiffly with pain, Vidal looked for his precious high-crowned black hat, and found it lying in a dry dusty curled-up mud puddle. The Smiths were stirring among the garbage cans, moaning and grunting. Bottles and cans rolled everywhere.

I grabbed Vidal by the sleeve and pulled him out of the alley. He reeked of garbage too—his jacket was all grainy with coffee grounds.

"Where's your bike?" I said.

"Up by Brown's."

"My car's here. Get in."

Vidal leaned back heavily against the car seat, still panting raspily. I drove quickly on down Placer Street, then turned left at the next corner, around the back of City Hall.

It occurred to me that, in a trivial kind of way, I was aiding and abetting a flight from justice. But it thrilled me too. Vidal's presence there in the car became something overwhelming in a curiously physical kind of way. Jesus had said that if you did something for the least of His children, you did it for Him. For almost the first time in my life, I had a frighteningly real sense of His existence right there in the car beside me.

Vidal's nose was bleeding down onto his shirt and his silver necklaces. So, at the next corner, I stopped the car again and wordlessly gave him my handkerchief.

Vidal mopped his nose with it and winced.

"Broken?" I asked, feeling as if I had touched the Holy Grail.

"Dunno." He wiggled it. "Don't think so." He grinned. "A nose as gorgeous as mine shouldn't get broken."

Like last night, he reeked of sweat, beer, leather and pot, only worse. But somehow it didn't offend me. A half ounce of the stuff was even sticking out of his jacket pocket in a worn Baggie. It must have come out in the fight.

"For chrissake, hide your dope," I said, pushing it back in his pocket. "Are you asking for trouble?"

He sat staring ahead as we stopped at the second red light on Main Street, by the corner of the Cottonwood Bank and Trust. He was still holding the handkerchief to his nose. The handkerchief was soaked bright red, and for some reason the sight of his blood horrified me.

Then he said softly, "No, I'm not really asking for it."

"You shouldn't smoke that crap," I said. "One reason, plain and simple. It takes away your motivation. And you already told me motivation is your big problem."

The light changed to green, and we turned out onto Main Street. The marquee of the Rialto Theater was still lit—there was only one show on Sunday evenings now. The cosmetics and boxes of candy in the drugstore window were lit with a gruesome fluorescent clarity of pink, blue and yellow. Main Street was just as deserted as before—except that Winter's squad car was now shooting down it with the red swivel light flashing. We watched it go by.

I pulled up by his bike, which was parked in front of Brown's.

But Vidal didn't get out. He kept sitting there, slumped, his breathing a little easier now. The wad of wet red hanky was forgotten in his hand.

"You're right, Father. I tell myself that every day."

"Drinking takes away your motivation too. And so does fighting."

"It passes the time," he said.

He looked at me with that same strange dark look as in the church last night. In the dark of the car, you couldn't tell his eyes didn't match.

"I get into fights because there's . . . happiness locked up inside me," he said.

"Ask God for the key," I said.

He smiled a little. "You make it sound so goddam easy."

He reached out and plopped the soggy ball of the handkerchief into my hand, as if he were giving me a present instead of giving back something of mine. "Thanks," he said.

I still had my eye anxiously on the rearview mirror, watching for Winter to maybe come back. "Get going now," I said. "Hurry up. See you tomorrow."

He grinned. "Why, Father, don't you *want* to see me punished?"

He got out and slammed the car door shut. He tromped on his starter and the big bike roared into life. The roar shattered the stillness of Main Street. The sound was almost like an angel's trumpet waking up the beautiful embalmed goods in the glass coffins of the store windows. With a little wave at me, he pulled his high-crowned hat firmly down on his head, and shot off down the street.

I walked into the rectory at five minutes after ten.

"You're late," barked Father Vance.

"Sorry, Father," I said. "My mother was having such a good time, I couldn't tear myself away."

"These kid priests who think they can gallivant around at all hours," ranted Father Vance, "like a bunch of no-good hippies . . ."

I went to my room. The bloodstained handkerchief was still balled in my hand. It felt as alive and as incomprehensible as the Incarnation. Something had definitely changed in my life. Something had become real.

I raised it slowly and reverently to my lips, and kissed it.

3

Monday went by slowly. I was like a little kid waiting for the last day of school to let out.

That evening, I assumed Vidal would be late. After all, he had a sloppy life-style. But I was wrong. His motorcycle came roaring up to the rectory ten minutes early. He sat in the waiting room up the hallway, while I finished talking to a young girl, Margaret Shoup, who was in serious trouble.

Meg had said she wanted to confess and had missed on Saturday. She looked so adult that she wouldn't have been asked for proof of age down in the Main Street bars. She was a curly brunette with glitter clogs on her feet, attractive in a pudgy kind of way.

"How old are you exactly, Meg?" I asked.

"Fourteen," she said, looking up at me from where she knelt.

I was floored.

"I know, Father. Everybody always reacts that way. Even my boyfriend did."

"How long have you been pregnant?"

"Oh," she said, "five months, anyway."

"Why in God's name did you wait so long before coming for help?"

"Because I didn't miss any periods, so I thought I was okay."

So much for the success of the sex education course being taught in the Cottonwood high school, I thought.

"Do your parents know?" I asked.

"If they knew, they'd kill me. I've been pudgy like this since I was eleven, so they don't suspect a thing."

I could well imagine her parents' reaction. They were two of the stuffiest, most puritanical people in town. Her mother was the self-appointed head book-burner of Cottonwood, and the bookseller on Main Street always shook in his shoes whenever he saw her coming. She had been in a bad mood ever since the court had knocked down her effort to have Salinger et al taken out of the bookstore.

Meg went on with a feverish rush. "Father, I don't know what to do. I'm too far gone to have a clinic abortion. It'd have to be in a hospital. But I'd have to have my parents' signature for that. Anyway, I don't have any money. I tried to borrow some from my girl friends, but they told me I was crazy to have an abortion now."

"Your girl friends are right," I said. "Where's your boyfriend?"

"He went to Seattle. He said he was looking for a job. If I knew where he was, I'd go find him and get him to help me."

Abortion dilemmas always distressed me. It always seemed like the cases I got were the messy ones, where people either obeyed the Church's teachings and the result was disaster, or they obeyed those teachings out of purely selfish reasons. But here was one of those rare cases where disaster loomed no matter whether the teachings were obeyed or not.

48

"Your boyfriend is being smart," I said. "He knows that when your folks find out, they'll have him busted for statutory rape."

Meg started to cry.

I patted her pudgy hand. "Listen, honey, there's no point in giving you a big moral lecture right now. The Church says that abortion is murder. But in your case, we've got to be practical. You haven't got any money, and it'd be dangerous for you to have one now. I can get you into a house in Helena where they help girls like you to have their babies."

Meg was still crying when she'd been absolved and left. I wasn't sure she was going to do what I said. She said she'd let me know in a few days. It made me very depressed.

Peering into the sitting room, I managed to smile at Vidal.

"Okay, you come in now," I said.

"Does everybody leave your office crying their eyes out?" he said.

He came in looking around shyly. His face was a little swollen and bruised from last night.

My "office" was an afterthought that hadn't been in Father Vance's original living plan for the rectory. When I came, and when I finally convinced him that I couldn't do counseling in my bedroom, he grudgingly had the storeroom off the pantry converted into a working space for me.

The room wasn't much bigger than the confessional. One wall still had the curlicued old wire hooks for hanging aprons and dustpans. The ancient furniture was salvaged from an empty classroom in St. Mary's Academy —a desk, a bookcase with a few scratched Walt Disney decals on it, and two chairs with schoolboys' initials carved in them. On the wall, the cheap crucified Jesus (also a relic from the academy) wore a peculiar agonized expression, as if He had just opened the envelope containing the Montana Power Company's electricity bill for the month.

The tall window had a gruesome green shade, so cracked that it let in quite a bit of light. When it was raised, I could see the dense jungle of lilac bushes outside. The old gas fixture was still on the wall. I had tried to give the room some comfort by putting cushions on the chairs, and hanging up a couple of old prints my parents had given me from their attic.

As I closed the door, Vidal sat down a little gingerly in the initial-scarred chair on his side of the desk. I sat down in mine. We looked at each other.

The first important thing in counseling is to make the counselee feel that he is truly cared for and loved, not just another name in the appointment book. These rules I had always followed, but they were easy with Vidal.

Vidal cleared his throat. He had combed his hair, and wore clean Levi's and a white Yucatan wedding shirt embroidered with pastel flowers. A Cottonwood redneck wouldn't dare to call him a pinko hippy fag if he wore that shirt into a bar, because he would know that Vidal would exact a terrible revenge.

Vidal seemed to be having a fatal attack of shyness. "How was Helena?" he said.

"Same as always." I couldn't help teasing him for this lame opener. "It's still the capital."

Vidal looked down at his silver-conchoed hat and laughed softly. "Pow, you got me. Your family live there?"

"They settled there in 1887 and they never moved."

"Oh, pioneers," said Vidal wryly.

"Your family are the pioneers," I said. "You're from up at Browning, aren't you?"

Vidal leaned back in his chair. From the flush on his face, he'd had a few drinks. From his half-shut eyes, he'd probably smoked a little pot too. All to get himself loose enough to talk to me again.

"Yep," he said. "I'm only one quarter Indian, but it's enough to put me on the tribal roll."

"What part of the reservation were you born on?"

"Oh, hell, I was born right in Browning there. My folks are town Indians. The fullbloods up in the hills over at Heart Butte kinda look down on us. I went to high school right there in Browning."

"You have brothers and sisters?"

"Two married sisters. Mary lives in L.A., and Jean moved to Denver with her husband and her kid. And I've got a brother, John, he's married too, and working in the oil refinery at Billings. We're kinda scattered all over."

I could see he was relaxing a little. One of the things I'd learned in my first year was roundabout gentle questioning.

"What does your father do?"

"He's one of the tribal policemen."

"You went to college, didn't you?"

"Yeah," he said. "I was class salutatorian and on the basketball team and that sorta shit, and I won a scholarship to Montana U. But that was where things kinda started to go wrong, there at Missoula."

"How do you mean?"

His mismatched magnificent eyes moved up from the hat to my face. "Oh . . ." he said evasively. "I don't know. I wanted to study education, be a teacher back on the reservation. Not many Indian teachers. That was why I was really happy to go to Missoula. But . . . the pressures, maybe. Something got to me. The first year I studied hard, and I even got engaged to this girl, Georgia Keough. Her dad's in the state legislature."

"Oh, yeah, Mike Keough. My dad knows him."

He looked back down and tossed the hat gently in his hands.

"Maybe I studied too hard. Anyway, that summer I went up home to Browning, and I kinda fell apart. I got real wild. My dad tried to knock some sense into me, but he couldn't. Drinking and fighting and gambling. Indian kids have got a special way of being wild. I used to lose a lot of money playing Hand. Lost a lot at the horse races over at Starr School. I don't know any more about race-horses than I know about saddle horses!" He laughed ruefully. "Broke up with Georgia. One thing led to another, I owed a lot of money, and then I did a real dumb thing. I robbed a liquor store, and I got caught by one of the regular town cops. My dad had a fit. They sent me to Deer Lodge for three years. Got out in two on good behavior, because of my school record, I guess. . . ."

He trailed off, then started up again, as if the booze and dope made it hard to collect his thought.

"Didn't feel like going back to Browning, lost my scholarship. So I went down to see my sister in L.A. for a couple weeks. Didn't like L.A. but I met my wife down there. When I came back, the prison placement service found me the job here."

I sat there just letting him talk. He was talking without prodding now, and I kept wondering what horrible (to him) sin he was going to come out with.

"And, well, Father, the thing is, I'm a young man on the way down. It's not just that I drink a little too much. I smoke a little dope too, but it's really the whiskey that's getting me. I want to stop. But I want to turn my life around too. Somehow I want to get my feeling of commitment back. I've tried by myself, but I just can't seem to . . ."

Commitment. The word hung in the air in the little office. It wasn't merely a strange word from a grease monkey. It was a strange word to be linking with a horrible mysterious sin. What was so horrible about drinking a lot, compared to, say, rape or murder?

52

He sat there waiting for me to say something.

"Is that all?" I said.

He nodded and sighed heavily.

"I don't believe you," I said softly.

He smiled. "Okay. You don't believe me. What else do you want to hear?"

"Where the hell do you get hard drugs in this one-horse town?"

He retrenched hastily. "Oh, there isn't much hard stuff in Cottonwood, Father. Why, I bet you'd have to go clear to Chicago for heroin. Not even much acid around—you gotta go to Missoula for that. But hell, Father, Cottonwood is the grass capital of the Northwest. Tons of the stuff come in on the railroad."

I had to laugh at his pitiless picture of the big dope scene in town. "What is it, Mexican?"

Vidal grinned. "It's mostly that stuff that grows wild over in the Bitterroot. You smoke, Father? I'll get you some."

I had to grin back. There we were, grinning at each other like a couple of college students. Again I had that eerie feeling that I hadn't grinned for ages.

"I used to, a little," I said. "I even admit to toking once when I was in the seminary. But now I'm straight. You can't offer mass if you're buzzed. Besides, Father Vance would have me crucified if he smelled pot in the rectory."

Suddenly we were lapped in that conspiratorial warmth of the "younger generation." At that moment, nothing linked me to Father Vance but the sacramental mark of the priesthood on my soul and the cassock he made me wear. Since it was obvious that Vidal was going to lie to me for a little while, and hold back his sin, we just talked.

"The sixties, Father, they weren't so bad, were they?"

"They were all right," I said. "But the party's over."

"I'll say," he said. "How did you spend the sixties,

Father? I don't know why the fuck I'm calling you father, we're the same age. How old are you, Father?"

"Twenty-eight."

"I'm coming twenty-seven in July."

"Well," I said. "I didn't do much different from you. I was class president at Helena High, and I played football, and I studied music for about ten years."

"You play the organ real nice."

"I've just about forgotten how to play. My parents had a lot of fights about where I was going to go to school. Only thing I can ever remember them fighting about. My father wanted me to go to Harvard business school and play college ball—"

"Harvard," said Vidal. "Lah-de-dah, whoop-de-do."

"My mother wanted me to go to Juilliard and be another E. Power Biggs. I couldn't stand the arguing, and I had other things on my mind. I went a year to Montana U. and then I dropped out and joined VISTA."

"We must have been at Missoula together. Funny I never met you."

"Well, you were in education, and I was in the music school. Not too surprising we didn't meet."

"VISTA. Christ, where'd you go, New York or something?"

"California. And that was where I decided I wanted to go home and be a priest."

Vidal shook his head. "Everybody knows the Catholic Church is on its last legs. Why does anybody want to be a priest?"

I sat silent for a moment. He really didn't have any business asking me that question yet, because he didn't know me well enough. But strangely enough, I wanted to answer it. Something in me fumbled around for the right words.

"Isn't that like saying that it isn't worth being a president after Watergate?" I said.

54

Vidal kept after me stubbornly, and I sensed that there was some motive behind his questioning.

"Do you really believe in all that old shit, Father? About abortions and divorce and sex?"

I looked at him studyingly. "To be honest with you, the way things are right now, I believe that the only thing a person can do is follow his conscience. The only real judge of that is God, isn't He?"

"So if I had sex with a person, and it was against what the Church said, and if I really believed I had done the right thing, then everything would be okay?"

I searched in his eyes and his face for the anxiety that ought to be there. What I saw was not anxiety, but just a peaceful, stoned curiosity. So he was really asking me what my attitudes were.

"If you really believed you were right, you would be okay," I said.

I rolled my eyes up toward heaven and said, "Father Vance would crucify me if he could hear that. But that's what I think."

My watch said eighty-thirty. We were getting nowhere fast, and I had to go to a meeting of the parish council pretty soon.

"What's really on your mind?" I said. "You didn't come up here just to tell me you smoke Bitterroot weed. In the church the other night, you acted like somebody who's pretty disturbed about something."

Vidal turned his head to one side for a moment, as if considering whether to spill it or keep it back. I was struck by his profile, so fine that it might have been pried off a Roman coin. Even the wavy hair, which brushed his rumpled embroidered collar, gave him a classical look. But he was no pretty boy for Hadrian. He was too old, and too scarred, and too wild, and he was tainted by the touch of woman.

He looked around the office uneasily, then back at me.

"This place is almost as bad as that little box in the church. I don't like talking in here."

"Maybe you'd like to talk somewhere else."

"Do they let you have supper with people?"

"Sure they do. I'm not a prisoner, for chrissake."

"How about you come to our house for supper tomorrow night?"

"No can do. Tomorrow night is bingo night. How about Wednesday?"

"Okay. Wednesday." He got up. "I've sure wasted your time, haven't I, Father?"

I got up too. "Not unless *you* think you have."

No one else was waiting for counseling, so I walked Vidal out.

The sun was just getting low over the mountain range to the west. The clouds looked as if some heavenly neon sign maker had gone crazy and wired them all for colors: reds, coppers, yellows, pinks. We walked slowly along the winding flagstone path, toward the street. The lawn around the church needed mowing already. We were too cheap to hire a gardener now, so I would probably have to do it myself.

Vidal's bike was parked by the church. We stood for a moment looking down at the wonderful view of Cottonwood and the valley in the summer evening.

The Catholic buildings dominated a little hill on the east side of town. If Cottonwood was Rome, then this was its one sacred hill. Across the street, surrounded by huge old cottonwood trees and cinder playgrounds, stood the shaky brick hulk of St. Mary's Academy. The rain had washed away the children's footprints on the playgrounds.

Up the street was another, bigger, brick hulk—St. Mary's Hospital. This hulk looked alive—lights at nearly all the tall curtained windows. Father Vance said his low mass in the chapel there every morning. You could almost hear rosaries clacking as the nuns hurried down the corridors, and smell the pain and the cotton swabs soaked in alcohol.

Behind us was the rectory; beside us was the church.

Before us, Cottonwood spread out its several thousand roofs in the evening glow. Dogs barked here and there. The streetlights and neon signs were already burning on Main Street, and so was the garish orange tower of the new McDonald's. The Safeway supermarket was lit up like a Christmas tree—the ranch people came in the evening to shop. Beyond Main Street, the tower of the grain elevator was stately and glowing pink as a triumphal column in the sunset. The winding line of willows and cottonwoods told where the river cut through town.

West of Cottonwood lay the hayfields, cut into squares by the fine lines of barbed-wire fence. The one grove of trees out there was the cemetery. Farther on, the runway lights winked on at the little airport.

As we stood there looking at the scene, hoofs came clopping along the street. An old cowman, white-haired and frail-looking, came riding on a big rangy sweat-dried black horse. He didn't give us a glance as he rode by. It was a contemporary of Father Vance's, Pinter Brodie, the oldest cowman in the valley. He, like Father Vance, was another of those living fossils of the old manly virtues. He had probably been up in the hills to look at his cattle.

"There goes old Pint," said Vidal, laughing. "When he goes home, you *know* it's time to quit."

"Kind of spooky, isn't it," I said, "to think that he can remember all the stuff that you and I have to learn from books?"

"Yeah," he said. "I used to get that feeling with some of the old folks up on the Blackfoot. I was never much of an Indian, though."

"How come?"

Vidal shrugged. "Like you said, I had other things on my mind."

"Where do you live, Vidal?"

He straddled his bike and clamped his hat firmly down on his head.

"Cross the river and turn left on Willow Avenue. It's the last house at the end of the street."

He tromped on the starter and the bike roared into life. He grinned at me.

"Good night, Father. I'm gonna buzz old Brodie and tell him to get a horse."

He circled out onto the street, threw a little wave at me, and gunned the bike down the hill. By some miracle, his hat stayed on his head—his guardian angel must have been sitting on it.

≡

With that smile still on my face, I jumped into the Triumph and gunned off down the hill myself. Next on the evening schedule was the meeting of the parish council. It had gotten so I dreaded these meetings, because we always ended up squabbling.

The parish council was one of the few real innovations that I'd been able to start at St. Mary's. Like others in the United States, it was composed of both clergy and laymen.

It was supposed to help provide solutions to problems for both the parish and the community. With the pinch of inflation these days, most of the problems seemed to boil down to Caesar's money or Christ's money. Father Vance supposedly belonged to the council, too—but he was mistrustful of it, so he usually delegated the meetings to me.

The council met once a week, on Monday evenings, at a different member's home. Tonight it was being held at the home of Meg Shoup's parents. I had really been sorry for Father Vance's decision to let Mrs. Shoup join, as she had started her book-burning crusade shortly afterward.

She had tried hard to make pornography one of our major problems, when it simply wasn't.

The Shoups lived on Daly Avenue, one of the "nice" streets in town. I had to park down the street from their handsome brick house, because the other council members were already parked in front. As I walked up the flagstone walk, I could look through the tall windows in the masses of Virginia creeper and see the council already sitting around the living room.

"Oh, Father, we'd almost given you up," Mrs. Shoup told me at the door. She was never diplomatic about telling me I was late.

Laura Shoup was a big busty woman who always wore brocade suits in the evening, no matter what kind of an affair she was going to, and patent leather pumps no matter what time of the year it was. She wore a lot of good-quality jangling costume jewelry, and as far as she was concerned, rouge and powder had never gone out of style. Her broad high-colored mask of a face was brought to life violently by her restless, burning black eyes.

I sat down and listened. Vidal's voice was still in my ears, and his face was still drifting in front of my eyes. Sometimes I found myself losing track of the discussion.

The council members were arranged around the plush living room like living pieces of the bric-a-brac that Mrs. Shoup loved. Mrs. Shoup had a Victorian's taste carried out in new things. She had that same love of drapes loaded with ball fringe, but hers were lilac chiffon. The pink velvet sofa and armchairs looked as if they were lost somewhere between the Gay Nineties and Danish modern. The room was cluttered with little tables, and the tables were cluttered with china collectables—mostly Chinese ladies and dogs. On the mantel stood a shiny brass 365-day clock that insurance man Dick Shoup had been presented by the Elks as last year's "Businessman of the Year" in Cottonwood. Mrs. Shoup's two yappy white toy poodles rushed around the room like more live china.

The council members sat bogged down in the pink armchairs. They reflected the age spread within the parish, and in the town itself. They were either very young, or they were middle-aged-to-old, with nothing in between. At my insistence, we had included two Catholic high-school seniors, Jamie Ogilvie and Sissy Wood, who had made (as far as I was concerned) a big contribution. I was literally the only member in the twenty-to-thirty-five age group. We had had one fine couple in that age group, the Murchisons. But they had gotten so involved with trying to start a flying service at the Cottonwood airport (he was a pilot) that they'd had to drop out.

"Well," said Mrs. Shoup crisply, "now that Father's finally here, we can start."

She nodded at the council president, Mrs. Ida Shaw, with the air of a famous conductor ordering the symphony to get ready.

Mrs. Shaw was exactly the opposite of Mrs. Shoup. She was the salt of the earth of my parish ladies, and if Father Vance, the Bishop of Helena and the Pope would have allowed it, I would have made her a deacon. She was spiritual, hard-working, no-nonsense, kind. She was head of the local Bicentennial Committee and the Cottonwood Historical Society, and had once confided to me that she'd like to run for mayor someday. She was a handsome widow in her mid-forties with warm brown eyes, a fondness for sweater outfits, a single strand of real pearls, and warm brown hair that uncharitable people suspected came from a Clairol bottle. When the council had elected Mrs. Shaw to be its president, Mrs. Shoup had said out loud that the forces of liberalism would have to be carefully countered.

"Well, the first thing on the agenda is the Bicentennial, of course," said Mrs. Shaw in her soft voice. "And our progress on same. Father, last week we discussed if the St. Mary's Home would be open in time for the Bicentennial. Do you have any more information this week?"

"Well, Beaupré told me the other day that the shipment of two-inch lead pipe finally came in," I said. "With a little bit of luck, the plumbing can be in and we can open in August."

"One of your first patients is going to be my mother," said Mrs. Pufescu. "She's gotten to be impossible. I just can't look after her at home anymore."

"You'll be lucky to get her in," I said. "We've got quite a waiting list."

"Please, no out-of-order discussions," said Mrs. Shaw. "We've got a lot of ground to cover tonight. Father, what about the float for the parade?"

More than a year ago, when the town had to make the first decisions about how to celebrate the national Bicentennial, Mrs. Shaw had stood up at a town meeting and reminded everybody of how Cottonwood spent half a million dollars on a historical pageant for its own Centennial in 1968 and now had nothing to show for it.

"Let's do something to improve the quality of life in Cottonwood," she had said. "Let's honor the past by doing something to ensure our future."

Everybody had cheered her suggestion. The block of the oldest buildings on Main Street, the Landry block, was falling into decay. The town decided to restore them and attract some new businesses. As a result, construction people in town had gotten some badly needed jobs. This summer, Cottonwood would have its first antique shop, a singles bar and a garden center, plus an elegant little tearoom to compete with the town's three dingy cafés and two fast-food joints. Mrs. Pawling, who refused to spend a nickel on repairing the church roof, had offered to plant two hundred new young cottonwood trees along Main Street—"It's getting so there isn't a cottonwood left in town," she said. "All the old ones are dying."

Shortly after I came to St. Mary's, Father Vance and I had made our own decision about the Bicentennial. On one of my first parish rounds, I had visited the county old-folks' home, and was shocked. The building was like a bare barn, with staring sick old men and women in bedrooms like little stalls. I had no trouble persuading Father Vance that we could celebrate God and America by creating a decent home for the aged.

One of the finest historic Victorian houses in town, the Mathers house, had been taken over by the bank on a mortgage foreclosure. We talked the bank into donating the house to St. Mary's. One of my very first money-raising assignments had been to get parishioners to donate work and materials.

The decision that St. Mary's would also have a float in the Bicentennial parade did, admittedly, have a worldly motivation. But the council members, in their gut, felt they wanted it, and we decided not to spend much money on it. The theme of the float would be the local settlers and the Indians working together to build the church.

"I've put a crew of volunteers to work on the float," I said. "Jamie is the head of the crew. Jamie, do you want to tell us about it?"

Jamie's face lit up as I singled him out. Suddenly, with a rush, I was reminded of talking to him Saturday evening in the sacristy, which reminded me of Vidal. That feeling of giddy frightened joy went over me all over again.

"Well," Jamie was saying, "me and three other kids in art class are going to make the thing out of heavy cardboard. We can scrounge the cardboard from Bissell's—the big boxes they get refrigerators and washing machines in. We're doing it in our garage, and it'll be light enough to lift right onto a truck. Mrs. Fulton says we can borrow some canned lilacs from the nursery to stand around it. The costumes will be easy—some paint and feathers and fringes on shirts and pants, and stuff. It shouldn't cost more'n fifty dollars."

Everybody smiled and nodded.

"Well," said Mrs. Shaw, "it sounds like we're moving right along. Does anybody have any more comments before we move on to the next item on the agenda?"

"Yes," said Mrs. Shoup. "No bare chests on the Indians on the float."

Suddenly I felt devastated by aloneness, there in that cluttered living room. I was a priest of God, of Divine Love. I should be like a holy high-tension wire, humming with the shock current of love, carrying love from God to man, and back. But I felt alone, and empty.

The council discussed a few more pet projects, and I tried hard to pay attention. Mr. DiSaronno had gloomy news about our county job-finding project—the sawmill was planning to lay off fifty men, because of a government decision to stop clear-cutting in the national forests. For us, that meant the Cottonwood, Elk Creek and Helena National Forests.

Finally Mrs. Shaw asked, "Now are there any new problems that anyone wants to bring up?"

"Yes," said Mrs. Shoup.

My mind snapped back to reality, and I groaned inwardly. She was still smarting from her recent rebuff by the court on the bookstore issue. Now she was looking for a new hotbed of obscenity.

All the other members' eyes fastened on her, a little wearily.

"The other day I visited the high-school library," she said. "I am a member of the school board, so I could demand to see the card files. And I was shocked to find that some highly unsuitable books are on the shelves for our children to read."

The minute Laura Shoup said anything, parliamentary procedures went out the window.

"Laura," said Mr. Meade, "you just lost a case, in court."

"The court is not infallible," said Mrs. Shoup.

"Are you appealing?" insisted Meade.

Mrs. Shoup didn't hesitate a moment. "Frankly, no," she said.

"Why?"

"My lawyer thought it would be a waste of time," she said. "Anyway, with the school library, we don't have to go through the courts. It's a simple matter of frightening the principal and the rest of the school board enough to take the books off the shelves."

"What books are you talking about?" asked Mrs. Shaw.

Mrs. Shoup had a long list. "Salinger, Baldwin, Hemingway—"

"Hemingway?" said Mrs. Shaw.

"It was Hemingway that got me to the problem," said Mrs. Shoup. "My daughter Meg brought *The Old Man and the Sea* home for an English assignment. I was shocked to find that there's a little scene where the old man, uh, relieves himself over the side of the boat."

"But that's not pornography," said Mrs. Pufescu.

Mrs. Shoup kept on listing books as if she hadn't heard. "Oscar Wilde—" she said.

"What's wrong with Wilde?" Mrs. Shaw said sharply. "He's one of my favorite authors. Goodness, all my children have read him."

"People *think* those stories are for children, but they're not," said Mrs. Shoup. "The author was a homosexual, and the stories are full of sick depravity and decadence."

I broke in too. "But Mrs. Shoup, they're very Christian stories. There isn't anything depraved about 'The Selfish Giant.' "

"Homosexuals aren't Christians," said Mrs. Shoup bluntly, turning the fiery blast of her black eyes on me. "Surely, Father, you aren't defending homosexuals."

Mrs. Shaw cut in. "What about other classics in the school library?"

64

"What about them?" said Mrs. Shoup.

"You haven't listed anybody earlier than 1900, except Wilde."

"Oh, I'm not after the old classics," said Mrs. Shoup. "I'm after filthy modern writing."

"Why not? There's plenty of seamy stuff in the classics," said Mrs. Shaw. Her eyes did not waver before Mrs. Shoup's gaze. "Shakespeare—the senior English class gets that. The Bible. Goodness, Laura, if you don't like toilet stuff, read *Gulliver's Travels* someday, that's on the senior reading list . . . And *Candide?* That's in the library too. It's loaded with sadomasochism."

Mrs. Shoup opened her mouth, but I cut her off.

"I agree with Mrs. Shaw," I said. "You're going to throw out half the library. What are the kids going to study?"

It was always a mistake to have a public head-on collision with Mrs. Shoup, and now I made that mistake, deliberately. Maybe it was the mood I was in. Father Matt was right—I was a shell of a priest.

Mrs. Shoup turned the full blast of her wrath on me.

"Father, our society is awash with swingers and polymorphous perverts, and with books by these people. I can't think of anything more practical or moral to do for the Bicentennial than helping rid Cottonwood of these things. And America."

I looked her right in the eye, thinking of what her daughter Meg had told me that very evening.

"Mrs. Shoup," broke in Mr. Meade, "you have the kind of mind that would see incest in *The Bobbsey Twins.* That isn't going to help our country—"

The meeting now broke up into the typical kind of squabble that I had gotten to dread. Everybody was talking and yelling at once. If the Holy Spirit had been hovering anywhere near, He was now flapping off in dismay.

Mrs. Shaw didn't have a gavel, but she kept pounding on the coffee table with her hand like a judge. "Order, order, everybody," she kept saying. "Please!"

Everybody quieted down. Mrs. Shoup looked flushed and sullen.

Mrs. Shaw looked around at the council with a spark of wrath kindled in her own gentle brown eyes.

"I think," she said, "that the simplest way to approach this issue is by our usual way. Voting. Do we or don't we want to be involved in the activity that Laura proposes, namely, getting books removed from the high-school library? Will someone make a motion to that effect?"

"I do," said Mr. Meade.

"I second the motion," said somebody else.

"All those in favor of Laura's proposal, say aye."

"Aye," said Mrs. Shoup.

"We have one vote in favor," said Mrs. Shaw. "All those opposed, say nay."

"Nay," said everybody else in the room, including myself.

"One in favor, six opposed. The majority vote wins, and the proposal is defeated," said Mrs. Shaw crisply.

"Misguided liberals," said Mrs. Shoup.

When the usual coffee and goodies were served, it was with very bad grace that Mrs. Shoup brought out her famous chocolate cake. If there was such a thing as a culinary obscenity, this cake was it: three layers of meltingly good devil's food held together by real fudge frosting and decorated with fancy little squiggles of white icing. That cake, and Mrs. Shoup herself, were the Jesuit Baroque of Catholic housewifery.

With all that bad feeling in the air, nobody said much as they ate. Through the kitchen door, I could see Meg eating a huge wedge of cake and ice cream. No wonder her mother didn't notice anything strange about her waistline.

On the pretext of giving me a piece of cake to take to

Father Vance, Mrs. Shoup waved me into the kitchen, and waved Meg out.

"Father," Mrs. Shoup said icily as she jerked a length of plastic wrap out of a package, "you must have something against me."

"No," I said.

"Then you must have something against the Church's teachings on sexual morality."

For a minute there, I had the childish and unpriestly impulse to pick up her cake and hit her in the face with it, like a custard pie.

"How could I?" I said.

"Of all the people here tonight, you are the one most responsible for whether Holy Mother Church is obeyed," she said. "It was your obligation as a priest to vote for my proposal."

Mrs. Shoup was busy cutting a big wedge of cake, much bigger than the one she'd given me, and putting it on the piece of plastic wrap. Out of the corner of my eye I saw Meg listening out of a doorway down the hall.

"I'm very sorry, Mrs. Shoup," I said as pleasantly as I could, "but I don't know of any dogma that obliges a priest to vote for removing Ernest Hemingway or Oscar Wilde from a high-school library."

"If you can't see the connection between dogma and applying dogma to real life, then I feel sorry for you, Father," she said. "Your life as a priest is going to be a difficult one."

Mrs. Shoup was wrapping the piece of cake with brusque angry gestures. Her pride was a wreck. Her pet crusade had been put down in her own home, with her own cake waiting in the kitchen. Hell hath no fury like a good cook scorned.

"Tell Father we miss him at the meetings," she said crisply, handing me the cake. "I hope he starts coming again."

She probably felt that Father Vance would put his foot

down on my youthful heresies. What she didn't know was that even Father Vance saw her as an extremist.

———

Mercifully, in a few more minutes, I was out of there. It was now past eleven, and I still had an hour's work on the parish books. Father insisted that we keep neat old-fashioned ledgers, because he was always afraid the Bishop would want to see them.

As I sat over the ledgers in the glow of the battered office lamp, the thought of Vidal returned to haunt me. Would Father give me permission to have supper at their house? I was curious to meet his wife—even Father Vance had mentioned something about how she wasn't very bright. Just a couple of hours ago he had been sitting there, his necklaces catching the light. I wanted very much to talk to him right then, to confess to him a few things of my own—my oneness, my sense of being tired at twenty-eight. At the moment, being a priest seemed less like a divine vocation and more like a special kind of treadmill. Priests were supposed to be detached from human relationships—but wouldn't God forgive my need for one good friend of my own sex? It had been so long since I had been able to talk easily and warmly to a man—since the seminary, in fact. But that friendship with Doric Wilton had ended unhappily for both of us. I wouldn't let it happen again.

It was after midnight when I got in bed and sat saying the Divine Office for the day. Father Vance insisted that it was supposed to be said before midnight, but he must have been the last priest in America to have this scruple.

I fell asleep with the light on and the black book open on my chest.

4

At supper the next night, Father Vance sat considering my request for permission to eat at Vidal's.

On his plate were the last crumbs of Mrs. Shoup's chocolate cake, and his *Messenger* was open before him. He was deeply engrossed in getting his swollen fingers to roll one of his handmade cigarettes. His pouch and his package of La Riz rolling papers lay beside the magazine. He had switched to home-rolled as part of our cost-cutting program, after he added up how much cigarettes cost him a year.

He looked doubtful about my request.

"We made some progress at the first counseling session," I said. "But he seemed a little stiff in the rectory. Maybe it'll help if we talk at his home. Because I do have the feeling that I can get somewhere with him."

"Well, I suppose it'll be all right," he said. "But you be home by ten. And I trust you won't come home drunk."

Father Vance never touched any liquor except the wine at Mass, and he was fond of saying that he wished the

Lord had used milk at the Last Supper. He highly disapproved of the fact that I sometimes accepted a drink when I went on parish visits, though I never had more than one.

I left the table feeling uneasily happy. I had lied to Father Vance. But it was a Jesuitical kind of a lie, partly truth. What I hadn't told him was that Vidal was becoming as much a friend as a penitent.

"I'm lonely," I wanted to tell Father Vance. "I have so little in common with Vidal, but it's worlds more than I have in common with you."

But there was no telling that to the old priest, of course. Because he would have lectured me on the pitfalls of becoming emotionally involved with parishioners' problems. "A good priest is like a good dentist," he was always saying. "He drills without hearing the patient say ouch."

The next evening, I put on my social uniform—the black pants and turtleneck and sports jacket. About six P.M. I drove across town. Once again I felt the same giddy apprehension as when I was driving to Helena.

The weather had changed, and it was a typical cold rainy June night in the Rockies.

Vidal lived on "the other side of the tracks." My windshield wipers swiped aside the spattering raindrops as the car bounced over the railroad crossings. The Milwaukee and Northern Pacific railroads cut Cottonwood in half. Behind me, on the east side of the tracks were the "nice" residential areas and the business district. Ahead of me on the west side was the not-so-nice area, which ranged from lower-class to shantytown.

I drove past the weathered red depot and the deserted yards. The two Amtrak trains a day didn't stop at Cottonwood—they just highballed through, blowing their whistles.

I drove across the concrete bridge. The little Cottonwood River was running bank high with the last of the melt waters from the mountains.

I turned the Triumph onto Willow Avenue.

In Cottonwood, Willow Avenue was synonymous with "poor." The homes were every kind of poor. Some trailer homes and cheap prefab houses had tiny overgrazed pastures behind them, with underfed horses that the local ASPCA was always making noises about. There were even a couple of ancient log houses that dated right back to the early days of the town.

At the end of Willow Avenue there was a dreary little clapboard house known as the Allerton house, though all the Allertons were in the cemetery now. Blizzards and cloudbursts had scoured the paint right off it, and the bare silvery wood had the clean look of bone. A tangle of Virginia creeper covered the porch, so that the lone rocking chair with no seat was in a cool green cave. By the front step, one huge old peony plant was in full bloom—it was probably planted by the family that built the house seventy-five years ago. The rose-pink exotic blooms, bent over on the steps by the rain, only made the house look shabbier.

The backyard was just an alkali flat, bordered by the willow brakes at the next bend of the river. The stains and crumbling of the house's granite foundation showed that, in years of higher water, the house had been flooded.

Vidal's bike stood on the porch, out of the wet. It was secured to the wall of the house by a heavy chain and padlock.

Vidal rented this house for $150 a month. The lights in the windows looked warm and inviting. I was a little cold from the rain, because we didn't keep the temperature very high in the rectory. The prospect of a warm supper and some casual talk was nice.

For some reason my stomach was churning with nervousness. I knocked on the door.

After a couple of minutes, Vidal opened it. He was wearing Levi's, an undershirt, and no shoes. His hair was damp. His bare arms and shoulders were as faintly patchy as his face. But you forgot that fault when you saw how well muscled they were.

"Hi," he said, grinning. "I just took a shower. Come on in."

Then he added in a low voice, "Now don't pay any attention to my wife. She can't help the way she is."

I looked around the living room, and my giddy anticipation melted away into the rain streaming down the windowpanes.

Few homes in Cottonwood were as squalid as this, of the ones I'd made house calls to. Vidal made a good wage as a mechanic, so it couldn't be poverty. It had to be because neither of them cared about the way they lived.

Two muddy mongrel dogs slept on the sagging sofa. The chintzy fake Oriental rug hadn't been swept for a month. Well-chewed bones, even a corncob or two, were scattered on the floor, along with baby rattles and seeds from the parakeets' cage by the window. The cheap old TV was blaring loudly. A bundle of greasy mechanic's overalls and dirty diapers lay on one of the armchairs.

Vidal's wife had decorated the walls by cutting a lot of color pictures out of magazines and pasting them up. It was a mural celebrating a consumers' Garden of Eden: wild animals, movie actresses, glimmering glasses of jello, flowers, bombs bursting, American Beauty roses.

Through the doorway, I could see into the kitchen. Dirty dishes, glasses, cups, cereal and cracker boxes stood on the table, and one of the wooden chairs was tipped over on the floor.

Vidal turned down the TV a little.

"This ain't the Ritz, is it?" he said. "Sit down, Father. Just kick those mutts off the couch. Now, I've got whiskey and wine."

"Whiskey," I said.

Vidal unearthed a bottle of Jack Daniel's from a cabinet by the sofa, and a couple of tumblers that were pretty clean. He poured us two shots.

"Cheers," he said, and poured his down his throat.

Just then Vidal's wife came wandering out of the kitchen. She was carrying a baby over one arm, and a ratty beaded handbag over the other, as if she was going out. She was wearing absolutely nothing but an old peach-colored taffeta slip. It was too big for her, except where her swollen breasts and slumped stomach stretched it tight. Her nipples had to be oozing milk, because there were two dark stains over them. Her rumpled ash-blonde hair was pinned back from her face with about twenty bobby pins.

She must have been around nineteen years old, but the early sag in her body made her look much older. To judge from the vacant look in her gray eyes, Father Vance had not been cruel, just truthful, when he said she was an idiot. If I had been the kind of priest who was freaked out by the sight of raw womanhood, she might have made me faint.

Vidal took one look at her and groaned.

"Just an hour ago, I had her all cleaned up," he said.

Gently he propelled her into the bedroom. "Father, would you help me with her?"

The bedroom was as sad as the rest of the house. The "bed" was an old double box spring and mattress right on the bare floor. It was unmade, with cheap flowered sheets. A huge old veneered dresser disgorged tag ends of clothes. On the floor in one corner lay a squashed sanitary napkin stained with fresh blood.

On three of the bedroom walls were more magazine cutouts. On the fourth wall, over the bed, a huge poster was tacked up.

It was one of those posters that head shops will make up for you from a snapshot. On it, a young Indian was performing in full dance regalia. As a blurred frozen crowd watched in the background, he was frozen in the middle of a bend and a twine, his moccasined feet stamping up a little white dust. He was wearing an eagle-feather bonnet, a red satin shirt, a beaded vest, a beaded loincloth, and some kind of feather bustle strapped over his buttocks. Around his bare brown legs were wound strings of bells.

Vidal was busy dressing his wife. He was pulling a drip-dry blouse up over her arms.

"Now Patti Ann," he said musically, "we've got company. So it's very important to keep your clothes on. Do you hear me, Patti Ann?" She kept trying to pick the baby up, and he kept prying the baby away from her, so that he could button the blouse. "Father, grab that hairbrush over there and take a few cracks at her hair."

I did as he asked. It was the first time in my life I ever brushed a woman's hair. If only Father Vance could see this.

The baby was a plump, smiling little thing, very re-laxed about what was going on. His diaper was coming off, so I fixed it while Vidal pulled a skirt up over his wife's legs. Up close, Patti Ann had a rank unwashed female smell that almost made me gag.

"Who's the poster?" I said, trying to make conversation.

"That's me," he said. "I had it made up from an old snapshot my dad took. I was about nineteen then. I was a fancy dancer."

"What's a fancy dancer?"

"Oh, it's a dance the Indians do. You know—when they have tribal get-togethers, or when they perform at rodeos. There's the war dance, the fancy dance, the eagle dance . . . That's about the only Indian kind of thing I ever did. That and playing Hand. Hell, I can't even ride a horse. I used to fall off my horse sometimes in the parades. But I was a good dancer. It didn't make me feel like an Indian. But it made me feel free. Real free . . ."

"You don't dance anymore?"

"No. But you know, I can still think about it and get that old feeling. Like for instance, sometimes when I dream, I'm fancy dancing in slow motion, and I feel happy as shit. I wake up and the feeling of that dream stays with me all morning, even when I'm under a car at the garage . . ."

Vidal finished buttoning Patti Ann's skirt. He patted her gently on the cheek.

"Okay, honey, you're all set now," he said. "You go on out to the kitchen and start cooking those tamales."

She put the baby back over her arm, and the beaded bag over the other arm, and shuffled out like a sleepwalker.

Vidal and I sat there hunkered on the edge of the unmade bed and looked at each other. Vidal tiredly ran one hand over his face and shook his head.

"There's times," he said, "I wish the fancy-dancing is when I wake up."

"What's the trouble with her?" I said.

"Hell, I don't know," he said.

"Have you taken her to doctors?"

"I don't think there's a doctor alive can do anything for her."

"How does she manage? Does she go out of the house?"

"Not much. I go to the laundromat and the store."

"But don't you worry about the baby? Isn't she alone with him all day long? She might drop him on his head or burn him on the stove or something."

"I know. Sometimes I've thought of putting him up for adoption. I'm not up to raising a kid myself. But you'd be surprised. She's pretty careful with him."

I was amazed. "You'd put your own son up for adoption?"

Vidal sat there staring at the magazine cutouts on the wall.

"Father, I've told you a few lies," he said.

"I know," I said.

"Everybody in town thinks she's my wife. Well, she's not. And the kid's not mine either."

This jolted me. I hadn't thought this was one of the lies.

"Ran into her when I went to Los Angeles to see my sister. She was living down the street with a bunch of other kids. Never did get the story straight, whether she walked away from some institution and got taken advantage of, or whether she dropped a ton of acid and went loco. Anyway, she latched on to me for some reason. Wasn't going to stay in L.A., got awful homesick, and the Montana prison people were finding me a job. So I brought her up here with me."

He was still gazing at the poster.

"Man, did I have a good time in L.A., though. What a craaazy place that is. I couldn't believe some of the things they . . . But I'm a small-town guy. And I thought Patti Ann would be a real good . . . what the hell do they call it in the spy movies . . . a real good cover. She doesn't know what's going on, and she doesn't ask questions. So I take real good care of her. You understand, Father?"

"Cover?" I said. "For what?"

"To keep the rednecks in town off me," he said.

"But why?" I said.

"So they won't get any funny ideas about me."

"You've already got quite a reputation as a wild man."

"I'm not talking about that," said Vidal violently. "Boy, are you thick, Father."

"I'm sorry," I said, "but I still don't know what you're talking about."

"That's another lie I told you," he said. "I didn't come to see you because I'm a bum. I came to see you because I'm the biggest queer in the state of Montana."

When he said those words, the smells and sights of that awful little bedroom rushed in on me like an implosion. I felt panicked, for no reason that I could think of. Probably it was because, in my single year-plus of counseling, I had never run into this problem yet. Cottonwood had officially presented to me just about every facet of human behavior but that.

I tried frantically to think through what the Church's teachings on homosexuality were. But I knew very little in depth about either the teachings or the condition.

"Well," I said numbly, "I guess the first question is, Do you want to change?"

"There was the time I did. But now I like the way I am."

"But do you *want* to want to change?"

"No."

"Then I don't see what I can do for you," I said.

"You can talk to me," he said. "There's a lot I want to know about the Church's attitudes. Let's leave it for next Monday, okay? Patti Ann should have those tamales about ready."

As we sat down at the kitchen table, I was a little dazed, partly by the shock of what he'd told me, partly by whiskey, partly because of the surreal impact the house had had on me.

Patti Ann had managed to clear the table off and set out four paper plates and a handful of cheap stainless ware. Who the fourth plate was for was anybody's guess. While she dreamily poured some steaming canned creamed corn onto the plates, Vidal fished a bunch of frozen supermarket tamales from a pot of boiling water.

We ate in silence, rolling the steaming tamales out of their paper wrappings and their corn shucks. If only Father Vance could see this, I kept thinking, he'd never let me set foot off the premises of St. Mary's for as long as he lives.

"You're shocked, aren't you?" Vidal suddenly asked. "And you told me you weren't going to be shocked."

"Not exactly." After a minute I added, "I'll be honest with you. It's something I'm pretty green at. I haven't counseled a homosexual before."

"Look," said Vidal, "call me gay. Don't use that awful word homosexual. It's so goddam clinical."

"But you called yourself a queer."

"Oh, hell, *I* can do that."

"Gay," I said. "What a funny word for something so . . ." I caught myself before I said the word *sad.* At this stage, it was probably better not to insult him.

But Vidal had read my mind with uncanny precision.

"You think it's sad? I guess I have to educate you." Suddenly there was fire in his eyes. "You explain to me the Church's attitudes and I'll explain to you about faggots. That's another good word, Father. Do you know why they call us faggots? It means the firewood they used to pile up around us, when they burned us at the stake back in the Middle Ages."

———

By the time supper was over, Vidal was pretty drunk. It was nearly nine anyway, so I told him I had to get back to St. Mary's.

He walked me out to my car. The rain had stopped. The town was very still—we could hear the rushing of the river, the sound of a TV from a nearby house, a car honking over on Main Street.

"So you don't want me to come next Monday," he said.

"Did I say that?"

"You're scared of me."

"Did I say that? Or is that what *you're* scared of?"

He reeled a little, leaning against my car. "Oh . . . I'm not scared to be me. But I'd be scared to be open around this town. Let's face it, Cottonwood is ready for McDonald's, but it ain't ready for gay liberation yet. Cruising around L.A. is different, nobody remembers your name, you're just one of a million humpy numbers. But around here . . ."

"Well, people won't hear about it from me," I said. "I'll

see you Monday at seven-thirty. And try to get there sober."

To show I wasn't repelled by him, I slapped him gently on the arm. His skin was hot, as if he had a fever from anxiety.

He grinned and punched me back on the shoulder.

"Sober as a judge, Father," he said.

I drove back to the rectory with my head reeling. The smells and the images of that house haunted me. The smell of dirty diapers and old bones and menstrual blood, and a half-breed fancy-dancer jailbird who talked of the cruelties of the Middle Ages.

The rectory seemed eerily normal after Vidal's house. Mrs. Bircher was rattling dishes in the kitchen. The air smelled of vanilla, lemon detergent and Father Vance's cigarette smoke.

Father Vance was in his office. The room was not luxurious, but it was big and comfortable, with leather chairs and filing cabinets and framed prints of Raphael madonnas on the walls. He peered at me over his bifocals.

"Well?" he said.

I tried to look as though the evening had been as dull and predictable as a low mass.

"It broke the ice, and I'm pretty hopeful. I'd like to get him to go back to school too. Once he gets himself straightened out, it'll be the logical thing for him."

"So far so good," said Father Vance. "Off to bed with you now."

In the dark of my bedroom, I lay on my hard single bed in my blue pajamas, arms behind my head, and stared up at the ceiling. The whiskey was wearing off, and I couldn't sleep. Outside the open window, the breeze rustled in the dripping lilac leaves.

My bedroom was another afterthought—it was next to the kitchen, and had once been a live-in room. Mrs. Bircher's home was three blocks away, so she didn't need it. The old potbellied stove still stood by the wall, and the floor was covered with worn ancient red linoleum. I had covered it with some rag rugs to take away its chill.

There was a small closet for my clothes and books, a table and chair for reading, a wastebasket, and a little portable Sony color TV my folks had given me. On the wall there was a crucifix, and a framed reproduction of Van Eyck's St. Cecilia playing the organ, which my mother had given me. On the other side of the narrow bed, the old lace curtains moved gently at the window.

The image of Vidal returned to haunt me in that room, with more force than ever before. I began to feel it not just in my mind, but in my bones. He was defending himself from the faith that I represented with the following weapons: an imbecile wife, a baby not his, a motorcycle, a whiskey bottle, and a poster of a fancy dancer. And he said he was happy.

My job as a priest would be to convince him that he was unhappy. Did I have the right to do that? I was hungry to see him again. But our friendship would have to seem as respectable as possible to my pastor.

Sleep was impossible, so I finally reached out and turned on the little TV and watched the "Late Late Show" for a while. The volume had to stay down, or Father Vance would complain. The movie was *Paths of Glory* with Kirk Douglas. But even the carnage in the trenches didn't seem too real to me.

One of the best-kept secrets of the Catholic priesthood is the number of priests who watch the late movie when they've got something on their mind.

5

When Vidal came for counseling the next Monday, I still hadn't heard from Meg about whether she'd go to the home in Helena, and I was a little worried.

Vidal had the flu. I was impressed by the stubbornness and sincerity that impelled him out of bed and up to St. Mary's. He sat hunched with aches and chills in the schoolroom chair.

"You must really have a lot on your mind," I said, fishing a bottle of aspirin out of my desk drawer.

"I do," he said. His eyes were dull with fever.

Going back to the kitchen, I got a glass of water for him.

He tried to kid me. "Will you play the organ at my funeral, Father?"

"Get out of here and go home to bed," I told him. "Call me when you're better and we'll make another appointment."

It was just as well he went, because the materials hadn't come yet that Father Matt was sending me in the mail. The very next morning after that strange evening at Vidal's house, I had called him frantically in Helena with my SOS. To deal with Vidal, I felt I had to know a lot more.

"Homosexuals are the toughest cases," Father Matt had said over the phone. "You've got to have a heap of patience and compassion to bring them around. And firmness. You have to be firm with them. But don't expect results overnight. Frankly, just between you and me, the success rate is pretty low. The only ones I've had luck with were priests who could be motivated to protect their ministry."

"Priests?" I had said.

"Good Lord, Tom, are you that naïve? We have priests who drink and chase women and even a few who use dope. Why shouldn't we have priests who are homosexuals?"

"I just never thought about it," I said.

"Well, I have a couple of things here that I can put in the mail to you. Then the next time you come to Helena, we can talk about it in detail. Oh, and Tom?"

"Yes, Father?"

"Pray for him. Pray hard."

On Tuesday morning, when I dropped by the post office, the packet from Father Matt was waiting in the St. Mary's box. Over lunch, I managed to read some of what Father Matt sent.

One booklet was "Principles to Guide Confessors in Questions of Homosexuality," and it was put out by the National Conference of Catholic Bishops. It summed up the Church's position very neatly and, as Father Matt would have said, very firmly. Since the genital relationship of two homosexuals cannot attain to procreation, and since the natural expression of love is between a man and a woman, these homosexuals have *ipso facto* committed a grave sin against nature and against God's law. The Catholic homosexual who persists in his or her sin may not receive the Sacraments.

The booklet went on to marshal all the Old Testament objections to homosexuality, as well as those in the writings of Paul. It said that lasting homosexual loves were rare. It finished up by recommending the proper pastoral approaches to helping homosexuals change, especially those who were married, or those who were in religious orders and the priesthood. Homosexuals who couldn't be interested in heterosexual relationships would just have to give up sex.

It was written in much the same stern, crisp language as similar official publications on divorce and abortion. If it had had a sound track, you would have heard the bishops' hands briskly dusting themselves of the problem.

I sat there drinking my coffee and feeling vaguely dissatisfied. The materials hadn't told me anything that I didn't already know (which wasn't much).

That same morning, Meg's parents had learned that their daughter had run away from home and they were turning the town upside down. Meg's hard-boiled little girl friends refused to tell the police anything except that Meg had been to see me. That afternoon Police Chief John Winter came to call at the rectory, and it wasn't to have coffee.

"Yes, Meg did come to see me Monday evening," I told Winter. "She wanted to go to confession."

"Did she say anything that would give us a clue why she ran away?"

"I'm sorry," I said, "everything she discussed with me falls under the seal of the confessional."

Little Meg had been pretty shrewd. She had known that she was sealing my lips. Like Vidal, she was an expert on covers.

"You can't possibly . . . I mean, her parents are going wild," said Winter. He was too good a Catholic to press me any harder than that.

"Well, before she confessed, she did say that she knows someone in Seattle. No address or anything. Just —Seattle."

"You should have spoken to her parents about it," said Winter.

"I couldn't, for the same reason I can't discuss it with you," I said.

John Winter left to telephone the Seattle police to put out an APB on Meg.

Father Vance eyed me. "Good boy," he said. "You've got more backbone than I thought."

But that afternoon we heard from Meg's parents. They marched up to the rectory and jangled the bell. When I came back from a hospital call, they were settled in Father Vance's office ready for a good long fight.

Mrs. Shoup did most of the talking, while her big good-looking husband with the tweed jacket and the salt-and-pepper crew cut just sat smoking his pipe. I now saw another side of Mrs. Shoup: a very emotional and primeval mother who, in the most sincere and misguided way, would have walked through the flames of one of her own auto-da-fe's for her child.

"Father Meeker," she said, "how did you dare not to inform us immediately that our little girl was in trouble?"

"I'm sorry," I said, "but I can only tell you what I told Chief Winter. Anything she told me during confession is confidential."

"If anything happens to her, we will hold you responsible," Mrs. Shoup said.

"I didn't think she was in any immediate danger," I said. "She didn't talk about running away. She was supposed to come back and talk to me this week."

"Surely you can tell us something! Was it drugs? Was

84

it . . ." There was one part of her mind, less fanatical, that was willing to admit the possibility. ". . . Was she unhappy at home?"

"If the police find her, she can tell you if she wants to."

"Mrs. Shoup," drawled my pastor, "I have to remind you that my curate is strictly within his rights and his sacred obligation to uphold the seal of the confessional."

"Sacred obligations!" yelled Mrs. Shoup. "A child's life is in danger, and you talk to her mother about your sacred obligations. I have a notion to have you both prosecuted for withholding information from the police. Especially priests like you who say nothing about the immoral books in our school."

Father Vance lifted his eyebrows. "St. Mary's does not have an imprimatur on what books can be put in the library, or sold in the Safeway . . ."

Mrs. Shoup turned to me, her eyes blazing. For the first time in my life, I looked into the kind of eyes that must have lighted the faggots in the Middle Ages.

"Father Meeker," she said, "you are one of the frivolous young priests that our seminaries turn out nowadays. You have no sense of what's right and what's human. I intend to expose you if it's the last thing I ever do in this town."

She stormed out, and her pipe-smoking husband strolled absently out after her.

Father Vance looked at me and lifted his brows again. At that moment, I came close to a feeling of affection for the old man.

"With laymen like that," he said, "who the hell needs the Holy Office?"

But the incident troubled me. I now had a deadly enemy in the town—one who made the school system, the newspaper, even the police cringe.

On Wednesday evening, Vidal called me up.

"I'm okay now," he said. "When can I come see you?"

Checking my appointment book, I found it booked up solid through the weekend.

"Tell you what," said Vidal. "Why don't you have breakfast with me tomorrow morning? I always eat at Trina's about eight-thirty."

Trina's Café was on the bar side of Main Street, about five doors north of the movie theater. Behind the silver-and-red name TRINA'S painted on the dusty window stood a rubber plant so big that Adam and Eve must have shoplifted it out of the garden of Eden. Inside, in the pink glare of the fluorescent lights, at the big formica tables, all sorts of people got a big breakfast under their belts.

Having breakfast with someone in Cottonwood is as solemn a rite as having lunch or dinner in the big cities. The only difference is, no liquor is served. Ranchers and farmers, especially, have learned that it is the one time of day when they might be around town. Over the ham and eggs, real estate deals are closed, cattle bought and sold, horses discussed, sheepshearers contracted, ranch hands hired, farm machinery ordered. When the wheeling and dealing is done and the second cup of coffee is poured, everybody settles back for a discussion of the terrible state of the world.

When I walked into Trina's the next morning, Vidal was already there.

He was already having a cup of coffee, and pushed out a chair for me with his foot. He looked at my trousers and turtleneck sweater.

"What?" he said. "No skirt during the day?"

Vidal ate there every morning, so the waitress didn't have to ask him what he wanted. She brought him a platter of bacon and frijoles and eggs over light and extra toast.

"I'll have the same," I told her, "only with fried eggs and hold the frijoles."

After first looking casually over my shoulder to make sure no one was close enough to read the title, I pushed the little yellow booklet across the table to Vidal. The nearest men were three tables away, and they were talking in loud voices about the fifty-mile Helena–Cottonwood endurance race for horses that was going to be a feature of the Cottonwood rodeo and fair this September

"Did you ever see this?" I asked.

After a deliberate pause, Vidal also raised his eyes to make the same sort of paranoid reconnaissance around the café. Then he settled back in his corner and looked at it.

"I never read any theology and stuff," he said. "All I know was how I was made to feel. When I was thirteen or fourteen, I tried to talk about it to a priest that I really liked and trusted. But he screamed and yelled and abused me so much that he scared me off. I really felt betrayed."

He read the booklet right through, while his eggs got cold on the platter. The waitress brought my order, and I started eating. Now and then Vidal made a wry face, or gave a soft snort. One of the ranchers at the nearby table, a big man in a tan hat, went over to the jukebox. After pondering a little, he put in a quarter. The jukebox lit up, and Patti Page started to sing "The Tennessee Waltz."

Vidal finished the booklet.

"This thing blows my mind," he said.

"Well, if you want me to help you, this is what I'm supposed to tell you."

"You don't sound like you're much convinced," he said. "Hell, Father, how could you be? If you really believe that stuff you told me the other night about a person's conscience, then you have to throw this thing right out the window."

We were being careful to talk in low voices and not to use red-flag-type words that people at other tables might hear. I was intrigued to see how quickly I had picked up his paranoia.

"What statements stopped you dead?" I asked.

Vidal pushed aside his platter. He hadn't touched his breakfast. As he flipped back through the booklet, he looked so endearingly owlish that I could imagine what he must have looked like poring over education textbooks at Montana U.

"Well, for instance, this here about 'lasting and fulfilling relationships are not found very often.' And that's very true. They're not. But the reason is that the straight world puts all kinds of pressure on you, to break your relationship up. Man, I wish I could find a steady lover. I've never had one, and I've given up looking."

"Do you know any happy . . . lovers?"

"I know a couple just sixty miles from here. But I've never been that lucky. Then this bullshit here about prisons. 'Prisoners who frequently submit to homosexual acts under terror are not entirely inculpable.' The guy that wrote that was never in jail."

"How did you manage in jail?"

"I managed okay. It was either that or be a fish."

"Fish?" I said.

"Gang rape," he said. "Actually, people have made sex in prison seem very negative. It isn't *all* bad . . ."

I couldn't resist looking around a little. But the men at the next table were now talking about how poachers had killed off nearly all the pronghorn antelope in Cottonwood County.

"Why, I used to have two, three dozen of them on the Myers Place up there," said the man in the tan hat. "And then when I went up there this spring, there wasn't but two or three of them, and one fawn. Even the old buck wasn't around anymore . . ."

Vidal was still flipping through the booklet.

"And this stuff from the Bible. My dad and the priest both threw that at me when I was a teen-ager. When I was in college, I sat down with the goddam Bible, and I read all those passages. And I noticed that Jesus didn't say a thing about what we're talking about. And I noticed that the Jews hated it because all their enemies did it. Also, they had to have babies and survive. That's just politics, Father, it has nothing to do with divine truth."

The waitresses were still bustling around. But the ranch people were thinning out, and more town people were coming in. You could tell them by their clothes and shoes and their pale faces. The jukebox was now playing "She Wore a Yellow Ribbon."

Vidal pushed the booklet back to me, cover down.

"What I'm saying is, I read this crap, and I can't fit it into the reality that I know," he said.

Father Matt hadn't been kidding me. This was going to be a tough one.

"So you've known about yourself for a long time," I said.

"Ever since I was ten or eleven." Vidal finally started to cut up his cold gluey eggs. "There's a moment that you know you are, and you know you always have been. You maybe don't know how you got that way, and maybe it's not important. But you know you are, and you know that it's real, and you know you can't change it."

"How do you feel about women?"

"I don't have anything against them. I'm just a lot more comfortable with men. It's more than sex. It's the whole thing, companionship, emotionally, spiritually. I balled a few girls when I was a kid, but it wasn't what it was cracked up to be."

"How about Patti Ann?"

"Are you kidding? I might as well fuck a corpse."

One of the ranchers near us said, ". . . I'm not against poaching if you're hard up and hungry, but some of these guys, they do it just so they can show off. They think they're real big men . . ."

Vidal got up and fished a quarter out of his pocket.

Muttering something about goddam golden oldies, he went over to the jukebox, put in the quarter and punched some buttons. Then he came back.

A waitress came bustling by and poured us second cups of strong black cow-country coffee.

"Do you feel guilty about the way you are?" I asked him.

"I used to. I went through an awful thing there, for a while. And you know where I finally got my peace of mind?"

"Where?"

"In jail, of all places. It dawned on me that a lot of the others were doing it just because they were horny. But the rest of us, *we* were doing it because we liked it."

The jukebox started to play Vidal's song. It was the Beatles singing "Rocky Raccoon." There isn't any heavy-metal rock on the jukeboxes in Cottonwood.

"So you're happy," I said.

"I'll bet I'm the only con ever came out of Deer Lodge singing like a lark. One little problem, and that was a job, but they found me one."

I finished my coffee and leaned back, and grinned at him. "It's going to be *my* job to make you unhappy. Real unhappy."

"Oh, it is?" He grinned. "You gonna do an Inquisition thing?"

I shook my head, serious now. "I want to give you what your conscience wants. Is that fair?"

"That's fair," said Vidal.

"If your conscience tells you to change, I'll try to help you. If your conscience just tells you to try to know the Church's teachings better, I'll help you."

Vidal was nodding. "That's real fair."

"Even if I tried to take a hard line, and threaten you with eternal hellfire, I'd run up against your conscience anyway," I said. "And so would the guys who wrote that little book."

90

Vidal was now smiling, wistfully.

"Father, I sure wish I'd met you ten years ago. You could have saved me a lot of grief."

The ranchers near us were now on their fourth cup of coffee, and they'd circled back to the big endurance horse race.

"Gonna be some local horses in that race too," said one. "Vern Stuart has been out working his Bobcat. That'll be a horse to beat. And a couple guys over at Drummond have got a stud horse . . ."

Vidal grinned. "You know, I know those guys at Drummond. I fixed their horse trailer one time when they came through here and broke down. I'll take you over there some time and you can meet them. That horse of theirs is really something."

I looked at my watch.

"God," I said, "I'm almost late for my adult-education class." We signaled the waitress frantically for the check.

Trina came out of the kitchen, and threw an eye around the place to see if everything was okay. She came sauntering along the row of tables. She was a tiny Chicana with her black-lacquer-hair up in a bun. She wore a red silk dress at eight in the morning, and little gold-bead earrings in her pierced ears.

She stopped at our table. "'Allo, Vidal, you gorgeous bike man, you." She winked her long fake eyelashes at him kiddingly. "When you take me out on your bike, eh?"

Vidal grinned at her. "I'll have to ask my wife's permission."

She pretended to pout. She looked at his plate, where the eggs and frijoles were half-eaten. "Watsa matter, Vidal, you no like them today? They no okay?"

"I had the flu, Trina. Guess my appetite didn't come back yet."

Trina was now looking at me, winking, one hand on her hip. "'Ey, *padre*, you gonna make a monk out of this gorgeous *hombre*?"

Trina loved to tease me because she knew I dug Chicanos.

"He's so fond of his wife that he's already a monk," I said.

We all howled. Even laughter could be a lie.

We paid and walked out onto the street. The stores were opening. On the theater marquee, a kid was putting up the black letters for THE GODFATHER II.

"Well, see you tomorrow," said Vidal.

"Tomorrow?" I said.

"I eat here every morning," he said softly. "Any reason why you can't? It's easier to talk here than at your office."

"Well . . ." I said.

He stood there, his leather jacket on now, hands shoved in pockets. In his eyes there was something like an appeal. He must be as lonely as me for someone young and relaxed to talk to. Or far lonelier, maybe. I was the only person in town who knew what was real for him. When he was with me, he could drop what I already recognized as the mask that gay people wore when they were out in the heterosexual world.

I wondered if he had a lover in Cottonwood. He hadn't mentioned one.

". . . No," I said. "No reason I can't."

As Vidal walked away up the street toward Snow's Garage, the letters ME glinted on the back of his jacket. Now I knew what they meant. It was as open a statement as he felt he could make in Cottonwood about his private reality.

6

Meeting at Trina's for breakfast was how Vidal Stump and I became friends.

The prayer mood of the seven-thirty low mass, and that half hour of looking God in the eye, had always been hard to protect from the exhaustions and distractions of parish work. But now this got a little harder, because at the end of the half hour was the sight of Vidal's face through the dusty café window and the leaves of the rubber tree.

Sometimes, during that half hour, voices came back to me from the seminary. "Beware of friendships that distract you from the love of God." "The priest's loneliness exists to be filled with the love of God." "You have no friends for the same reason that you have no wife and children." "You belong to no one, so that you can belong to everyone."

Sometimes those eerie voices, coming to me as if down some long hallway, filled me with a feeling of subdued panic.

But when I walked into Trina's, and the smell of frijoles and frying ham hit me in the face, I was happy.

Safe and private amid the public clatter of plates and

93

cups, and the boom of the jukebox, and the raucous laughter of cowmen telling rowdy stories on each other, we sat at a table along the wall in the back, and we talked.

Sometimes I did worry about Mrs. Shoup. Surely she wouldn't go so far as to have me watched or bugged. Vidal wasn't too worried, though. We did change tables every day. Anyone who'd had human territoriality in mind would have thought this strange.

My lies to Father Vance stayed Jesuitical white lies: Vidal and I did talk about the Church's teachings at breakfast. He grumbled about what an Injun scallywag Vidal was. But, hoping that the scallywag's soul would be saved, he didn't object.

Sometime during our second breakfast, Vidal stopped calling me "father." He didn't ask my permission to change, and I didn't protest, when he called me "Tom."

He was by far the most delightful human being that I had ever known.

First of all, he had the wry Indian sense of humor. He could have me half hysterical with laughter on the other side of the table. I hadn't laughed so much since I was in grade school and my elderly eighth-grade teacher's petticoat fell off one day when she was marching around in front of the blackboard.

When he told a story, he had a talent for turning into everyone in it. If it was a story about some famous bronc up on the Blackfoot, his face got long and equine. If it was about some effeminate type gay that he'd met in a bar in L.A., his eyes flashed and his voice rose an octave and his shoulders moved suggestively, and I could visualize a real "queen" without ever having seen one. But I always had the feeling that his talent for mimicry had something to do with eat or be eaten, like the tan of the antelope that matches the tan of the dry hills around Cottonwood.

In front of everyone else, he put on a face of tough straight guy. Around the garage, when I went there to buy gas or get my car fixed, he was Clint Eastwood in greasy coveralls, squinting, silent, mysterious, somber. But in Trina's every morning, he shed much of this, and let me see his anxieties, and his fantasy, and the little peace of mind he had.

I learned that his violence didn't come naturally to him. It wasn't just a directionless Indian-reservation kind of violence. It was also his frustration at having settled his sexual orientation but not his existential problems. I could imagine how he would look some day, all calmed down, in a classroom somewhere, wearing a cheap business suit, teaching history to eighth-graders and making them crack up with laughter.

One morning I asked him: "Don't you ever leave town and kick up your heels? I mean . . . aren't there any other gay people in this part of the world?"

He smiled a little.

"There are six gay bars in Montana," he said, "and all of them are at least eighty miles from here, and if it was a couple years ago, I'd be crazy enough to drive there. There's a few gay people over in Missoula, and a bath in Great Falls, and there's even a gay dude ranch up at Ronan. But I'm sick of that whole scene. Sick of tricking, sick of games, sick of catting around. I don't even like straight bars anymore. I'm kind of on a high lonesome for a while."

"You must be living as celibate as I am," I kidded him.

"Yeah," he drawled, "except I can masturbate and you can't."

In the next couple of weeks, I got to care for him more than for any friend I'd ever had—even Doric Wilton. The feeling for him went so wide and so deep that sometimes I wondered if I felt the same way about my parents.

The fact was, I'd never felt that way about anyone in my life. I'd always been so turned on to people in general that I never got turned on to anyone in particular.

That last week in June, the Seattle police finally located Meg Shoup. She turned up at a shelter for street kids, and one of the personnel there recognized her from the bulletin. She was broke, and hadn't found her boyfriend, and she was scared to death.

Her parents were so glad to have her back that they gave her less hell than they might have. Quietly they packed her off to the home in Helena without anyone knowing about her (read: their) disgrace. They told people that they'd sent her to camp for the summer. The police search for the boyfriend went on, and Mrs. Shoup swore with the wrath of a passionate mother that she would have him prosecuted for statutory rape to the full extent of the law.

Most of her wrath, however, fell on me.

"If I didn't already know the name of the father," she thundered, "I would suspect you, Father Meeker. We all know what these young priests are like nowadays."

Luckily, she said these things to me right in front of Father Vance, and lost a little more credibility with him. Father took it that she was accusing him of sheltering a Good-time Charlie in his rectory.

"That woman is a maniac," he told me when she'd left. "I've tried to talk to her about some of her doings, and she even says *I'm* a modernist. You be real careful now. Don't let her catch you in some kind of scallywag silly stuff."

"I wouldn't put it past her to make up something," I said.

In Cottonwood, people noticed idly that the curate of St. Mary's and the half-blood ex-con mechanic were spending some time together.

Mrs. Shoup, who seemed to have ears as sensitive as a radar telescope, heard about it. She complained to Father Vance that his curate was engaging in a most unsuitable friendship. Father Vance told her bluntly that he didn't see anything wrong with our acquaintanceship, especially since I'd had such an edifying effect on Vidal. He'd already made his stand with me, that first day, and he had to stick with it now.

One day John Winter stopped me on the street and said, "Say, Father, can I have a word with you about Vidal Stump?"

"Sure," I said, half-panicked. I wondered if Winter had found out what was behind Vidal's cover marriage.

But Winter had the nice mild look on his wide face that he saved for social pleasantries.

"You're doing wonders with Vidal. He's a changed man."

"Oh?" I said, trying not to show that I was limp with relief.

"Darn right," he said. "The guys at the garage say he's a lot more friendly and relaxed. They kinda kid him about how he's got religion. But they respect him too, so they don't carry it too far."

"I didn't know that," I said. "Nice to hear it."

"Best of all, Father, the guy hasn't been in a fight for weeks now. Matter of fact, people say they don't see him around the bars much anymore. The back-room poker game at Brown's has plumb fallen apart. It's mighty good of you to take him under your wing. I really believe in rehabilitation, and I've always thought Vidal had a lot on the ball."

I grinned, and got right into the spirit of the conversation.

"Just between you and me, he's going to waste fooling around with those souped-up drag cars of yours."

"Oh, izzat so?" said Winter, grinning right back.

"That's so," I said. "When I get done with him, he's going to be back in school."

"Does he know that?" laughed Winter.

"You bet he does," I said. "I've threatened him with it."

"That's real nice of you to let him in on your plans for him," said Winter.

"Well, God and I thought it was only fair," I said.

Winter had to crack up laughing then, and he leaned back against the fender of his squad car, pounding on his thigh right below his pistol holster.

"Seriously, Father, so many of these young guys go right back to prison in six months. Vidal's made it through his parole, and even now he's got nothing more than a little drunk and disorderly. He might make it all the way."

"Let's keep our fingers crossed," I said.

"You know, Father, you're quite a hand with guys that have got themselves in trouble. Maybe we could work up some kind of program. I can think of a few kids in town, delinquents, that I'd sure like to see you do that kind of magic on. Maybe we could get the little Meg Shoups before they happen."

"It sounds like a good idea," I said. "The trouble is, I'm half-overworked already. But why don't you talk to Father Vance about it? He has the say-so."

Winter must have dropped by the rectory that same day and had a cup of coffee with Father Vance, because the next day my pastor called me into his office. He seemed grudgingly pleased.

"I've heard some good things about you from John Winter," he said. "Of course, Vidal's not in heaven yet, so don't let up on him. And this idea of Winter's, the program for delinquents, well, you'd have to fit the program into your spare time. And as near as I can see, you don't have any. Unless you'd like to give up your trip to Helena once a month."

In the middle of the first week of July, there came the first really traumatic day of that summer.

Cottonwood had celebrated the Fourth of July with a few firecrackers, a firemen's barbecue, and a parade by the Veterans of Foreign Wars. Now the ranch people were starting the haying operations. I knew a little bit about ranching from my father—much of the bank's business was still in agricultural loans. The last week in June, the ranchers shut off the irrigation water, and by the first week of July, the fields were dry enough to cut.

Along toward noon that day, a lady called to cancel a counseling appointment. So it looked like I would have my thirty-minute lunch hour free for once. Father Vance was on call for emergencies.

So I called Vidal down at the garage. "Why don't you grab us a couple of sandwiches? It's a beautiful day—let's get out of town for a few minutes."

He came roaring up the hill on his bike, his hair blowing in the hot breeze. He was wearing his greasy coveralls and clutching a paper sack.

"Whatsa matter?" he kidded me. "You got church fever?"

"Church fever?"

"That's when a priest gets cabin fever," he said.

We laughed, and I climbed on the bike behind him, and held on to him. I was in such a hurry that I kept my cassock on. In one more minute, we were out on the flats on the east side of town. We passed Fulton's Greenhouse. Then we were sweeping up the long slope of Powderhouse Hill. The road was bounded by two barbed-wire fences and one power line, and an eternity of dry hills and ravines on either side.

We went howling and popping up past the old powderhouse, where they had stored ammo for the cavalry detachment garrisoned in Cottonwood until 1902. Then we passed the abandoned brickworks, which had made all the brick for Cottonwood's early buildings, including St. Mary's. The earthquake had hit it hard, and the kilns and the stack had caved in.

At the top of the hill, we hit another flat, or "bench," that lay along the east side of the valley above the river floor. Up here there were thousands of acres of wild hay, dry-land wheat and native pasture. Here and there you could see hundreds of scattered dots in a pasture—cattle —and the toy buildings of some far-off ranch. I knew the griefs of many of those ranches, for the owners were parishioners of mine.

Ten miles away, the mountains lifted from the eastern edge of the bench. Their peaks were streaked with the last of the snows, which would vanish in the hot days of July.

Wind and dust stung my eyes, and my hair blew wildly. I wrapped my arms hard around Vidal, glad to be sheltered behind him. He was taking the full blast of the wind, but I knew he loved it. He was driving the big bike flat out, at about eighty miles an hour. I could feel his hard back against my chest. It was good to be tearing off down that long road with this strong friend.

Now and then the road bent at right angles, and Vidal had to slow sharply. The land up here was laid out in neat sections. At one ninety-degree curve, we spotted three antelope standing about a hundred yards from the road. They must be some of the last left in the country. They bounced off into a nearby gully, flashing their snow-white rumps.

Suddenly Vidal slowed the bike down. Ahead was a vast hayfield—it must have been three hundred acres. Along it, near the road, stood a lonely little clump of quaking aspen trees. Vidal turned the bike off the road there, and shut it off. The entire wild trip had taken about five minutes.

The silence was deafening.

"How's this for a picnic spot?" he said.

"Yeah, and no Mrs. Shoup around," I said.

The hot sun beat delightfully through my cassock. It was amazing how fast my feeling of physical well-being could come back when I got away from St. Mary's.

I looked around. A little ditch of sparkling green water ran along the edge of the field, past the trees. The field had been mowed, and the grass lay drying in windrows. The men would come back and bale it in a day or two, if the good weather held. But right now no one was around. The air had that classic smell of drying clover, alfalfa and wild grass.

"It's not bad," I said grinning.

Vidal was looking at my cassock, laughing. I looked at it too. It was gray with dust. We both howled.

"I'll have to get into my clean one before Father Vance sees that," I said.

Feeling silly as a little kid, I ran gently off across the field, jumping over the windrows. Vidal chased after me. We started playing tag. As we tried to dodge each other, our shoes would slip on the stubble, and one of us would fall flat. In no time, the curate of St. Mary's was not only dustier, but stuck with bits of dry grass.

We wound up having a wrestling match on the ground, gasping and laughing our heads off. Since we were pretty evenly matched, neither of us could keep the other one down. Finally we gave up and just lay there, tangled together, Vidal half on top of me. Our arms were around each other, and we were panting.

The July sun poured down on us from a cloudless sky. His whole body seemed to pulsate against mine. Even his thigh, which lay heavily across my legs, moved with a deep, tidal rhythm. His head lay on my chest, and the breeze stirred his hair against my face. I could feel the sweaty heat of him through my clothes. A dizzy contentment went over me like a single gust of breeze.

But then it passed. Somewhere back in my mind were the urgencies of who I was.

"We better eat," I whispered. "I gotta get back."

Slowly we got up and brushed ourselves off.

We sat under the little aspen trees, and leaned on their gnarled green trunks. The leaves fluttered and twisted in the breeze in their typical way, making a shade that seemed to sparkle with light. We could smell the moist earth along the ditch.

Vidal's sack yielded two cans of beer, still cold, and four meat sandwiches made to go at the drugstore counter near the garage. We ate and drank, not saying much. Vidal was sitting close to me. When he finished, he stretched and yawned. Then he lay down against me again, and pillowed his head on my chest.

"Shut-eye time," he said.

I laughed a little. "Nothing doing. We have to leave in a couple of minutes."

His hair still had grass stuck in it, so I brushed it out. The waves and loose curls were hot and had a rainbow iridescence where the sunlight dappled them. When the grass was gone, I just ran my fingers through the curls gently. Vidal's eyes were closed.

"Did you hear me?" I said.

"You're doing a good job of putting me to sleep."

He slid one hand up and rubbed my arm in its black sleeve, slowly, fondly. I studied his broken black fingernails and remembered seeing those fingers clenching through the lattice of the confessional.

"Come on," I said. "Shake your ass, fancy dancer."

He raised his head until his face was opposite mine, and almost touching it. His eyes were still shut. "No," he said with soft defiance.

Just then he kissed me on the mouth, gently, almost chastely. It would almost qualify for a kiss of peace between two cardinals. For a moment, my mind went almost blank. Nothing was there but comfort and

102

brightness. I didn't turn my lips away. His hand was still rubbing my arm slowly.

Then his hand slid up to my shoulder. Without really moving, his body tensed until the tendons creaked like rope. His fingers moved over to my chest, to the buttons of the cassock.

My responsibilities rushed back into my mind.

I drew back. "What's going on here?" Out of habit, I tried to sound like I was kidding.

His eyes were open now, looking directly into mine. The pupils were very wide and black with excitement, like a cat's are before it pounces. For the first time, his eyes looked the same color.

Now I was feeling a strange and terrible panic, which I covered up by looking at my watch. "Look, I'm late," I said. "Let's go back."

Without a word, Vidal drew away, then got up. He didn't look at me. We picked up our lunch papers, got back on the bike and went back down to Cottonwood.

All the way down, I was cursing myself. I had only meant to express my friendly feelings for him, and he would interpret my innocent action in his own way. How could I have been so dumb? I held on to him less tightly now—just tight enough to stay on the bike.

He dropped me at the church and said, "See you tomorrow." He looked hurt, but also a little amused as he drove off.

At the rectory, Father Vance was waiting for me, furious. His eyes took in my dusty cassock. "Where have you been?"

I looked at my watch. We'd been gone only thirty-five minutes.

"I wasn't on duty, so I went off for lunch. I'm only five minutes late."

Father Vance had the kit with the holy oils, and looked like he'd just been leaving in a hurry. He shoved the kit at me.

"Get right up to the Malley ranch," he said. "You've got a faster car. Clem Malley just had a terrible accident with a baling machine. His wife called."

Panic-stricken at the mess I was in, I jumped in my sports car. In another five minutes, I was out on the north side of town and gunning up Interstate 10. This was certainly a day for moving fast around the county.

Six miles north, I went off the exit with a shriek of wide-track tires, and onto a long stretch of county road, and then into the barnyard of a small ranch. Clem Malley's weeping young wife was waiting in front of the frame house, and she jumped into my car.

"Out in the west hayfield, Father," she sobbed.

We jounced along a dirt road. In two more minutes, I was back in a hayfield, with the same hot sun pouring down on me. The baling machine sat still halfway along a windrow, with a half-loaded wagon hitched behind it. The ambulance and the squad car were there, red lights blinking. Clem's teen-age son and two ranch hands were standing stunned while the medical people bent over the bloody form on the ground.

Clem's body was so mangled that it no longer looked human. Even his head had been hacked nearly in half, and his eyes were falling out of their sockets. A blood-soaked packet of Bull Durham had been torn out of his shirt pocket and lay gently on an exposed lung. Baling twine was tangled around him.

I nearly gagged. No auto accident that I'd ever been called to was as hideous as this. But, recovering myself, I went through the rubric of the holy oils.

John Winter had taken Clem's wife and son aside and was questioning them gently.

"He'd been having some dizzy spells," she said. "I wanted him to go to the doctor. But he was too busy. He was only thirty-two years old . . ."

"We didn't really see what happened," said his son. "Stu and I were back on the wagon, stacking bales. I guess he must have had a spell and fallen off right in front of the conveyor. By the time we noticed, it was too late. The conveyor took him up into the cutters there . . ."

I looked at the machine. The conveyor fed the windrow up into powerful choppers that whacked the hay into lengths, then into a ram that made the bale and tied it. The whole apparatus was splashed with black sun-dried blood.

The ambulance took Clem Malley's body into town. I stayed a while with his family. Then I drove slowly back to Cottonwood, feeling dizzied and drained.

At the rectory, Father Vance was still mad as a hornet.

"You were five minutes late coming back," he said. "The soul stays in the body for fifteen or twenty minutes. The faculty of hearing is the last to go. Clem might have heard you if you'd been there to confess him sooner. Your carelessness might be the difference between his going to heaven or going to hell. Or the degree of grace he might have in heaven. Or the amount of time he'll spend in purgatory. Take your pick, young man."

I was upset enough to lose my temper.

"May I ask why you didn't take the call? You were on duty."

"I went out on a sick call. When I got back, Mrs. Bircher told me that Mrs. Malley had called five minutes earlier. I was just leaving when you came. If you'd been here . . ."

"Wait a minute," I said. "With all due respect, Father, not even the Pope knows how long the soul hangs around in the body before it takes off. Second, I was not on call. You were. Your judgment in leaving was just as bad as mine was in coming back late."

"Get out of my sight," he raged, "and don't let me see you for the rest of the day." As I left his office, he fired a parting shot at me. "You're running around just a little *too* much with that half-breed gunsel friend of yours."

I turned to offer the usual lie. "We were talking about . . ."

"Counseling, my foot," said Father Vance. "You smell of beer. I've probably lost a soul because of you."

———

Late that night, I kneeled in the dark church for a long time. The place was lit only by a few flickering votive candles, and silent as a tomb. I prayed for Clem Malley's soul.

Then I repented heartily of my error in judgment with Vidal, and expressed to God the hope that I hadn't done him any harm. Since I hadn't meant him any harm, I probably wasn't guilty of a grave sin, just a venial sin. If I ever committed a grave sin in Cottonwood, I would have to carry it around with me for a month until the next trip to Helena, or else make a special trip there. Meanwhile I would be compounding the sin by saying mass, receiving communion, absolving penitents, et cetera, while fallen from grace. Luckily my next trip was coming up next week.

All the neat theological phrases ran through my head. It had been a close call. I prayed for Vidal, and decided that maybe it would be better not to see him for a few days.

But when I'd locked the church and gone to bed in my lonely little back room, I remembered those few minutes of warmth and closeness out in the field, and a lump came into my throat.

The "Late Late Show" that night was *The Thing*.

7

On Thursday and Friday I didn't go to Trina's for breakfast. I didn't go on Saturday either. Too yellow to tell Vidal why, I simply stayed away.

Father Vance must have noticed that on Saturday morning I ate breakfast at the rectory for the third time in a row, but he didn't comment—partly because he still wasn't speaking to me. All I could think of was splitting for Helena on Sunday to see my parents. There wouldn't be much comfort in seeing Father Matt either, because I hadn't decided whether or not to tell him about my slip with Vidal.

At lunch Saturday, Father Vance said, "John Winter told me that Vidal got drunk as seven hundred dollars last night. He got in a big fight in Brown's, and he damn near wrecked the place. John had to put him in jail for the night to cool him off."

At that, I exploded again.

"Doesn't *his* soul matter, Father? I haven't seen him

since Wednesday out of respect for you, and he probably thinks I've abandoned him."

"You can't baby him along the rest of his life," said Father Vance calmly, spreading mustard on a hot dog. "Sooner or later he has to stand on his own two feet."

I was so mad that I got up and left the table.

Striding into the church, I knelt in a corner by the altar rail and put my head in my hands to think. The thing to do was to go see him. Winter would have released him in time to go to work. Or at least I should call him up at the garage.

But suddenly I realized that I was afraid to see him again. Just the sight of his face, the sound of his voice, might call up that feeling of warmth again. Worst of all, the sight of me might stir him up, and as a priest I had no right to tempt him.

Strictly speaking, I couldn't see him anymore, ever—not if I was going to be true to the things I believed in.

That night my confessions were from eight to nine, and I wasn't even in the mood to play the organ. In the state I was in, I was a little harsh with a couple of penitents, and slapped them with heavier penances than usual. The hour dragged on, and I was just thinking that there were only fifteen minutes to go, when the next voice at the lattice made my stomach jump like an antelope.

"Tom."

My whole physiology reacted violently. My heart pounded, sweat sprang out all over me, my nerves buzzed with emotional electricity.

"Vidal, I've stayed away from you for your own good . . ."

"I'm not in the mood for any of your priest bullshit tonight."

We were both whispering, when we might have been yelling at each other. Father Vance's anger was nothing compared to the almost Biblical blaze of wrath that Vidal poured through the lattice at me. After I'd heard a few sentences, I was so stunned that I didn't speak anymore.

"Don't you give me that Catholic morality bullshit, you faggot. You're as big a faggot as me, but you don't have the balls to admit it to yourself. My own good, huh? You love me, don't you? You're a Christian, you love everybody, you love God, you love people, you love the world. What the fuck do you know about love? You don't even love yourself, because if you did, you could be honest with yourself. I just dare you to get in bed with me, you holier-than-thou faggot, and I'll show you what love really is."

He delivered this boiling little sermon in such a controlled whisper that none of the penitents waiting in the pews outside would have thought anything unusual was going on in the confessional. Vidal had been smart enough to trap me in the one spot where I couldn't get away from him without making a scene. I sat there pressed into the corner of my booth, feeling as trapped as if I were being fed into the cutting knives of a baling machine.

"You're crazy," I said. "Get out of here and leave me alone."

"You know I'm not crazy. You know I'm right, don't you? All these weeks I've been playing along with you, waiting for you to wake up and realize that you were attracted to me. And the other day up there, I kissed you and you liked it, didn't you? You didn't stop me, did you? And the only reason you didn't let me go any farther was that you were scared."

"So you lied to me," I said. "You didn't want help at all. It's the oldest trick in the book. Women play it on priests all the time."

"At first I wasn't after anything. At first I thought you were probably straight, and I just wanted to be near you. I saw you walking down the street one day, and you were looking so butch and so free, with your skirt and your blond hair blowing in the breeze, and I fell for you. I went crazy thinking about you, I drank, I got in fights. But I didn't go around you because I don't go in for rough trade—"

"Rough trade?"

"That's when you throw a pass at some stud and you don't really know if he's gay, but you're willing to take a chance. I don't go for rough trade, see? But finally I got so crazy I thought I'd just try hanging around you. Do you know how gorgeous you are? If you went to Hollywood and walked down Highland Avenue in that cassock of yours, you'd have every queen in town chasing after you . . ."

"Will you shut up?"

"You shut up, or everybody in church is gonna hear us. So I got to know you, and at first I didn't have any intentions. But after a while I could see you warming up to me and I thought to myself, Holy Christ, this stud's as gay as I am, and he's coming up to that big moment. Remember I told you about that minute that comes, when you *know?* Maybe it happens when you're fourteen, and it doesn't happen to some guys till they're nineteen or twenty, and guys like you till they're twenty-five or thirty. But it comes, and when it does, you have to decide which kind of lies you like better. Even being a closet queen is less of a lie than knowing you're gay and staying straight. Don't talk to *me* about *lies* . . ."

He stopped to catch his breath. His head was leaning against the lattice, and the dark wavy hair was pressed through, just like on that first night. In his breathing I could feel the enormity of the emotion that he'd built up all through these weeks.

I sat there in a state of shock, my fingers playing idly with the fringe on my bitterroot-embroidered stole.

"And you liked it when I kissed you. Didn't you?"

110

I closed my eyes and put my hand over them. A fine trembling was going up and down my body. One time last fall I'd been driving too fast to Helena, and the highway was wet, and the Triumph spun off into a ditch. The trembling I felt at that brush with death was the same as now.

"Yes," I said, in such a low voice that he probably had to strain to hear me.

"Did you ever have any kind of sex with a guy?"

"No."

"But you must have had sex with women."

He questioned me as pitilessly as some Inquisition lawyer. All that remained was the formality of confession before being burned at the stake. Wounded into a state of shock, I answered his questions.

"I was engaged once, like you. She was a Helena girl, you wouldn't know her name. I'd really convinced myself that I was in love with her. And I felt that everybody expected it of me. Sometimes I felt real horny too, and I thought she was what made me feel that way. A couple of times I almost went the whole way with her, but somehow I just couldn't get into it. I realized that if I married her, everybody would expect me to perform. And I also thought that it was religion holding me back. Later on I looked back at it and thought it was my vocation beginning. I thought it meant that I had a vocation to be celibate . . ."

"So you must have had feelings about men."

"I had friends . . ."

Something was cutting into my head like a huge chopper.

". . . a couple of friends that I loved, maybe not what you'd call love, but it was the most feeling I ever had for any person . . ."

Something was chopping my chest open, tearing out my lungs. Surely the penitents waiting outside could see the blood pouring out of my side of the confessional from under the musty red velvet curtain.

"Tell me about them," said Vidal.

"One, in high school, Eddie Machin, he was on the football team with me and he went to the same church I did in Helena. I would have died for Eddie. And you know, one day, I put my arm across his shoulders and the parish priest saw me do it and he told me that men who do things like that, even little things, just automatically are damned. He told me it was the unforgivable sin . . ."

Voices came whipping at me out of a long dark corridor, voices like knives.

"Any more?"

"A boy in the seminary, Doric Wilton, we got to be friends . . ."

From somewhere, the tears had come up, to dribble down my cheeks, hot as blood from a cut. The mention of Doric's name brought them up. I'd trained myself not to think of Doric for such a long time that he'd almost become like something I'd read about in a book.

"Go on . . ." said Vidal.

"We never touched each other. But Father Matt could see that something was going on between us, he's no dummy. He was pretty kind about it, but he told me that he thought it was a dangerous friendship, without being specific about what he meant, and he must have talked to Doric too. Because without saying a word to each other about it, we decided to be less friendly. Doric is somewhere in Colorado now. After we were ordained, I never saw him or heard from him."

It was hard to talk in a whisper and cry at the same time.

"Any more?" asked Vidal.

"No. Except you."

We were silent for a moment.

"Listen," I said, "you'd better get the hell out of here, or people are going to start wondering."

"I'll see you at breakfast tomorrow."

"I can't. Tomorrow is Sunday. I'm going to Helena to see my folks."

Vidal thought a minute.

"All right, here's what we'll do. I'm sick of seeing you half an hour here, fifteen minutes there. Tomorrow we'll meet somewhere and talk for a couple of hours."

"I can't. I'll be with my family, and then I have to see Father Matt, and then I have to come back here."

"Then we'll meet on the road to Helena somewhere." He thought a minute. Obviously he had a lot of practice at fixing up things like this. "You know the Holiday Inn on the pass?"

"Yeah."

"I'm going to drive up there tonight and get a room. If I do it tomorrow morning it'll look funny. So I'll go home now, grab my knapsack, and go straight there, like I've been traveling all day and I'm played out. I should be there by eleven. So you be at your office phone at eleven tonight, and I'll call you and tell you what the score is."

"Vidal, we shouldn't . . ."

"No more bullshit from you. You be at that phone when I call."

"And if I'm not?"

Vidal laughed softly, and put on his queen voice:

"Then I'll sit in the Holiday Inn and I'll make a little bitty voodoo doll with a little bitty cassock on it, and I'll stick my hatpin right through it."

He got up and pushed out through the curtain. I could here his footsteps going away along the side aisle.

There were two more penitents. I hardly heard what they said, and they must have wondered at the little penances they got.

As eleven o'clock neared, I was sitting in my little office with a cup of coffee, pretending to be balancing the parish books. The total collections last Sunday were $149.50, which was very disappointing. Father Vance was still in his office, writing a couple of letters.

I was so exhausted that I could hardly keep my eyes open. My eyes wouldn't focus on the columns of figures written down the ledger pages.

If I went to the Holiday Inn and visited with Vidal for a couple of hours, it would be a classic example of putting myself in an occasion of sin. Tired as I was, I saw it with terrible clearness.

At exactly eleven o'clock, the phone on my desk rang. I stared at it, mesmerized. It rang again. All I had to do was not answer it, not see Vidal, tomorrow or ever. On the other hand, I could make sure that all we did was talk.

The phone rang again. If I let it ring too long, Father Vance would notice.

I picked it up.

"Coward," said Vidal's voice. "You were sitting right there, and you were too chicken to answer."

"Don't rub it in," I said.

"I'm in Room 203. You don't even have to go in the front. Just park in the lot and go in the side door, like you're going to your own room. There's a million people here, nobody'll notice you. Go up the side stairs there. You come right out on the corridor where my room is. It's the third door on the right. Got it?"

"I guess so."

"What time do you leave there in the morning?"

"About ten-thirty. So I should be there about eleven. You going to sleep now?"

"I think I'll go down to the bar and get a little drunk. See you tomorrow, Tom. Sweet dreams."

His voice hadn't softened at all—it still had that ironic tone in it.

"Yeah, sweet dreams yourself," I said in the same tone.

When midnight came, I was still sitting there, with cold coffee in the cup, playing with the ledgers. Outside the window, the lilac bushes whispered in the cool night breeze. I was only the fourth priest in nearly a hundred years to listen to their sweet and senseless rustling.

In my mind, I was rehearsing the virtuous conversation we'd have tomorrow morning, during which I'd convince him to just continue being friends.

The late show that night was some nineteen-thirties musical that I didn't pay much attention to. I should have been praying for my life. *Pray,* Father Matt had said.

8

The next morning, my head was spinning with exhaustion and guilt. I felt drunk.

At ten-thirty, just as I was leaving, Father Vance said, "Oh, Tom, on your way out of town, drop by and see Missy Oldenberg. She's in pretty poor shape."

This would delay me—I was furious.

Missy Oldenberg and Clare Faux lived on what had been an old dairy farm at the edge of town. The barn had fallen in, and they now sold their crocheted and knitted things to handicraft shops in that part of the state. Missy had been ailing from a gallbladder problem for some time.

Obsessed with the thought of Vidal, I spent a bare half hour with Missy and Clare. Then I roared on out of town.

This time the car radio was turned off. I drove grim and tight-lipped.

The country had changed since the last trip to Helena —the green grass had now burned into a sun-cured tan. The phlox and wild roses were gone, and the milkweed had already turned into silvery white umbels that blew apart in the hot wind. The yellow sweet clover bloomed tall and rank along the highway.

The Holiday Inn sits where the Interstate crosses over the Continental Divide, at thirteen thousand feet. Its bland modern architecture, picture windows, patch of lawn and parking lot are a curious insult to the bare grandeur of the timberline country around it. Behind it were a few patches of stunted pine, and the dizzy rock slopes of Mt. Magan.

Before the Inn, on the other side of the highway, the land falls away in a terrifying thousand-foot cliff called the Magan Wall. Below, the timbered Rockies roll away in one of the most spectacular views you could find anywhere between the Tetons and Glacier Park. From the Holiday Inn parking lot, you can see a million square miles of mountain peaks. The locals like to say that when God got done making the world, He dumped the tailings here.

As Vidal had said, the parking lot was crowded with cars, and a few people came and went. But the place was eerily quiet, and a cold wind whipped down off the bare rock faces above.

My body shivering with nervousness, I walked straight in the side door, trying to look as normal as possible, and up the stairwell. The hallway was carpeted with plush red rug, and smelled sweetish and stuffy after the alpine cleanliness outside.

I knocked softly on the door of Room 203.

After a long, awful moment, during which I thought it might be the wrong door, Vidal opened it. His face wore the same look of strain that mine must have. I went in fast and he shut the door.

Motel rooms always manage to exist outside of time, space, history and humanness. This one had plush red

118

wall-to-wall carpet, a phony Spanish bed with a caissoned headboard, a color TV, and the usual bathroom as sterile as a hospital.

On the other side of the room, the picture window gave a view up the tumbled granite slope, where a little melt stream gushed down over the moraine. The breeze would smell of old snow and nude rock and emptiness. Here we were shut away from it, hermetically sealed behind the thick plate-glass window, smothered by air conditioning that seemed to circulate the cigarette smells from other people's rooms into ours.

Vidal was strangely silent. He walked over to the window and leaned against it, looking out. He was wearing Levi's, and his feet and torso were bare. His body seemed as hard as the rocks beyond, and as twisted as the pines.

"What's the matter with you?" I said.

He turned his head a little, his face coming into profile against the moraine.

"I thought you'd stood me up."

"Father Vance stuck me with visiting an old lady on the way over."

"You could have called."

"I'm sorry. I just figured you'd know that something made me late. Don't you trust me?"

"I trusted you Thursday, Friday and Saturday," he said bitterly.

At the sight of his sad, handsome head, cut like a coin profile into the rock and snow beyond, all the theology went out of my head. I felt an agonizing need to try and recapture the good feeling of the day before. Maybe it was too late now.

Unsmiling, expressionless, he watched me as I walked over to him. Though I didn't look at it directly, his torso made me very aware of its nakedness. It had the brutal beauty of a man who lifted and shoved heavy metal all

119

day long. It was softened only by the dark silky curls of hair across his breast, and the carelessly hung silver necklaces. I was even aware of the pulse beating in the side of his neck, of his navel moving as he breathed. Up close, the intensity of him was almost terrifying. It was like standing at the rim of a volcano about to erupt.

The complusion to touch him was there. Wasn't I a very fond-of-touching person? Part of my ministry was patting the hands of old ladies, jouncing screaming babies at the baptismal font, putting an arm across the shoulders of the despondent—all gestures devoid of sex, but all full of caring and feeling.

Slowly I put both my hands up and held his face like a chalice. He hadn't shaved, and his thin cheeks were hot and harsh. Almost without thinking, I felt his cheekbones with my fingertips.

"I just want to talk to you," I said.

My voice was so low that I wondered if I'd only thought the words.

He smiled a little. "Talk away," he said. That shade of irony in his voice again.

A kind of revelation stilled my mind, as if an eighth seal had been opened. What I saw, in that silence that went through heaven, was Vidal's face as it had always been, down in the deeps of my mind, even before I met him. I was the void, and he was the spirit moving over the face of the deep. In my beginning, his face and his body were the Word made flesh.

His warm hands closed around my wrists, and I had to close my eyes. The heat of his face came close to mine. My fingers found their way into his hair, to the hot nape of his neck. At some moment that I hadn't thought of, the grace of God had already gone out of me—for that is the belief, that the grace goes out as fast as when my mother puffed out her birthday candles.

I kissed him on the mouth, and learned that kissing was everything it was supposed to be, providing you did it freely and not out of duty.

At another moment I hadn't noticed, his arms were around me hard and we were straining together as if our muscles would pull out by the roots. Now that I had gone this far, though, the habits of years kept dragging me back. When he tried to get his hands inside my clothes, I kept shrinking back.

"Not yet. Not so fast."

"You're not getting away with the Princeton rub," he said. "Not with me."

That first time was less a textbook lovemaking than a free-form stop-and-start exploration. Vidal was wise enough to let me find my way with it. But, to turn Father Matt's phrase around, he was firm too. After last night in the confessional, he knew now that the only thing that worked with me was shock. He shoved me straight to the bottom of the water and made me find myself there, drowning and fighting for life.

I was a naked Jacob wrestling a naked angel on the deep red carpet. All the caring in my life was there, in my hands, my mouth, my body. I drew from his all the heat that I had tried for years to take from people, from God. His hands, his mouth, his pressing straining body stripped me of every shrewd and stubborn lie that I had ever hidden myself in.

Over us rose the mountain, impassive and serene. Only the mountain saw us, through the window.

———

Afterward we lay there still loosely embraced, unwilling to give up the touching yet.

"I'm surprised," he said softly.

"At me?" I said. "I didn't put up much of a fight, did I?"

"No," he said. "At me. Usually I like to get rougher and raunchier. I felt like I was dancing again. Only I left my fuckin' feather bustle back up on the Blackfoot." He smiled dreamily.

"You don't connect that dance with anything Indian, do you?"

"Nope. The tribal council'd shoot me if they could hear me say it. It reminds me of—I'll tell you what. It does remind me of a kid who was my first lover, up there. We discovered the whole thing by ourselves without even knowing it had a name. He was a beautiful dancer."

"What happened to him?"

Vidal laughed softly and raised up on one elbow, looking down at me. I looked up at him out of my sudden amnesia. The past, the priesthood, even the fact that I had ever worn clothes, had all fallen down a cliff somewhere.

"When he woke up to what he was doing, he got scared to death, and he got married. He's still up there, living at Starr School with his wife and kids. I used to see him at the races at Starr School sometimes. He won fifty dollars off me one time but he could never look me in the eye."

"Did anybody know about it?"

"My dad figured it out."

"Did he threaten you with jail or anything?"

Vidal laughed again. "No. But he kidded me so much, it was one of the reasons I left. That was always the way the Indians did things. They never forced you. They just kidded you until you got back in line."

"What was the old-time attitude toward it, I wonder?"

"Oh," said Vidal carelessly, "from the little I read, they were pretty relaxed about it. If a guy wanted to cross over and live as a woman, they let him. What the warrior studs

122

did in the secret societies, I don't know. Who cares? It's all in your head, anyway . . ."

He kissed me again.

"In case you didn't notice," he said, "you're my lover."

Far at the back of the mind, the urgency of who I was waited to come forward again.

"You didn't tell me you love me," I said.

Vidal shook his head and started laughing. "You're very free with that word love," he said. "You'd think it's a basketball, the way you bounce it around."

"But . . . "

"Look," he said, "you're still very green at this. You'll learn. You've got lots of time, so don't jump in with both feet."

I was very disappointed at his reaction, and began to remember that I was a damned sinner, and naked. My clothes were scattered nearby, and I reached for them. Vidal stopped my arm by grasping it with his hand.

"Now your feelings are all hurt," he said. "What do you want me to say? I never waited so long and so hard for someone in my whole life, and it was worth every minute. And I need some breakfast."

That made me feel better. "You're not only a pervert, you're a glutton," I said.

He got up, walked naked to the phone and dialed room service.

"But they'll have to come in the room," I said.

"Take your clothes and hide in the bathroom, dummy," he said. "Yeah, this is Room 203. I want to order a real big breakfast. Four eggs over light, a lot of bacon, a lot of toast, and coffee."

When room service knocked on the door, I cowered in the bathroom while Vidal wrapped himself in a towel and went to answer. The lies start in again, I thought. Finally he told me the coast was clear. The waiter had gone, and there on a big stainless steel tray was enough breakfast for two.

We ate off the one plate, and drank out of the same cup.

"You're pretty good at this sort of thing," I said. "You think of everything."

"You'll get pretty good at it too," he said. "You'll have to be better than me."

"Yeah," I said. "I think I'm gonna be a genius at it. You realize what'll happen to me if somebody finds out?"

"I've got a vague idea."

"They bar you from mass, confessions, everything. They ship you off to a retreat house somewhere and try to shrink your head. If you say you won't go, they throw you out. The only thing they can't take away from you is that mark on your soul from when you were ordained. You wander around with that thing stuck on you like the mark of Cain."

"It isn't any worse than what everybody else goes through," he said. "So don't make a big production out of it."

"Holy Christ," I said, "what time is it?"

My watch said nearly three in the afternoon.

"My folks'll be going crazy," I said. "I told them I'd be there around two. And I'm going to miss the appointment with Father Matt. Doesn't much matter, I guess. What am I going to tell him?"

After thinking a minute about what kind of story I was going to tell them, I dialed my parents' number in Helena.

"Tom!" my mother cried. "Where are you? We've been worried sick."

"No sweat, Mom," I said. "I'm calling from a garage in Amberville. I had some carburetor trouble. Luckily the mechanic was around, and we got it fixed. I'm leaving right now."

124

"You should have called sooner!"

"I know. I'm sorry. It took longer than I thought. Look, Mom, I'm a little short of change because of the repairs. Would you do me a favor and call Father Matt? Tell him what happened. I'll make another appointment with him."

"Oh, I'm so relieved! We always worry about you. You drive so fast . . ."

When I hung up, the tender amnesia had started to lift a little, and the guilty nervousness was coming back.

"You're improving already," said Vidal, drinking the last of his coffee. "And speaking of money, we've stayed past checkout time. So I'll owe for another day."

"How much is the room?"

"Thirty bucks."

"I'll pay for half of everything, okay?"

"Okay."

My worn black cowhide wallet yielded four ten-dollar bills, which I put on the tray. When I got to Helena, my financial state wouldn't be a lie.

"We won't be able to afford this *all* the time," I said.

"No," he said. "We'll have to figure out some things. I'll have to start climbing in your bedroom window."

"God, don't do that." The very idea made me break out in a scalding sweat.

No one paid any attention to me as I walked out of the side door and unlocked the car. The mountain air smelled good after the sickly stuffiness inside. I got in, started the car, and wheeled out into the Interstate with a screech of tires.

Now that I'd left him, images of him rushed back to warm me and haunt me; laughing in Trina's cafe, looking sad by the picture window, angry and icy behind the confessional grille, gasping in abandon on the deep red rug, changeable as the weather over those mountains.

There wasn't even any point in repenting of my sin, because I knew I would do it again. Only now that I'd given in to it did I know how deep was my need to love a man.

———

At my parents' house, we had supper instead of dinner. The everyday Irish linen placemats were on the table, and Mother lamented the nice prune whip that Rosie had ready in the afternoon. For once I didn't have much appetite, but I choked down the food so that they wouldn't think something was wrong.

But Mother said, "You're looking awfully peaked, Tom. Don't you think so, Frank?"

"If it was spring now," said my father, "and *my* mother was around, she'd dose him with sulphur and molasses."

"It's the work," I said. "It's getting me down a little."

"Father Vance has no right to run you ragged like that," said my mother. "I'm saying a word or two to the Bishop next time I see him."

"For Christ's sake, don't do that," I said irritably.

"Why not?" said my mother. "Don't you lose your temper, Tom. I was only trying to help."

"Tom means that things aren't done that way," said my father, who had more savvy for politics.

"My goodness, I feel like an idiot," said my mother. "How *are* things at St. Mary's, Tom?"

"Pretty much the same," I said. "We're still half-broke and running around giving the last rites to people who get chewed up in baling machines."

It now seemed like I had to lie every time I opened my mouth. The shock of that intimate encounter was still in my system. Mother solicitously watched me butter a hot biscuit, and I wondered how she would feel if she knew what those hands of mine had been doing all afternoon.

If this had been a normal situation, I could have sat there at the table glowing and joyful and said, "Mom, Dad, I've met this wonderful person that I think I'm in love with." All my life they had shared in the milestone experiences: baptism, birthdays, first communion, high-school commencement, my engagement to Jean, my announcement that I wanted to be a priest, my ordination when I lay flat on my face before the altar and the Bishop of Helena made me a priest forever.

"Maybe you should get out a little more," said my mother. "Socialize a little. You're allowed to do that, aren't you? Maybe you should take a little vacation?"

That evening, before I drove back to Cottonwood, I called Father Matt. It felt safer to talk to him over the telephone.

"Sorry I got hung up today," I told him. "We'll just have to leave it for next month."

"How are you, my boy? Everything okay?" Father Matt asked.

I wondered if he'd picked up any strange vibes from my voice. "Well," I said. "I'm trying to pray."

"Prayer isn't always sweetness and light. Sometimes it's like throwing a pebble at God's window and wondering when the hell He'll ever hear you and get out of bed and open it."

The memory of that feeling of genesis came over me again, and I wondered how I could have possibly felt that way. It was a sacrilege to think of Vidal as my own private Word.

"Have you heard any news about the secretary thing with the Bishop?" I asked.

"I saw him the other day. He said he might call you in for an interview sometime soon."

As I hung up the phone, I wondered what exotic lies I would have to tell the Bishop. On the other hand, maybe that job would be my salvation. It would take me away from Vidal without my making any effort of my own. This was a very unspiritual thought, of course. A serious Christian was supposed to be willing to make efforts.

On my own, I knew, I would never be able to give up my lover. I'd drag him straight into hell with me, and we'd flutter forever through the flaming murk, clutching each other like Paolo and Francesca. I tried to remember if Dante had put any homosexuals into his *Inferno,* but I couldn't.

9

The church behind me was full of rustlings and creakings of pews and the soft flipping of missal pages. The usual hundred-odd Sunday regulars were there, plus one new face. The church reeked with incense, and the stained glass glowed in the light of a hot August morning.

Usually I saw only the backs of the Sunday high-mass-goers, since I played the organ and saw those backs in the mirror over the keyboards. Father Vance had always jealously guarded his celebrating that high mass. But today he was down in bed with a rotten summer cold, so I was saying the Mass. Since there was no one to play the organ, the congregation was just singing the responses *a capella*. They must feel that their voices sounded thin and off-key without the rich chords of the organ.

At the altar I was coming down to the Consecration.

The vestments I wore were the white ones, from the set made by Clare Faux and Missy Oldenberg. Amid the liturgical symbols, the two old ladies had worked a graceful tracery of native summer wildflowers and birds:

meadowlarks and mountain bluebirds, Indian paint-brush, larkspur and wild geranium. But there was no joy in wearing those vestments—they felt like they were going to choke me.

Behind me, everyone was on their knees, waiting for that moment when, at my words, the thin wafer of bread on the paten before me would become the real and present body of Our Lord. They were behind me because in Cottonwood we still said Mass facing the walls, thanks partly to the church's layout and partly to Father Vance's hatred of modernism.

I bent over the wafer, holding it in those hands of mine that had fondled Vidal's face, explored his body, touched his genitals. The liturgical words, as they came from my mouth, seemed to be a terrible secret affirmation of my guilt.

"This is my body," I said.

I slowly raised the wafer so that the people could see it. Sometimes I was sure that through some kind of inverted miracle, they could see Vidal in the wafer instead of Jesus.

Bending again, I said the words over the chalice.

"This is my blood."

Behind me, soft footsteps shuffled up to the altar rail, as people came forward to receive Holy Communion. In the silence, off down the hill, we could hear the deep echoing blast of the Amtrak train as it barreled through the Cottonwood station without stopping.

Now I was coming down the altar steps to that row of my unsuspecting parishioners, holding the ciborium of consecrated wafers. It seemed impossible that they couldn't see the blackened, twisted state of my soul. Any one of them was in better spiritual shape than I was probably. They didn't know it, but their priest was be-traying them.

I went along that row of kneeling people, slipping wafers into their opened mouths. One by one, they rose and shuffled back to their pews, heads bowed, hands clasped, carrying in their mouths that treasure that stayed miraculously unstained despite my having touched it.

Though I didn't raise my eyes, I knew that my lover was sitting there shamelessly in the very front pew. Vidal wasn't devout enough to go to communion, and I didn't pester him to go. It was a curious reality of my dilemma that I, a shepherd, should actually want one of my sheep to stay away from the Holy Sacrament. Slipping that wafer into Vidal's mouth would have been too painful a ritual parody of our relationship.

That face of his seemed to have been formed in my consciousness long before my birth, as much a part of me and human history as original sin. Sometimes I felt that I had been born with that face marked on my soul, as sure a fiery stamp as the marks of baptism, confirmation and ordination that came later. In the Bible somewhere was a line, "I am thine from my mother's womb." That was me.

He sat there quietly watching me, that mask of indifference settled firmly on his face. I knew very well that he wasn't there because he loved God. He was there because he wanted to look at me. Every morning he was there now, even at the low mass I celebrated every weekday morning. It meant that he had to get up forty-five minutes earlier, but he did.

That being physically together in the same church, thirty feet apart, not speaking to each other, with the lie on both our faces, was one of the few times during the week that we could see each other.

=====

Even after the Mass, we couldn't get together right away. Vidal went home, and I kneeled at the prie-dieu to make a thanksgiving. It wouldn't look right for Vidal to hang around the sacristy waiting for me.

I had always made my thanksgiving in front of the altar

131

of Mary. In recent years, Catholics' devotion to Mary had slackened a little, just as their devotion to a lot of older forms had slackened in the face of obsession with new issues and new ideas. But from the time I was a teen-ager, I had always had a very real (I thought) devotion to the Mother of God.

Now, however, after these sacrilegious masses of mine, my "thanksgiving" was full of black and guilty thoughts. Staring at Mary, I had to rethink my devotion to her, and what it meant in terms of my sexual orientation.

The fact was, several of Mary's tears at the cross must have fallen because of me personally. By rejecting heterosexuality and the Church's teachings on sexuality, I now rejected her divine motherhood. The Incarnation, and all the events that followed it, were God's keystone in the arch of heterosexual sex.

Not only that, I now realized that I loved Mary because she, of all women, threatened me least. A virgin who bears a divine child has to be the ultimate comfort for a man who shuns mortal women.

It all made me think again about that dubious virginity of mine that had survived twenty-eight years, only to be lost to Vidal. I had always assumed that I had kept it because of my feeling that I would be a celibate priest. A couple of times, with Jean, I had made stabs at losing it. We had done some heavy petting, and she was ready to go all the way with me.

Now it dawned on me how worthless and phony that virginity of mine had been, and how it was nothing more than the cover for the deep unacknowledged homosexual feelings that would someday come pushing up. Even my vocation was phony—it was a running away into an oc- cupation where I couldn't be pressured to perform as a heterosexual. I was a fraud.

Vidal had talked a lot about closet occupations. "Either they help you hide better," he said, "or they give you better opportunities." Surely the greatest closet job of all was that of the celibate in any religion.

═══

The logistics of a closet affair in a small town can be compared to planning a major military invasion of the Far East.

Discipline and split-second timing and original thinking are very important. I began to understand why so many gay people want to lose themselves in the big cities. In a place like Cottonwood, the straight line from prying eyes to disaster is a lot shorter.

Father Vance was grudgingly edified at Vidal's regular church attendance. He also noticed that Vidal frequently came to confession on Saturday nights. This was because the ten minutes spent together in the confessional was part of our cover, and it was one of the few chances that we got to talk.

We didn't want to be seen in public together any more frequently than before. So we started skipping breakfast together at Trina's. My explanation to Father Vance was that I was trying to improve my spiritual life, and was staying after Mass to make a thanksgiving. And I did kneel at the prie-dieu awhile, torturing myself about my sins.

Instead, I went to Vidal's house for supper a couple of times a week. Since Father Vance was so edified, and since I wasn't eating breakfast with Vidal anymore, my pastor didn't have any objections to this. I drove publicly right up to Vidal's house and parked. He, I and Patti Ann had supper in the brightly-lighted kitchen, with all the shades up so the neighbors could see. Then, for fifteen precious minutes, we would go in the bedroom, close the door, make sure the shades were down. We would throw ourselves down on that box spring and mattress, in front of that poster, to make love. Then I would take a quick shower so I wouldn't smell of semen, being careful not to wet my hair. An hour later I would be back at the rectory. No lingering anywhere was one of the keys of our tactic.

Patti Ann could be counted on not to say a word about what was going on. Not even the CIA could have gotten information out of her.

Vidal got himself further into Father Vance's good graces by offering to take charge of St. Mary's seedy lawn and hedges. For no charge at all, he came up once a week, and mowed and clipped and raked. The place looked neater than it had since I came there. He even offered to whack down the lilac bushes that were overrunning the grounds, but Father balked at that.

Vidal's greatest coup, however, came when Father Vance actually asked him to take a look at his car. My pastor had always had his ancient 1955 black Buick serviced at the other garage in town, Farrell's. The car had developed a mysterious tendency to veer to the left, and the left front end was dropped. When Farrell's told him the trouble was a bent axle and that the job would cost him $250, Father was horrified. He brought the car to Snow's and Vidal put it up on the lift. After tinkering with it, he announced that the trouble was a bent torsion bar, which would cost only $110. Father was delighted, especially when the car came back to him driving perfectly again.

After that, I was sure that if Mrs. Shoup had actually come to Father and whispered to him that his curate was having a homosexual relationship with the garage mechanic, Father might not have believed her. Any parishioner who did things for St. Mary's for free couldn't possibly be that wicked.

In fact, I was discovering that—providing we were careful—I had a terrible freedom to violate the century-old sexual ethic of that town.

134

Clergymen of all faiths are often suspected of many other things, from hitting the bottle to embezzling church funds. Nowadays Catholics in particular keep a sharp eye on their priests' tendency to go roving off after girls. But homosexuality is seldom suspected, rooted though it is in the priest's liturgical loneliness and his being bound in a brotherhood that is exclusively male.

I learned how free I was in August when Jamie Ogilvie's parents started pushing me at him. They had noticed their teen-age son's doglike attentiveness to me, and they interpreted it in a way that suited them. They were sure that Jamie had a vocation for the priesthood.

After Sunday mass, they always lay in wait for me. "Father, why don't you take Jamie backpacking?" "Father, if you go on a trip, why don't you take Jamie with you?" "Father, please pay some extra attention to Jamie, maybe he'll get a vocation."

To Jamie himself, they must have said the same thing. "Try to get Father to take you on trips." If he had been a girl, his parents would never in a million years have shoved him at me like that. I later learned that this was a common experience, and a very hair-raising one, for priests who are closet gays. The temptations that Satan rigged up for Jesus, taking him up on the mount and showing him all the cities in the world to rule, are as nothing compared to the temptations for such a priest when parents shove their sons at him.

Their pushing didn't panic me, because I wasn't attracted to Jamie. But it must have panicked Jamie, because the poor kid finally talked to me about it.

One Saturday night in August, Jamie came to me for his regular confession. After the usual recital of little sins (inattentive while serving mass, nasty to his little sister), he hesitated a few minutes, then stammered:

"Father, you're the kind of guy that people can really talk to. So I've got to tell you something that's really bothered me a lot. I know the Church says it's evil, and I

135

hope you don't take it wrong. Anyway, Father, I've got a crush on you."

He had to know that this fact wasn't exactly news to me. Was this a play for my attention, but a less tortured and elaborate one than Vidal's? I would have to handle this very carefully, putting him off without crushing him.

He waited on the other side of the grille, a handsome but owlish seventeen-year-old boy who wore bifocals that magnified his blue eyes. He always wore a sweater vest over his shirt and tie, and was the best chemistry student in Cottonwood High.

He took my pause for moral indignation. "I hope you're not shocked, Father."

"Jamie," I said gently. "I'm not shocked, just thinking. This is something that a lot of people go through. Especially getting a crush on a person who's a little older. Girls go through the same thing. Don't let it worry you."

"Did you have crushes when you were my age?"

"Sure, I did. The thing about crushes is, you get over them. A year from now, you kinda laugh at yourself, and you think, Boy, what did I ever see in *him?* or *her?*"

"Supposing I never get over it? I mean, there are guys who never get over . . . having crushes on guys."

So this might be the real thing. Jamie was not playing for attention. He was scared to death about himself, and the only person to whom he could scream for help was the object of his affections.

"That's true," I said. "There *are* people who never get over it. Men and women both. Either they don't want to change, or they can't . . . But just because of one crush, it doesn't necessarily mean that you're that way. A crush is one thing, love is something else. Part of growing up and being a man means that you learn to handle your feelings for other men, and you decide what place those feelings are going to have in your life."

Now that Jamie was sure I wasn't going to threaten him with hellfire and damnation, he relaxed a little.

136

"For a long time I was afraid of losing control," he said. "Then I realized that I picked you because I didn't have to be afraid of losing control. Around you, I was safe, Father."

My head reeled. He really thought I was straight, when the only reason he was safe with me was that I didn't go for what Vidal called "chickens."

"My parents are pretty naïve, I'm afraid," he said. "They keep nagging me to hang around you. Be a priest like Father Tom. Be a priest like Father Tom. And you know, Father, I respect the priesthood and everything, but I want to study biochemistry."

I had to smile again, at the awareness and maturity that the boy had, compared to the moral simpleminded-ness of his parents.

"Would you feel better not serving Mass anymore?" I asked him. "Maybe we're putting you in an occasion of sin by keeping you there under my nose every day."

He sounded relieved. "I'm awful glad you thought of that, Father. I wanted to ask Father Vance to replace me, but I was scared he'd wonder why I wanted to quit."

"Don't worry," I said. "I'll fix up something. You'll be going away to college anyway. Can you hold on till we train someone else?"

"That's great, Father."

"And just remember that Our Lord is merciful and ready to help you when you stumble—more merciful in His judgments than people are in theirs. Now say a good act of contrition, and for your penance ten Our Fathers. . . ."

I pronounced the absolution while he mumbled his act of contrition.

My mind was still reeling at the hypocrisy and sacrilege of me, a priest fallen from grace, absolving this boy from mere thoughts of a sin that I myself was actively engaging in. Every time I absolved a penitent, or baptized a baby, or gave Holy Communion in the state I was in, it compounded my guilt to a monstrosity of mathematics that I'd already lost track of.

As the days went by, I started to realize exactly why the Church was so stubborn about celibacy for its priests. It was a kind of flesh-hating manichaeism that shrank from the idea of my hands touching the Body of Christ after having touched the body of a human being.

The strange thing was that my guilt was making me more cautious, sensitive and skillful in dealing with people's problems. It was burning out of me the last shreds of first-year brashness and seminary bookishness.

I began to wonder about other gay people like Vidal who had gone through the terror and anguish of seeking a sexual identity out there in the rural reaches of America.

Vidal's only touch now with the gay scene outside the state was the magazines he got in the mail. They came discreetly wrapped, to his post-office box, looking no different from *Backpacker* or the *Montana Livestock Reporter*. He had piles of them in his closet. There was the nationwide gay newspaper *Advocate*, a few glossies like *Mandate*, and the Canadian think magazine *Esprit*.

I started sneakng them into the rectory in my briefcase and reading them late at night when Father Vance was asleep, and they made me realize there was a whole homosexual universe in America. It existed in the same place and time as the heterosexual universe, and in apposition to it—something like the universe of antimatter that the physicists like to imagine.

This search for identity was tough enough in the urban areas, where the gay man or lesbian could find companionship and help. There were not only gay bars and baths, but private clubs, theaters, church groups, stores, consciousness-raising groups—even gay travel agencies and insurance companies. And there were gay switchboards if you wanted a shoulder to cry on, or someone to talk you out of committing suicide. But if you were gay in Browning or Cottonwood, or any one of a million other small towns on the American map, you had to "hang and rattle," as the cowmen said.

I started to be curious about these hidden, lonely people, crying out in their small-town wilderness.

"I know just about every faggot in the state," said Vidal. "They're pretty amazing people, some of them. They went through the whole crock without any help from anybody. Talk about moral courage."

"I wish I could meet some of them," I said. "Except that people might find out about *me.*"

So now and then, on July afternoons when I could arrange to be free, Vidal and I would take off on some crazy lightning trip. Even Father Vance was getting worried that I was overworked, so he grudgingly let me take a breather now and then. He was a realist—if I conked out on him, he'd have to do more work himself.

Our cover was backpacking. I had done a lot of it when I was in high school and college, and now rescued the old packs and boots from my parents' attic in Helena. Vidal got himself some cheap second-hand equipment too. We'd roar out of town quite publicly on Vidal's bike or in my car. When we came back, we had to be prepared with convincing stories about the two grizzlies we'd seen in the Bob Marshall Wilderness, or the awful way hikers left litter in the Swan River National Forest.

It was strange—our relationship had begun with the fiction that I was the confessor and Vidal the penitent. But now he led me. Vidal was my Virgil, taking me deep into the landscape of a *Commedia* said to be undivine.

===

One day he said to me, "Remember I mentioned those friends of mine who raise horses? They're getting that horse ready for the Helena–Cottonwood endurance race. I think you ought to to meet them."

It was a hot clear afternoon in mid-July. We roared

north up the Interstate with the radio blaring Crosby, Stills and Nash. Our hair whipped in the breeze. For a little while my guilt and fear were sucked right out the window like a piece of paper. I loved those trips, out on the road with him—free, going somewhere, anywhere.

At Drummond, we took the exit off the Interstate. On the other side of that little cowtown, we took a gravel county road.

It wound up through dry empty hills dotted with lonely junipers and cedars. A few grade cattle grazed here and there. On top, we came out on a bench like the one east of Cottonwood. This one, however, was all native pasture—a sweep of dry grass. In the distance, at the end of a lane, was a cluster of ranch buildings.

The lane was lined with young cottonwood trees. Since cottonwoods ordinarily wouldn't do well on a dry place like that, these were carefully watered with a little pipeline, and they were thriving green.

While a few of the sheds were old, the barn and the corrals were new. The house was a rambling brick affair with picture windows overlooking the bench. It was beautifully kept, shaded with young mountain ashes and weeping birches, flanked by beds of pansies and red geraniums. The lawn was freshly mowed and gave off that hayfield smell. A sprinkler whirled on a spot where the grass had gotten dry and blue-colored. On the side was a flagstone terrace of pink native granite, set with lounge chairs.

The whole place had a look of a little Eden painstakingly grown on that dry bench, with the help of hard work and irrigation.

As we parked the car and got out, the silence and the immensity of the open country closed around us.

Just then a stubby little Australian blue heeler rushed around the corner of the house at us, barking. The front door opened, and a tall, spare young man in faded Levi's, work shirt and walking boots stood there, grinning. He had a round, weatherbeaten face, sideburns, and eyes so blue they looked dyed. He must have been in his late twenties.

"Lady, stop that racket," he yelled at the dog. He came down the flagstone steps, and shook hands with us.

"Let's have us a beer," said Larry. "My partner'll be along."

In another two minutes, we were out on that terrace lounging in the chairs, with the little blue dog now wiggling happily around us and icy cans of beer in our hands. The beer slid down my throat like a mountain brook after the long dusty drive. Larry was a relaxed, warm person with the goofiest kind of cow-country humor, and pretty soon he had us laughing our heads off.

But when I asked Larry what kind of horses they bred, he got quite serious. I'd expected him to say quarter horses or Appaloosas or something, but to my surprise he said:

"Mustangs."

"I don't know anything about horses, but I thought mustangs were extinct. Didn't the dogfood people kill them all?"

"They almost did," said Larry. "There's about fifteen thousand of them left in the West. They're running around in the back country on the public lands. They've gotten real man-shy, they've been hunted so much. The scissorbills in Washington finally passed a law that really stopped most of the hunting."

"But what are they good for? Aren't they wild and runty?"

"They're a helluva horse," he said. "They conquered the Americas. And they're a persecuted minority. That's why we breed them."

The words "persecuted minority" stuck in my ears for a moment. That was an odd thing to say about a breed of horse.

"Of course, some of them *are* pretty common looking."

Larry was saying. "They crossbred a lot with draft mares and other breeds that ran wild or the studs stole them. But those old Andalusian genes are real potent. Now and then you will see a horse that's the pure old Spanish-Arab-Barb type, with the back that's missing the lumbar vertebra, and everything. We used to make the rounds of all the dogfood auctions and pick up those typey horses for five, ten cents a pound, a stud here, a colt there. Boy, those horses would come out of the trucks looking like holy hell, half starved, crippled, blinded with buckshot. We put together our whole breeding herd for less than a thousand dollars, and that's counting shipping costs."

I was very moved. "Are any other breeders doing this?"

"A few," said Larry. "We've even got a studbook now. A horse can't be registered till he's dead and we can count his backbones." He grinned. "Of course, the bank thinks we're nuts. That's why we don't make our money on the horses. We've got a good commercial cow operation going here, and we make out as well as anybody else in the cow business—which is to say, not so good these days, but . . ."

He looked off across the barnyard and said, "Well, here come the other *two* partners. Will and our best stud."

"That's the horse that's going to enter the race," said Vidal to me.

"Damn right he is," said Larry. "He's going to put all those high-flyin' quarter horses right in his back pocket."

Will rode right up across the lawn with a grin on his face, a little cigar clenched in his white corn-kernel teeth. He was the same age as Larry, wore a battered leather vest and leggings, and was so swarthily handsome in an Oriental way that he looked more Indian than Vidal.

The stud came stepping softly over the grass, his silky hide stained with sweat. Will got off him by the terrace, and the stud stood quietly, bowing his neck and playing with his bit till his lips foamed.

He was a small horse, looking a lot like a wiry tough

Arabian. I knew enough to know that he was a blue roan. His head was lovely as an antelope's, and you could have put all the Church Fathers' wisdom into one of his dark eyes. His rippled salt-and-pepper mane fell clear of his narrow hard-muscled chest, though his tail was pulled short at his hocks the way ranchers do with a working horse. He was good-looking enough, but the overwhelming impression he gave as he stood there was one of diehard be-damned toughness.

Will popped open a can of beer, and we expected to see him gulp at it. Instead, he poured a foaming palmful and offered it to the stud. The horse lapped it politely like a cat and finished by carefully licking Will's fingers with his long pink tongue.

We all laughed.

"If Flint wins the race," said Larry, "maybe the Budweiser people will want him to do an ad."

"He looks like he's in great shape," said Vidal. "If he was a basketball player, I'd be scared to death of him."

"We've been training him careful. One day he'll do fifteen or twenty miles, the next day just eight or ten. Thing about Flint is, he's a natural pacer. Pacing's easy on a horse, so he has a big advantage."

All the time he talked, Will was gravely sharing the beer with the horse.

We walked around the ranch, Lady wiggling behind, and they proudly showed us their little operation. Will turned the stud out in a corral and he got down in the dirt and rolled around raunchily to scratch his sweaty back. Then we and Lady got in the truck and drove out to see their cows and their herd of brood mares.

The fifty mares and their foals ranged in three big pastures. They were in three harems, each under a stud. They were every color of the rainbow—pinto, dun, roan, gray, sorrel. The duns had zebra stripes on their legs. They acted nervous if we came too close, and the stud would come toward us in an unfriendly businesslike way while the lead mare edged the band away.

"All these adult horses were foaled in the wild," said Will. "They've never had a man on their backs, and we don't much care to break them. They just roam wild here like they was to home. The foals we got at the auctions, and the foals born here, are the ones we'll break and show and sell."

"Was Flint born in the wild?"

"Yep, he was. He's sort of our showcase horse. We got him right down in the Pryor Mountains on the Montana-Wyoming border, six years ago. There's a protected band of a hundred and fifty running up there, and they had a Bureau of Land Management sale to cull some colts."

I felt more and more moved. As a ranchland priest, I couldn't help liking horses, even though I was a little scared of them. Larry's and Will's breeding program was more like a crusade. If they succeeded, people would see that the despised mustang, whom many ranchers had wanted exterminated for years on grounds that they stole the grass from cattle on the public lands, was as good a working horse as any.

But I kept asking myself why Vidal had wanted me to meet these two guys.

We walked back to the house to have some lunch.

In the big kitchen, Will stirred a pot of homemade chili that was simmering on the stove, while Larry made a great big salad. The kitchen was beautiful, with copper pans on the walls. Obviously they both liked to cook, a thing that bachelor cowboys had to make up their minds whether they'd bother with or not.

"We've got homemade bread too," said Larry proudly. "We bake our own now. We got sick of that cotton store stuff."

It was in the kitchen that I started noticing a few

144

things. When I did, I asked myself why I'd been so dense.

Now that they were indoors, out of sight of the ranch hands, Larry and Will had a different, more intimate way with each other. It wasn't too obvious—just the way they stood at the counter with their arms touching as they argued about whether the avocados were ripe enough, or the way Will leaned against Larry as he reached up to the spice rack to get the chili powder.

These two men, who were living together so unspectacularly, thought of by their neighbors as the usual pair of bachelor cowboys, were lovers.

And if they behaved this way in front of me, it meant that they knew I was Vidal's lover.

We sat at the big pine table and ate. I found I had fallen strangely silent. Through the kitchen picture window, we could see the horses scattered across the bench and Flint standing in his corral swishing flies. Now, of course, I knew why, of all breeds, these two young men would pick the mustang.

I traded looks with Vidal. He knew I had finally figured things out, and he smiled.

After lunch we sat in the living room with one more can of beer. Larry put a record on the stereo, Neil Young's *After the Gold Rush.* Young's haunting falsetto filled the room, and the peace of this place sank deeper and deeper into my bones.

The room was functional and comfortable, but planned with thought and taste. The huge fireplace was built of the same pink granite as the terrace and steps outside. The furniture was deep red leather, and there were magnificent old Navajo rugs everywhere, on the floors, hung on the walls, draped over the sofa. On one wall, a dozen Catlin prints were massed. Like the rest of the ranch, the room breathed the peace and purpose of the two individuals who had created it.

Sitting on the couch, Larry and Will were just a little

cozier—Will put his arm over Larry's shoulder, and they leaned together. Lady jumped up on both their laps and licked both their faces.

"How long have you two known each other?" I said.

"We met at the Billings rodeo eight years ago," said Will. "Larry was up in the bareback riding, and I was sitting on the arena fence, and he bucked off in front of me."

They both laughed uproariously, like they were sharing some secret joke.

"We took a notion to get drunk together that night," said Larry, "and we've been together ever since."

Vidal was laughing too, as if he knew more of the story than I did. "You'll never break up," he said. "The bank won't let you."

"Yeah," said Will, "let's hope the bank never finds out we don't use both the bedrooms in this house."

"Or the insurance company," said Larry.

When I excused myself a while later to go to the bathroom, the beer having taken its course, I saw the two bedrooms as I went down the hallway. They both looked lived in, with both beds more or less made. I was reminded of my own lies.

When we left, late in the afternoon, the shadows of the lonely cedars lay long across the hills. Vidal drove and I sat silent. I was still under the spell of that place and those two people, and knew it would haunt me for a long time. I would never be able to live with anyone and create a life like that.

≡

Back at the rectory for supper, I told Father Vance a few tales of an afternoon's hike through the Hellgate Canyon. I'd hiked it in high school and knew every foot of it, so I didn't have to fictionalize.

146

"By the way," said Father Vance, "Mrs. Shoup was asking for you this afternoon."

"She was?" I said. My stomach felt like it was sliding over a cliff.

"She was surprised you weren't around. I explained you were out hiking. She has a book she wants you to look at. She thinks it's obscene, of course, but she wants you to explain some of the music stuff in it to her."

I tried to pretend I was only mildly irritated.

"If God didn't command me to be charitable," I said, "I'd tell her to put the book in her left ear."

The creepy feeling came over me that Mrs. Shoup was trying to check up on me.

10

One night at supper, around the end of July, Vidal said to me, "Get ready to go backpacking again."

"Where to this time?"

"Oh, right over to Helena," he said.

"What natural wonders do we see?"

Vidal grinned. "The first drag ball in the history of Montana."

"I don't believe it."

"It's even got a Bicentennial theme. Everybody is supposed to come as the old-time lady or gentleman of his choice. It's going to be at the Broadwater Hotel."

"How did you find out about it?"

"It was advertised right in the Helena paper. Of course, the ad didn't say *drag ball,* but . . . I suppose some straights will show up that won't really know what is going on. Larry and Will saw the ad and told me."

"Are they going?"

"Nope. They're too busy training the horse and putting up hay."

I stirred my second cup of coffee moodily. "Drag," I said. "I'm not sure that's my kind of thing."

"You're a priest, man. Everything should be your kind of thing."

"And Helena . . . My God, that's a place where a lot of people know me."

"Maybe they wouldn't want you to know *they're* there. Come on, Tom, learn to project your paranoia on other people too. We'll dress up like everybody else. You can wear a mask if you want. I'm not gonna."

"You really want to come out, don't you?"

"Yeah," he said. "Any day now."

"We could go as the Lone Ranger and Tonto."

Vidal snorted. "That's not a very original idea. I'll bet you there'll be a dozen Lone Rangers and Tontos."

I smiled bitterly. "I could go in my cassock. Nobody would dream it was real. I could go as Father de Smet, and you could go as one of the Indians I converted."

For the next few days, I didn't see too much of Vidal. He was so involved in his costume, and the way it must relate to some fantasy of his, that he didn't seem very interested in making love. I wondered if he was already losing interest in me a little.

After all, I probably wasn't as sexy as he had fantasized me to be. I kept remembering the way he had described the first time he'd seen me walking down Main Street. It was hard to relate it to the way I saw myself. . . . *Looking so butch and so free, your skirt and your blond hair blowing in the breeze* . . . Was that me? He had probably expected to get that cassock off me and find one of the hot sweaty studs immortalized in photos and prose in his gay magazines. Instead, he had found me, the Rev. Thomas A. Meeker, and I didn't quite fit.

One night I again smuggled some of his magazines back to the rectory and sat brooding over them late in my room. Father Vance would sure get a surprise if he

150

searched my room and found them, so I would have to smuggle them out again tomorrow.

As I sat on my bed in the glow of the lamp, flipping the pages, the images of those beautiful and unreal men rose up at me, like a sexual litany, from the personal ads where hustlers and lonely lovers advertised themselves:

Rugged Viking stud
Horny Aussie nude
Black Diamond in the rough
Hairy Levi model
San Francisco Adonis
Kentucky cowboy
Young Texas lad
Rugged New York jock
Virginia gentleman
Cowboy leather master
San Diego moon child

There were bodybuilders, blond blue-eyed surfers, muscular athletes, hip students, clean-cut outdoor types and strong cats without claws. They were heavy hung, handsome and horny, well endowed, uncut meat, raunchy, with bulging baskets and beautiful buns, have hands will travel, shoot your load, hot, wild and ready. They said they had dancer's bodies, swimmer's bodies, runner's bodies. They were manly but sensuous, all man, young and ready for heavy action.

None of them was me.

On top of my religious guilts, I was beginning to feel another, more secular kind of guilt: that I couldn't live up to these fantasies of Vidal's. My sensuality was limited, or maybe it operated differently from his. Mine started with caring—his ended there.

Impatiently I threw aside the magazines—the *In Touch*, the *Mandate*, the *Entertainment West*—and picked up the *Advocate*. I felt more comfortable with this national gay newspaper. It had raunchy personals too, but it carried a

151

wealth of news and feature articles about my gay brothers and sisters out there beyond the isolation of Cottonwood.

I scanned the paper hungrily. Every page told me that in other states, other churches, the battles between the hierarchy and the gays were sharpening. In Tennessee, a Methodist minister was expelled from his church because he openly said he was gay. In California, gay people picketed an Episcopal cathedral where the bishop had made antigay remarks in a sermon.

Suddenly one headline riveted me. CATHOLIC ORGANIZATION EXPANDS.

I read the article with feverish speed. There was actually a national Catholic coalition of gay priests, religious and laymen who were openly challenging the Church's teaching on homosexuality. It was called Dignity. Its national headquarters was in Boston, but it also had a growing list of chapters in other cities across America. Avidly I scanned the list, wondering if there was a chapter in Montana.

No, there wasn't. But there was one in Denver. That was the closest one geographically. There were chapters in Seattle and Portland too.

I let the newspaper slide aside and sat there in a state of nervous excitement, thinking. The thoughts formed themselves into a wordless prayer that God might help me somehow to get to Denver so that I could talk to some of those people. Maybe talking to another gay priest would help me.

I wondered how I could possibly fabricate an excuse to go to Denver. It was farther away than anywhere I'd gone with Vidal. What else was going on in Denver that I could attend as a cover? Father Vance had mentioned an anti-abortion conference that was going to be held at Regis College in Denver in August some time. Maybe he would give me permission to go as a vacation.

I sat there thinking for a long time, in a stifled state almost like mental prayer.

Rugged blond blue-eyed priest, has hands, will travel.

Finally I bestirred myself and searched for my breviary. Let it be recorded that Father Tom Meeker, after reading forbidden magazines with suggestive pictures in them, did say his Divine Office.

≡

That Saturday, the ball wasn't supposed to start till 8:00 P.M., but we left Cottonwood around noon.

I had asked Father Vance for permission to do a few hours' hiking in the Hellgate Canyon near Helena, camp out there that night, then make my regular Sunday visit to my parents and Father Matt. Father was getting a little worried about my rundown look, and he said Sure, go ahead. I actually did plan to look in on my parents on Sunday—supposedly Vidal was nothing to hide, so they might as well meet my good friend from Cottonwood.

Vidal and I made a big show of loading our groceries and hiking equipment into the Triumph, and left town about twelve-thirty.

I was getting more and more nervous about the ball, and about the whole way we were living. Once in a while I'd have paranoid thoughts that Mrs. Shoup was following us around, writing down everything we did in a little black book. Or was having a private detective follow us.

We got to Helena around two, and got rooms in a cheap little motel outside of town, not too far from the Broadwater Hotel.

For the first time, we had several hours in a private place. But not surprisingly, I wasn't in any mood to take advantage of them. Vidal tried hard to get me in bed with him, and finally gave up in exasperation. We almost had a fight, and Vidal went off to his room and shut the door.

Deeply depressed, I lay on the bed and brooded for the rest of the afternoon. About six-thirty, with a feeling that it was my fate, I got up and started putting on the costume that I'd thought out. Then, in front of the bathroom mirror, I worked on my face with a set of Magic Markers of different colors.

At about a quarter to eight, my room phone rang. I picked it up.

"You getting dressed?" Vidal said.

"Thought I might as well," I said.

"I'm all ready," he said. "Look, don't get so uptight. Try to relax and have a good time. Nobody's going to recognize you, I promise."

"I know you're trying to understand," I said.

"We wasted the whole goddam afternoon," he said. "It could have been nice."

"I know," I said. "I'm sorry."

A few minutes later, he knocked on the door of my room. When he came in, we looked at each other and our jaws fell. Then we broke out laughing.

For a little over thirty dollars, Vidal had put together a really amazing costume. He was a fancy dancer. But neither I nor his father or the Blackfeet tribe would have recognized him.

First, he had bought a beautiful but very fake Indian war bonnet at the tourist shop. It had pink, blue and yellow feathers in it. Instead of with beading, the brow band was decorated with little shells, beads and seeds. Vidal had gotten some glue, glitter, sequins and thread and needle at the dime store, and added some extra touches to the bonnet. But the crowning touch was the insertion of about three dozen peacock feathers in the bonnet and in the part that trailed down the back.

Vidal was wearing little else: a skimpy vest, a pair of bikini briefs and a pair of cheap moccasins, also from the tourist shop. But these items had also been transformed into a wonder of sequins and glitter. The vest had hippy bead-and-shell necklaces and pieces of peacock feather sewn onto it like insane brocade. The eye part of one

154

peacock feather was sewn insolently over what I had learned to call his basket—two others accentuated his buttocks.

This absurd and magnificent outfit really set off the crude hard beauty of his body. You still noticed the patchiness of his skin, his callused hands, the scars from fights. It was the body of a gutter fighter who had come out in the trappings of his innermost Jungian fantasy.

"Good God, where did you get those peacock feathers?" I asked.

"At the hospital thrift shop. They had a whole vase of them there. Some lady had used them like flowers, and she got tired of them."

He was looking searchingly at my costume, trying to figure out what my fantasy was.

My clothes were simply some Western outdoors items, and they hadn't cost me a cent—I had fished them out of my own closet at the St. Mary's rectory. Walking boots, Levi's faded to baby blue, a leather belt, a pale yellow long-sleeve cotton shirt, and a straw cowboy-type hat.

There was just one bizarre touch to this outfit. I had drawn colored designs all over my face and hands and neck. My shirt was daringly open to the waist and sleeves rolled up to the elbow, showing that my chest and arms were designed too. I had even ripped out a small square in one thigh of the Levi's and put a design on the patch of skin that showed through. The suggestion was that I was tattooed all over with wildflowers, birds, butterflies and green leaves.

A big butterfly covered my whole face. The marks on the wings were my eyes, the body was my nose, and the smaller back wings spread over my cheeks. My fingers were green stems, ending in roses on the back of my hands. There was a pair of red lips on each of my palms. My neck was covered with stars. On my chest was a smiling angel with a pair of red lips in the middle of its chest.

"Holy Christ," said Vidal, "yours is even better than mine. Your own mother won't recognize you."

"Cheaper too," I bragged. "All it cost me was the Magic Markers, three ninety-five at the drugstore."

"You're making quite a display of yourself," he teased. "Didn't know you had it in you. After being such a virgin all afternoon." He was walking around me. "Every one of those things means something. They're like—embroidery on vestments, huh?"

This hadn't occurred to me, but right away I knew he was right. The vestments of those guilty masses I had celebrated had burned right through into my skin.

He came up to me and kissed me gently. "So we're not going as anybody else. You're going as you and I'm going as me."

As we walked out through the lobby, I heard my gayness commented on in public for the first time. An old cowboy type was leaning against the desk gossiping with the clerk, and he sang out, "My oh my, looky all the pansies goin' off to the garden party."

I shrank from the words, but kept walking as if I hadn't heard.

———

The Broadwater Hotel is a beautiful relic of Helena's gold-rush days.

It stands just off the highway south of town, in an immense park with old poplar trees planted along its avenues. The dark Gothic pile of verandas and towers rises mysteriously above the treetops, now darkened by a century of rain and storm. Abandoned and closed up for years, with the furniture still inside it, the hotel had recently been rescued by a history-minded group of Montana financiers. They had reopened it as a kind of exotic resort hotel with authentic Gay Nineties atmosphere.

156

There was even talk that they would put the famous old hot-spring swimming pool back into working order again. But for now the pool was still a weedy ruin.

As we walked up the wide front steps, where the carriages had once stopped, we could already hear the music through the open windows of the grand ballroom.

"I guess there's not going to be any rock music tonight," said Vidal, a little disappointed.

"Doesn't sound like it," I said. "That's a Strauss waltz called 'Wine, Women and Song.' "

Vidal laughed.

In the huge lobby, the fantastic costumes mingled with the regular guests, who stared a little but didn't say much. We were stared at, especially Vidal.

"My God, the costumes," I said. "Some of them must have cost hundreds of dollars."

We stopped in front of a Victorian-looking poster with all kinds of fancy script that was mounted on a stand. It announced the Silver State Bicentennial Ball, with entertainment, door prizes and contests. Down at the bottom, it said, "Sponsored by the Montana Calamus Committee."

"Who the hell is the Calamus Committee?" I asked.

"Probably a bunch of rich butch businessmen," said Vidal. "I'm dying for a drink."

We stood in the crowded bar, with its Art Nouveau stained glass and its red velvet booths and its flickering gaslights, and drank a whiskey. Now and then I remembered, with some surprise, that I was a Roman Catholic priest. Everybody was looking everyone else up and down, and it dawned on me that I might have my first experience being "cruised" or "groped" (words I'd learned from Vidal) before the night was over.

Some amazing-looking women drifted by us. One looked like Mae West. One looked like a classic dancehall girl. There were a couple of madams and an Annie Oakley. One plump young person with a china-doll face had squeezed herself into a real hourglass corset and looked hauntingly like the Jersey Lily.

One really caught my eye. She was a wraithlike thing, wearing a real antique gown of apple-green watered silk, with a froth of fragile old lace at the throat and at the wrists. Her hair cascaded in brown ringlets, and spit-curls framed her forehead. She wore a little green velvet hat with a veil. Her long-lashed hazel eyes looked drowned in belladonna. She looked the most authentic and might have floated out of some old photograph in a velvet-covered family album somewhere on Helena's West Side.

Slowly, with a feeling of muffled shock, I realized that most of these lovely creatures were male, or had been up to some point in their lives.

Vidal read my thoughts, and leaned over to explain in a low voice.

"Some of them just like to dress up. But some of them are transsexuals. Either they've had operations, or they were born that way, or they just feel they got stuck with the wrong body. Some of them are gay, some of them aren't. I mean, how can a guy be gay if he's convinced he's a woman?"

There were butch-looking men in the crowded bar too. Most of them were dressed up as tough Western types—gunslingers, gamblers, cowboys. As Vidal had predicted, there were a Lone Ranger and a Tonto. A few of the younger men were just wearing outlandish little costumes with more or less flesh exposure. One young guy was wearing white high-heeled kid boots laced up the knee, and a little brief with fringes of glass beads like you find on old lampshades. His mask was sewn with seed pearls, and on his head he had a big picture hat with pink ostrich plumes. He was drunk, and waltzing slowly all by himself.

It occurred to me that I was now looking at a whole hotel full of fancy dancers. In spite of the pressures on them, or maybe because of the pressures, gay people had found the ability to explore and express a richness of inner human experience that straight people had somehow missed. The Church would impoverish herself to the degree that She refused to tap this richness.

"This really blows my mind," I mumbled. The whiskey was starting to get to me.

"Don't drink too much now," said Vidal. "You're not in practice for it. Let's go in."

But my nervousness was getting worse. Supposing somebody I knew was there, and saw through the paint job on my face? Supposing . . .

The orchestra was wearing white tie and tails, and playing on a platform banked with palms. The crystal chandeliers glowed. Beneath them, all the butch gays, transvestites, transsexuals, lesbians and straights twirled and dipped to the strain of "Voices of Spring." Some of them couldn't waltz too well, so they just danced slow with their arms around each other. Colonel Broadwater would have done a war dance in his grave. In the adjoining room, a roast beef buffet was being served (which would make Montana cowmen happy), and people were heaping their plates.

Vidal turned to me, grinning, and held out his arms. His peacock feathers stuck up two feet over people's heads.

"May I have the honor of this dance?" he said.

"Dance?" I said. Somehow it hadn't occurred to me that we'd have to dance.

"That's what we're here for," said Vidal.

I was a little drunk, and very serious. "I haven't danced since I went into the seminary."

Vidal's eyes narrowed. His blue eye seemed to get bluer, and his green one got greener, in another fit of impatience at my hangups. "Okay," he said. He turned on his moccasin heel and disappeared into the crowd.

His action hit me like a bolt of lightning. There I was, alone and abandoned in the middle of Purgatory by my Virgil.

I stood forlornly on the sidelines and watched the happy crowd. The next time I saw Vidal, he was dancing close and slow with a glowering gunslinger type in black leather.

I went back to the bar and had another drink. What with my exhaustion and the fact I hadn't eaten any dinner, the whiskey was starting to do funny things to my biochemistry, but I didn't give a damn. The bar had emptied out a little, so I was rather conspicuous sitting there on my stool, nursing my shot glass.

"Well, well, what do we have here? A little wallflower?" said a deep male voice in my ear.

I looked up and saw a sunburned U. S. cavalry officer standing there, complete with sideburns, crop and spurs.

I turned back to my drink.

"What other pretty pictures you got there where I can't see 'em?" he said, laying a hand on my thigh and trying to put his finger through the little square I'd torn out.

I shook his hand off and looked him in the eye. "You're late for the Custer Massacre," I said.

He shrugged and walked off.

A few drunken moments later, there was a rustle at my elbow and a wisp of an herbal scent. There stood the girl in watered silk, looking at me with her great drowned eyes.

"Lonely boy," she said.

She didn't seem to be throwing a pass, so I motioned her to sit down beside me. "What'll you have?" I said.

"Gin, straight up," she said.

As the bartender slid the drink over to her, she said, "I can't bear to see people alone." She sipped the gin delicately, this creature of lace curtains, lilacs and old sheet music. "You have a fight with your lover?"

"Yeah," I said. "What about you?"

"Oh, no. He's just in there dancing," she said.

I considered this statement solemnly. "How do you feel about that?"

"I'm his slave, so it doesn't matter."

We strolled along the veranda, holding our drinks. A summer thunderstorm was blowing up over the mountains, and lightning flickered far off through the great old poplar trees. Her green silk skirt ballooned out, exposing her little slippers of white kid. I kept looking at her, wondering what the reality of her soul was, as God saw it. The illusion she created was so perfect for me—was it for her? Did she even fool God? But nobody fooled God. I remembered the tone of the bishops' booklet. How did they dust their hands of her? How would God condemn her?

I also remembered the bishops' statement about how homosexual loves were short and merry. Maybe the bishops knew something we didn't—Vidal and I were obviously headed for a lot of grief.

She took my arm. "You look so young under that butterfly face."

"I'm not so young."

"Yes, you are. A baby. I'm old."

I made a lopsided smile. I was getting pretty drunk. "How old are you? Sweet sixteen?"

"I'm a thousand years old," she said. "Touch me and I turn to dust."

She said it so convincingly that I halfway thought her face would shrink to a mummy's, then crumble under her veil.

She started to hum a waltz tune and spun slowly ahead of me along the veranda. I started to laugh with insane delight. The gaslights and the music and the lightning spilled at us. She waltzed back to me and drifted into my arms, and spun me into her slow motion. A puff of milkweed thistle could have moved a boulder into a waltz by blowing against it the way she blew against me. I was falling over my feet and laughing like an idiot.

"I'm an awful dancer," I kept saying.

She finally conned me into the ballroom. Drunk as I was, I knew my motive. I felt safer (i.e., less gay) with her because for all intents and purposes she was a woman.

We joined the crush and she taught me how to waltz. I looked for Vidal's peacock feathers, and saw him dancing slow and close with the Lone Ranger. It hurt me to see him catting around like that, to see him touching other men, but I kept laughing.

We danced past him. He saw us, and his face clouded.

Suddenly there was a drum roll. The music stopped and a hush fell over the ballroom.

"La-deez and gentlemen," said the MC.

"What's going on now?" I asked the girl.

"The contests," she said. "Mr. and Mrs. Montana, the best costume, the ..."

A flame of fright went through me. I didn't want to be singled out. Neither did she, apparently. We hovered in the background as the contestants filed before the crowd. It was just like a bathing beauty contest, except that here men paraded in the near-nude, in shimmering briefs. The crowd erupted with whoops and wolf whistles, especially when Vidal took his turn in the spotlights. He turned his natural-child grin on them, and the applause was deafening. They gave him second prize.

There seemed to be a stir in one corner of the ballroom. The MC said into the mike in a low discreet voice, "If there is a clergyman in the house, would he come to the bandstand, please?"

There was a note of urgency in his voice. "Wonder what happened?" I asked the girl.

My conscience told me I ought to go find out. But my fright held me back. For the first time in my life, I couldn't care enough to move into action. We kept dancing. *Someone needs help,* I told myself. *I should . . .*

We kept dancing.

Suddenly I said to myself: *What kind of a man of God are you? Get your anointed ass into gear.*

We pushed our way over to the bandstand.

"Oh, you're a couple minutes too late," said the MC. "Some old guy had a heart attack. He was scared to death and asking for a minister, any kind of minister, he said. They just took him out to the ambulance."

Just as he spoke, the siren started up in the park outside. We heard it fading away slowly into Helena.

I almost told him a lie, that I'd been in the bar and hadn't heard the appeal at first. But my teeth closed on this one just in time.

"Did anybody come?" I asked the MC.

"Nope," said the MC, shaking his head sadly.

I turned away kicking myself for being such a coward. Vidal had brought me there to show me the scene, and instead through him God had shown me the reality of myself. I had refused to help a lonely and desperate soul. Jesus would ask me about it on Judgment Day. "And when you were at the drag ball, did you not deny Me three times until the cock crew?" "Yes, Lord, I did." "Be cast out, then, into the darkness . . ."

I walked gloomily away through the swirling dancers. The brief euphoria was ashes now. The crystal chandeliers seemed to press down on me with a crushing despair.

In the bar, I ordered another whiskey. The girl ordered another gin. The gaslights and the Art Nouveau glass were starting to grind slowly around me like a merry-go-round.

"Are you a clergyman?" she said.

"Yeah," I said.

"Minister? Priest?"

"Yeah."

Her drowned eyes searched mine. A bright flush had come out on her cheekbones—she must be getting pretty tight too. Through an open stained-glass window, we could hear the thunder roll nearer and the whisper of rain along the verandas. I thought she was going to ask me why I hadn't gone to the bandstand sooner. Instead, she said:

"Does God love me?"

"Are you a Catholic?"

She took my drink away from me. "You're drunk and you didn't answer my question." Her eyes seemed to focus with a blurry anxiety.

"Yes, as a matter of fact, God loves you," I said. "If He didn't, I could walk out of here with a clear conscience."

She was looking at herself in the mirror behind the bar, her face almost lost in the rows of glasses. She put her kid-gloved fingers to her cheek as if to touch that fever spot on her cheekbone.

"God loves me," she said wonderingly.

"God loves everybody here, including my lover," I said. "He even loves me." I started to cry.

The Broadwater Hotel was tilting over, like a sinking ship about to go under water. The bar kept trying to rise up and hit me in the face. The Magic Markers were staining down my cheeks.

Then came a sickening car ride, a motel corridor, and vomiting in the toilet bowl.

≡

"Wake up, you crummy amateur sinner."

Vidal was bending over me.

My eyes seemed to be held shut by cobwebs, and my tongue was a mildewed velvet pillow. An ax of doom was splitting my skull.

"What time are you supposed to be at your folks' house? Twelve?" Vidal asked.

The bathroom mirror showed me a stranger's swollen face with a butterfly on it, all smudged under the eyes. I scrubbed at it with soap and water. Panic: it wouldn't come off. But finally it did. Shaking, I managed to wash up and shave.

Vidal leaned in the doorway, watching me coolly. He was wearing jeans and his Yucatan wedding shirt.

"I thought you were mad at me," I said.

He shrugged. "I can't stay mad at you, you're such a mess. But your hangups get me sometimes. And then you went off and danced with that goddam queen."

"You danced with plenty of people."

He grinned. "I'll be damned. The priest is jealous."

At twelve on the dot, we got to Stuart Street.

My mother was at the door with her usual little shriek.

"Mom and Pop, this is a friend of mine from Cottonwood, Vidal Stump," I said as casually as I could.

My parents looked him up and down, and smilingly said they were pleased to meet him. Rosie set an extra place at the table, and we ate dinner at one. My parents were very nice to Vidal, but I could detect a little strain in the air. But how could they possibly know, or even guess, what we'd been doing the night before?

When we were having our after-dinner Drambuie and my mother was showing Vidal some of her coins, my father said quietly, "Tom, you look awful tired. Can't you take a vacation?"

"I guess you're right," I said wearily. "There's a conference coming up in Denver. Maybe Father Vance will let me go for a week."

"A conference isn't a vacation," said my father. "Maybe you'd like to just come here and eat and sleep for a week."

"Believe me," I said, "just getting away from Cottonwood for a week will be a vacation."

"Well, you ought to do it," my father said. "I can't remember when I've seen you look so bad. You look like something the cat brought in."

After a moment, he asked, even more quietly, "Tom, maybe it's none of my business, but ... have you been drinking?"

———

Next I was supposed to drive over to Carroll College for confession. But I didn't have the nerve. I called Father Matt, told him I was exhausted, and canceled.

Father Matt said, "Tom, I've begun to feel that you're hiding something from me."

"Hiding something?" My stomach plunged with fright. "No, I'm not hiding anything. I'm just half-crazy from being tired."

I talked a lot into the phone about my fatigue and pretty much convinced him. Finally he said, "The conference ... that's the one at Regis College, isn't it? Why don't I give Father Vance a call and tell him *I* think you need a little breath of air?"

11

I came home to Cottonwood with a crushing sense of having been humbled. In His mysterious way, God had used the Silver State Ball to show me my weaknesses, and to show me that there was nothing infallible or automatic about my capacity to care for other people.

In the days that followed, as I rushed around doing the regular parish work, I made a resolution. Never again, with God's help, would I be guilty of a lapse like that.

Up until now, Vidal had been my guide. Finally I took my first shaky steps on my own. Vidal had insisted that gay people were my new "parish," and now, for the first time, I looked for the boundaries of that parish in Cottonwood itself.

An estimated ten percent of Americans are homosexual. So, even allowing for the fact that so many gays are concentrated in urban areas like New York City and southern California, it still meant that maybe two hundred of the 3500 people in Cottonwood had to be gay.

They were not visible, but logic told me that they had to be there.

So, who were they?

These secret gays of Cottonwood haunted my waking hours, my prayers, and even my dreams. What stores did they work in? What streets did they live on? Did they live on "nice" streets or on the "other side of the tracks"? What post-office mailboxes did they use? Were there any in the high school? The county old-folks' home? The sawmill? The jail? The small police force?

I had a wish that was raw and painful as a bruise, to reach out and touch their lives, know their thoughts and feelings, taste their guilts and their joys. Were any of them free spirits like Vidal? Not too likely. Were they racked with guilt like me? Probably.

People sometimes talked about Al Bovington, who owned the florist shop next to the bank, and played the organ for the Presbyterian Church. They said he was "kind of a fruit." But by now I knew from Vidal that being outwardly effeminate and gentle is not necessarily being gay.

Once, during those first days in August, I glimpsed the shore of that hidden continent of feeling in my town. And it turned out to be the most shattering experience I'd had so far as a priest.

═══

Missy Oldenberg was looking pretty poor, and her doctor and I both had the feeling that she was going to die soon. She had a bladder condition that subjected her to attacks of pain and vomiting. The doctor felt that Missy was already too weak to stand up to an operation.

So I visited Missy and her friend Clare Faux a couple of times a week, and spent an hour. Seeing the county old-folks' home had opened my eyes to the urgency of making old people feel cared-for.

The two ladies' dairy farm was on the north edge of town. It had been thirty years since the place sent any milk to the creamery in town. In the empty pens, the manure-rich soil grew every species of weed native to Montana. Tumbleweeds rolled across the trackless barnyard. The pastures were thick with quack grass, fox tail and tall Russian thistles. The huge barn had caved in, and its shingle roof was silvered by a half-century of weather. Along the creek, the big old cottonwood trees were half-dead, their branches torn out by winter storms.

But around the big white frame house with its green shutters, the two old ladies defended a square of life and order. A boy came to mow the lawn. In the back, Clare still tended a big vegetable and flower garden. She did the work alone now.

Inside, the house had that fragrance of old wood that always reminded me of my parents' home in Helena. The broadloom carpets with their fake Oriental patterns were worn, but always swept clean by Clare. The smell of fresh coffee always floated out from the big kitchen. There, the old curtained glass cupboards rose clear to the ceiling, and the yellow-oak wall clock made its soft deep chime. The two old ladies' hats hung on pegs by the door. Missy's was a black straw boater with a bunch of daisies on the brim. Clare's was a black straw boater with a bunch of red cherries.

The house was crammed with examples of the two ladies' artistry. The living room curtains were hand-crocheted, and as delicate as spiderwebs. There were antimacassars on the chairs, afghans draping the sofa, rag rugs on the floor.

One day Clare showed me an amazing patchwork "friendship quilt" that the two of them had made. They kept it on the bed in the guest room. It was patchworked in tiny squares of silk instead of the usual cotton, and it had a rosette pattern as rich and colorful as a stained-glass window in a Gothic cathedral. In one corner, the two of them had stitched their names and the date 1934.

I asked her the why of that year.

"Oh, it was the year that we moved in together," Clare said shyly. "We'd both been widows for exactly one year, and we decided that two could live cheaper than one."

Clare and Missy were very different, though you might have thought they were twins when you saw them walking to church with their identical black umbrellas. Clare was taller, bigger-boned, with a round apple face and a bulldog jaw, and a quiet blunt way of speaking that went with her features. Missy was more frail and more fey, with a cameo profile and faded green eyes that still hinted at the beauty of her young days. But forty years in the same house had so entwined their habits of thought that you couldn't pick out any individual philosophy, any more than you could pick out which stitches one of them had put in the friendship quilt.

On my visits, I always sat with them in Missy's bedroom.

Missy lay propped on several pillows, her thin hair carefully combed by Clare into a tiny chignon. She always wore a blue wool bed jacket that Clare had knitted for her. Clare would sit by the window in a creaky yellow-oak rocking chair, and I would sit on a straight chair by the bed and read to them from the New Testament. That was what they wanted. They especially loved the Beatitudes. Clare would rock creakily and knit, and Missy would listen, her watery eyes looking blindly, dreamily out the window.

"Blessed are the meek, for they shall inherit the earth," I would read. "Blessed are the . . ."

"When are we going to have a picnic on the lawn?" Missy would suddenly interrupt. "Clare, are there enough eggs in the house to make some egg sandwiches?"

"We used to picnic on the lawn a lot," Clare would say to me apologetically.

One afternoon, Missy interrupted by reaching out tremblingly for my hand. She held it in her own thin veined hands, which were warm and helpless as the paws of a newborn kitten, and she patted it.

She said in her high quavering voice, "I'm so fortunate to have Clare, you know, Father."

I put down the Bible and patted her hand back. "You are very lucky," I said.

"If it weren't for Clare, they would have come and put me in the county home," said Missy.

"Pretty soon St. Mary's is going to have its own nice home," I said.

She kept patting my hand. "But, Father, what will happen to Clare? When I go, who is going to look after her? They'll come and take her away to that county home, Father."

"Now, Missy, you don't worry about me," said Clare. "We've got our savings, and I'm still healthy and working away."

Missy wasn't listening. A fine silver thread of elderly monomania ran straight through her mind.

"We don't have any family anymore, Father," she said. "They're all dead now. My sister Fay is dead and buried, and Clare's sister and brother are dead a long time now. All we have is each other."

A couple of tears went jumping down Missy's cheeks from wrinkle to wrinkle. Clare had stopped knitting and was staring out the window, as if she was succeeding in holding back tears.

"Father," said Missy, "I'm going to say a very sinful thing."

"What?" I said, still patting her hand. A big lump was growing in my throat.

"If I go to heaven, there won't be any beatitude until Clare is there with me."

"But she *will* be with you," I said. "You'll be together through sanctifying grace."

But Missy wasn't listening. "I won't see God until I see Clare in heaven."

When Missy got tired, Clare and I left the room.

Clare always insisted on sending me away with a little fresh coffee and homemade cookies in my stomach, so we sat in the living room and talked a while. The conversation with Missy had impressed me, more deeply than ever, with their feeling for each other. I knew that Missy was right—Clare would be in an agonizing readjustment when Missy died.

"Mrs. Faux," I said, "can I talk frankly to you?"

"Yes, Father," she said. "Have I done something wrong?"

"Oh, no," I said. "Missy is right, the things she said back in the bedroom there. Have you made plans for the future?"

She was silent for a time, stirring her coffee in the old china cup with a battered sterling spoon.

"No," she said.

"You should," I said. "Both for Missy's peace of mind, and for your own welfare. You'll need something to be committed to."

She was silent again, her bulldog jaw working—whether from emotion or bad teeth, I couldn't tell.

"I'd feel guilty making plans," she said.

"Don't," I said. "Mrs. Oldenberg's days are going to be more restful now for knowing that your coming years will be safe and busy."

Clare was silent, stubborn. Then she said, "It would be a betrayal."

172

"No," I said. "You've given each other so much. After she's gone, you'd still be giving it to her, through others."

This time Clare was silent for the longest time of all. She was strong, but made weak at the core by the tiny crack of love.

Finally she said, "Yes, I do see what you mean."

"Please think about it. I'll give you any help you need," I said.

"All right, I'll consider it," she said doubtfully.

When I left the house, I looked back at it from the car. The lawn and the garden were a little oasis of life in that desert of a farm. It made me think of Will and Larry's ranch over at Drummond.

Suddenly, as vague and shifting as the leaf shadows falling through those windows onto the spiderweb curtains, the thought fell on my mind that the love of these two radiant old ladies might go far beyond friendship.

I drove away from the farm stunned by the thought.

Except for what I'd read in Vidal's magazines, I knew next to nothing about lesbians. Vidal himself couldn't tell me much about them.

That little booklet published by the National Council of Bishops had stated that lesbians were less physical in their relationships than gay men, in line with the myth that women in general are less physical. But I knew better. From a year and a half in the confessional, I knew that women were no less carnal than men, though they often felt they had to hide their desire. I wondered if that silk quilt once covered the bed where Missy Oldenberg and Clare Faux slept together.

I wanted to discuss the two old women with Vidal, but of course I couldn't—no more than I could discuss any other parishioners' problems with him. I was as alone with their problem as I'd been when Vidal walked away from me at the Silver State Ball.

One evening when Vidal and I were snatching our

173

fifteen minutes together in bed (we still managed it two or three times a week), he said, "You've got something on your mind."

I shrugged. "Nothing to do with us. A favorite parishioner of mine is going to die."

"That's just it," he said. "I always feel like there's some parishioner of yours in bed with us."

About midnight, one night during the first week in August, Clare called me at the rectory.

"The doctor was just here," she said. "He thinks you ought to come. And she wants to receive the sacraments."

"She should be in the hospital," I said.

"She doesn't want to go to the hospital," Clare said. "She wants to die at home, in her own bed, like decent people should."

Feeling the usual twinge of guilt, I dressed, got the bitterroot stole and the case of holy oils, and drove over there. Once again the poisoned priest was going to adminster his stained sacraments to his unsuspecting flock.

In the bedroom, I put on the stole and took Missy's hand. "Mrs. Oldenberg," I said.

After a moment her half-open eyes opened a little more, and she rolled her head feebly toward me. She didn't have the strength to pat my hand anymore. Her lips looked dried, and her face was a putty color. Her flat chest moved up and down under the embroidered sheet with a jerky uneven rhythm.

"Father?" she whispered.

"I'm right here," I said. "Do you want to confess, Mrs. Oldenberg?"

"Oh yes, Father, I've sinned some bad sins . . ."

I held my breath, patting her hand. Was she about to avow the sexual sin that I suspected? It was my duty to "be firm," as Father Matt had said. Dig it out, get her to repent, threaten her with loss of her immortal soul. But,

174

guilty as I felt about myself, I couldn't bring myself to do it to this gentle, dying old lady.

"Father, I confess to being snappish with Clare sometimes," Missy was saying. A sudden last rush of energy brought a little color into her washed-out face and eyes. "I haven't been well, of course, but I shouldn't be so snappish . . ."

She was silent for a while, moving her broken teeth weakly together, gazing at me blankly.

"Is there more, Mrs. Oldenberg?" I prompted.

After a few minutes, she said, "I've worried so much about what will happen to Clare, that I haven't trusted in God enough . . ."

Another silence. I felt as if my heart was going to break.

"Is that all?" I asked.

"Yes," she whispered, her voice fading now, like a radio signal. "So heartily sorry, Father . . ."

That lump in my throat was gagging me again. I had already learned the scent of a clear conscience, the way it only takes the young hound dog one lesson to know the scent of a mountain lion.

"Mrs. Oldenberg, if you can't say the act of contrition," I said, "just try to think it while I absolve you."

The lump in my throat made it hard to talk, but I choked my way through the words. Marking her forehead, hands and feet with little crosses of holy oil, I gave her the Sacrament of the Sick. Taking the single consecrated wafer from the pyx, I slipped it into her mouth, with those doomed fingers of mine that had touched Vidal's flesh. She closed her eyes, and her broken ivory teeth moved on the wafer a little.

Then she gave a little sigh and went to sleep, her chest still moving gently.

When I left the house, I sat in the car for a few minutes and tried to cry. But the lump just stayed there, strangling me.

The next morning around 8, Clare called me again. Missy Oldenberg had died quietly in her sleep around 4:30 A.M.

≡

Three days later, the doomed priest had to say Missy's funeral mass.

For the first time in my life, it struck me what an awful thing the Mass for the Dead is—awful in the old-time sense, with its root in the word "awe." In an age where Americans seem to have lost touch with death (though the headlines put it next door every day), the Mass with the Body Present doesn't fool around with soft lighting, cosmetics and plastic green grass. It rattles the bones right in your face. Even the modernization of this Mass, which had taken place in recent years, didn't soften it for me. The hair-raising *Dies Irae* isn't sung anymore, and the Church has tried hard to blow the stench of brimstone and burning flesh off this last rite—but my own guilty conscience put that stench right back.

All morning, I kept wondering obsessively what Missy's last judgment had been, and what I should have or could have done to change it. And what would my judgment be, if I died with that same sin on my conscience, plus my betrayal of my ministry? Even if I managed a last-minute repentance, would that be enough?

The Mass started at 10:00 A.M.

It was a furnace day, like a gust from the deep gulch of hell itself. Out in the hayfields around Cottonwood, any careless hayhand who didn't wear a hat would have a sunstroke by mid-afternoon. Even the church, which was usually cool, had a scorched dusty smell in it. The candles around Missy's bier burned straight up, with a sound like soup simmering.

In the sacristy, I put on the green vestments that Missy and Clare had embroidered. Black vestments weren't worn much anymore. Surely the two old ladies must have had the random thought that these things would be worn at their own funerals. They had chosen a design of wild-roses and crab-apple blossoms.

When Jamie and I came in through the front door of the church for the processional, I was surprised to see so many people. Usually the death of an old lady in a small town goes unnoticed by everyone except her peers. But here were several young people that I didn't recognize. They must be from out of town, maybe some of the handicraft freaks that Missy and Clare had corresponded with in other parts of the state.

The one important person who wasn't there was Vidal. He didn't know what this Mass meant to me, so he was down at the garage.

As I came in, the people rose with a rustling of hymn books and a clunking of feet against the wooden knee rests. Even Clare got shakily to her feet in the front pew.

She was alone. She had taken the bunch of cherries off her black straw hat and substituted a black net veil. Her huge old black silk umbrella with the yellowed ivory handle fell over, out into the aisle, and the clatter echoed through the church. One of the young people picked it up for her. She stood with her face tight and vacant, fanning her iridescent sweaty cheek with an old lace fan.

I spoke the first words of the rite. They were gentle modernized words, and they sounded funny coming out of that mind of mine, that echoed with the shrieks and the cries of the Last Judgment of gays:

"The grace and peace of God our Father and the Lord Jesus Christ be with you," I said.

"And also with you," said the people in the church.

The pallbearers had Missy's coffin there. The peculiar feeling came over me that it was my own defiled corpse that lay inside. I sprinkled the body with holy water. The pallbearers put a white pall over the coffin.

Then we proceeded down the aisle to the sanctuary.

Jamie carried the lighted paschal candle. The gospel book rode along on the coffin, over Missy's head. The congregation stood singing a hymn as we walked along slowly through them. Since I was not playing the organ, their voices had the usual naked, lonely, off-key sound.

I plowed my way through the Mass, my voice breaking. Everybody knew I had tended Missy in her last days, so they would put this down to grief. Yet every word of that Mass seemed to be a public announcement of my guilt, and Vidal's. I wondered if I would get desperate enough to think of killing myself.

When I came to the Scripture readings, I chose one from the book of Wisdom that suited my state of mind. It was almost like giving myself away:

> "He who pleased God was loved;
> he who lived among sinners was transported,
> Snatched away, lest wickedness pervert his mind
>   or deceit beguile his soul;
> For the witchery of paltry things obscures what is right
> and the whirl of desire transforms the innocent mind . . ."

Now and then, as I turned to face the congregation, I saw that Clare had her handkerchief in front of her eyes. I would have given anything to know what she was thinking about.

Odds and ends of thoughts fluttered through my head, like magpies that come flying to pick out the eyes of a dead cow. I thought of super-sensitive saints like Rose of Lima, who shook when the word "sin" was even mentioned. I thought of Roman martyrs of both sexes—some of them just children—who let themselves be torn by wild animals, beheaded, flayed, stabbed, roasted alive, rather than let their minds and bodies be defiled by the pagans. In my hotter religious moments, I had toyed with the idea of becoming a saint. It was just another of the long train of human fantasies, and it was a lot funnier than Vidal's fantasy about the sexy priest.

===

After the Mass, the six parish men carried the plain black coffin out into the hot sunlight. Their foreheads were already beaded with sweat as they slid it into the waiting hearse.

Grief had not seduced Clare Faux into spending her savings to quiet her conscience. She had made it plain to Bender's Funeral Home that the arrangements were to be as simple as possible. I had offered to be present at her discussion with the undertaker, to make sure he didn't con her into anything, but she handled it very well by herself. She had also asked for no flowers, only donations to the still-unopened St. Mary's Home for the Aged.

Father Vance, Jamie, Clare and I got into Father's car, and fell in behind the hearse. Everybody else piled into their own cars and followed us slowly through Cottonwood with headlights on. As we crossed the bridge, I could see the roof of Vidal's house through the willows.

I wondered how well Clare would be able to hide her grief during the burial service.

At the cemetery, we parked the cars just inside the gate. The heat struck down on us with savage force.

Clare had asked me to have a processional to the grave —the only touch of pomp in the whole funeral. So we formed up, Jamie with the cross, me, Clare leaning on Father Vance's arm, the six pallbearers with the coffin, and the little crowd of mourners. Then Father Vance's gravelly voice led everybody off with the hymn that Clare had wanted.

We started down the gravel road through the oldest part of the cemetery—you could tell it by the style of the tombstones and by the age of the trees. In the deep shade of the ripest old cottonwoods stood the earliest crumbling brick graves of the French and Métis builders of St. Mary's, and the weathered marble tablets of the mid-1800s, with good New England names on them.

But we headed on out into the new section. Here, the trees were just saplings, and the sun beat down on the broad lawn with its neat rows of new granite stones. Our voices, singing "O God Our Help in Ages Past," sounded even tinnier than in the church.

Halfway through it, we came to Missy's brand-new grave. It was a deep chalky rectangle. The bone-dry gravelly earth was piled to one side, on the grass. In that hole, we were going to bury a lifetime of devotion that the Church said was an abomination.

We all stood around the grave with our clothes and vestments hanging limply in the still air. A fine white dust seemed to cling to us. On the nearby hills, clouds of wild baby's breath were in bloom. From the little airstrip nearby, a small plane took off, climbing over us into the bald blue sky. On the hayfield across the road, a baling machine moved slowly along a windrow, and some men were stacking bales on the wagon hitched behind it. The farthest foothills shimmered in the heat like a mirage.

I glanced anxiously at Clare as I blessed the grave. She stared dry-eyed down into the hole. There must be no loneliness on this earth, I thought, like that of an elderly gay person who has lost a lifelong mate. My own eyes were dry and burning as I read the rites.

"Give her eternal rest, Oh Lord," I said.

"And may your light shine upon her for ever," the people answered.

The pallbearers lowered the coffin into the grave.

Clare stood leaning on Father Vance's arm, holding her big umbrella shakily over her head to keep off the sun. I had a sudden irrational desire for a cold beer, and thought of Larry and Will. Someday death would part them too. A ghostly roan stud and a ghostly gay rider paced slowly through my mind. I shook them away.

As the cemetery crew shoveled the dry dirt back down onto the coffin lid, a tremor seemed to go over Clare's body, like the barest breeze stirring the leaves of a quaking aspen.

When the hole was filled, she motioned one of the young people forward with a long box. From it, she took the only flowers of the funeral. They were from the garden that she and Missy had tended so lovingly. She must have moved slowly around the yard that morning, cutting the flowers slowly with a little pair of sharp scissors. It was a real old-fashioned bouquet—spikes of blue and purple delphinium, pinks, bachelor's buttons, sweet peas, roses, yellow snapdragons—all tied up with a black velvet ribbon.

She bent forward to put them on the mound of rubble, and nearly fell. Father Vance caught her arm just in time.

═══

That afternoon, I dropped by her house to see if she was all right.

Moving like one possessed by habit, she came out of the kitchen with the usual two steaming china cups on the tray. We sat with the coffee while the hot sunshine streamed through the spiderweb curtains on us.

"Now, Mrs. Faux," I said, "if you need anything, you let me know. Even if you have to call me up in the middle of the night."

She managed a little smile. "I won't be doing that, Father. But it's nice to know you mean it."

She held on to her cup and didn't drink much.

"I've thought about your suggestion, Father, and I've made some plans. Missy said you were right. She said, Now I don't want to hear about you living on alone here and being found dead by the milkman some fine day." She chuckled a little. "Missy got so confused. We don't have a milkman anymore."

"Are you going to sell this place and move to a smaller place?"

The creaky old farm would bring only pennies on the Cottonwood real estate market.

"Goodness, no," she said. "I'm going to stay here, and I'm going to be very busy. You'll see."

She took my hand and patted it gently, very much the way Missy did on her deathbed.

"You're a good priest, Father," she said. "And you're a very manly young man."

She smiled slyly. "And you're humble too. Goodness, I shouldn't say that. You can't tell a humble person that he's humble, can you?"

———

That night, Father Vance looked at me sharply as we sat at the rectory table. I was picking at my baked beans, and Father knew they were one of my favorite dishes.

"I've had a call from your confessor," he said. "He's concerned about your health."

I nodded dully.

"You look like we buried the wrong corpse today," said Father Vance.

I shrugged and nodded, and pushed my plate away.

"You've taken Mrs. Oldenberg's death much too hard," said Father Vance. "We have to set an example. Remind people that death is where we start, not where we end up."

Father Vance scraped the last bean off his own plate and rolled one of his powerful cigarettes.

"Your confessor said you were interested in this conference at Regis College in Denver. So I'm giving you permission to go."

This should have been happy news. But I was so wrung

out that the idea of traveling to Denver suddenly seemed impossible.

"But I can't give you much money for traveling," said Father.

My eyes were falling shut. "Oh, I'll manage by myself," I said.

But in bed that night, I tossed and turned. The stage had come where I was too tired for rest.

The late movie that night was *Born Yesterday* with Judy Holliday. But I didn't even watch it.

12

The next week was spent in figuring out how I was going to go to Denver on the cheap, without getting found out.

The first thing I did was write to the Dignity/Denver chapter, using Vidal's name and return address. I explained that a priest wanted badly to talk to someone there, and what did they suggest.

A few days later, the answer came to Vidal's mailbox in a plain white envelope. He gave it to me when we had supper at his house that night.

The letter said, "We would be very glad to meet with your friend. Tell him to call 745-7891 when he gets to Denver. That is the number of our chaplain, Fr. Doric, who will help him in any way he can." The letter was signed, "Love and peace," and the name of the chapter president.

Shakily I folded up the letter and hid it in my wallet. It didn't seem possible that this might be Doric Wilton, my old friend at the seminary. But I had always known Doric had wound up counseling in Colorado somewhere, not doing regular parish work. And Doric wasn't a common name. I wondered if this chaplain was gay. Many Dignity chaplains, I had read, were not gay, just concerned straights.

That phone number shone in my pocket like the pillar of fire that led the Israelites out of bondage. But a pillar of fire can be a very scary thing.

The next problem was transportation.

"Why don't you go with me?" I asked Vidal. "Visit your sister as a cover . . ."

He thought a minute. "Somehow," he said, "you and me going off in your car to the conference is too obvious. It's not the kind of thing I'd do, and Father Vance would know it."

"That means I drive down alone," I said. "I was hoping you'd help with the driving. It's a ways, and I'm too goddam tired to drive."

"I think it would be better if I went down alone on my bike. Why don't you bum a ride down on a plane?" Vidal said. "All these little planes flying out of here . . . Somebody'd give a priest a ride."

Vidal thought some more, musingly. "Denver," he said. "That's always been a big gay town. Some good night life there. Almost as good as California. You could see a few things you don't know yet."

I felt irritated. "You don't want to show me any bar life," I said. "You're just itching to go to bars alone."

Vidal looked me in the eye. "Maybe," he said.

The next afternoon, between a house call and a hospital visit, I drove out to the little county airport.

It was a single concrete strip, just long enough for a small plane to land on. It was sandwiched in between two alfalfa fields, with its magnetic compass heading 37 painted on the concrete at each end in huge white letters. The single small hangar, where a through plane could get repairs, was painted with the name MURCHISON FLYING SERVICE. The little office was prefab, with a counter, a desk, maps on the walls, a radio and a couple of sun-faded philodendron plants in the window. Dust and tumbleweeds blew across the strip, and the two planes tied down by the hangar moved their wings a little in the wind.

"Sure, Father," said Murchison. He was a husky rosy-cheeked man in his late twenties, with ragged brown hair down to his collar. "I'm flying to Missoula that week to have the annual checkup on the 170. From there you could pick up a flight to Denver with Bill Flavey. He's a businessman, flies there two or three times a week. I've got Bill's number, I'll give him a call to make sure he's got the seat free."

As I worked my way through the last few days before the conference, my stomach did tailspins every time I thought about Denver. Vidal was making some quiet arrangements of his own. The garage owed him some vacation, because he had worked some Sundays on police cars. He told them he wanted it to go visit his sister, and they said okay. He overhauled his bike for the long trip.

On the last evening, Saturday, Murchison called me at the rectory. He said to be at the airport by nine in the morning.

The next morning, I put on my social clothes, packed my little bag and said good-bye to Father Vance.

"Where are you going to be staying?" he said.

"I've got a couple of priest friends there. They're putting me up."

For once, Father Vance didn't demand the address and the telephone number. "Good," he said. "Cheaper than a hotel. Are you sure you have enough for meals?"

Father Vance stood at the rectory door as I climbed on the back of Vidal's bike. Vidal was taking me to the airport.

"Good-bye," the old priest said. "God bless you."

A lump rose in my throat. I was saying good-bye to everything I had known as a priest so far—perhaps to everything I had known as a person.

It was a hot, still August day. At the airport, Murchison already had the 170 untied. His skinny young wife leaned in the office doorway, wearing khaki pants.

"You get airsick?" he asked me.

"Not that I know of," I said. "But I've got Dramamine just in case."

The 170 was a four-seater, painted beige and pale green. Murchison threw my bag into the back seat, plus his own knapsack. As I climbed up into the front seat, Vidal was sitting on his bike over by the office. He just grinned and waved. When we had taken off, Vidal would drive back to his own house, tie his own knapsack on the bike, and hit the Interstate south for Denver. He would contact me there by calling that same phone number. I felt like I was going on some kind of undercover mission. James Bond would shoot me between the eyes and dump me out of the plane.

I slammed the little door and fastened the seat belt. As casually as if he was starting a car, Murchison turned the ignition key, and the propeller coughed around.

Murchison flicked on his radio, took his mike and called regional control in Missoula. "This is Zebra two-eight-three-nine-five at Cottonwood . . ." he said in that blah voice that pilots use.

He waved at his wife. I waved at Vidal.

The plane trundled lightly toward the end of the runway. That lump was sticking in my throat like a hunk of dry bread.

As we roared over the giant white letters 37 and then lifted off, I could still see Vidal sitting on his bike down there.

We went up dizzily over the alfalfa field, then the

188

treetops of the Cottonwood cemetery. You could even make out the bare spot in the new lawns that was Missy Oldenberg's grave. We climbed higher, passing a circling hawk. I looked back over my shoulder, and saw Cottonwood falling away behind us. On the little hill far back and below, the toy spires of St. Mary's poked up through the toy trees.

The feelings and events of the summer poured over my memory like the airstream outside. God would punish me. This little plane would crash in the mountains somewhere, and I would die a lingering horrible death and go to hell. Or Vidal would be killed on the highway to Denver, and I would suffer the guilt of his death for the rest of my life.

Murchison was an affable guy. Sensing my nervousness, he thought it was from flying, and tried to put me at ease.

"Ever flown in a small plane, Father?" he asked.

"No," I said.

We were already at fifteen thousand feet. The Rockies rolled out under us in every direction. Their tumbled peaks made a complete circle around our horizon. Since it was now August, they had shed the last of their snow. This vision of divine creation didn't make me feel inspired. Instead, it crushed me like a worm.

"You can see a long way from up here," said Murchison, trying to show me the sights. "See that farthest range way to the north there? That's the China Wall, up near Glacier Park. And you see those white peaks to the south there? Those are the Tetons, down in Wyoming."

I felt ill, and took one of my Dramamines. All I could think of was Missy Oldenberg's funeral, and the bouquet wilting on the mound of chalky dirt in the hot sun.

≡

In thirty-five minutes, we were touching down on the bigger runway at Missoula airport.

I had to wait two hours there for Flavey the business-man. So I passed the time in one of the small flying-service hangars, hanging out with the pilots, drinking coffee out of the vending machine and watching Murchison get started with the 170's inspection. I listened to the pilots telling tall tales and brooded about my fate. I could close my eyes and feel myself sitting behind Vidal on the bike, his strong back against my chest, his hair whipping my face.

Bill Flavey showed up right on schedule. He was a big stout florid man in a big hat. He looked like a Texas oil man, but the pilots had told me he owned several pulp mills.

Flavey and I climbed into his fancy little red and white two-seater Cessna and took off. Flavey didn't talk to me much, and didn't even seem to know I was a priest. I was glad to be anonymous. Yet a new kind of aloneness closed around me. I was like a voyager through space, lost beyond time. Cottonwood had burned out behind me, like an old star, and Denver didn't exist yet.

Two hours later, after a very bumpy flight and another Dramamine, we were circling in to Stapleton Interna-tional Airport on the north side of Denver. The city spread across its flats under us, shrouded in smog—you could scarcely see the mountains that ringed it.

"Okay, see ya in a few days," said Flavey. "Here's my number in case anything comes up."

He handed me his card and strode off, swinging his cowhide briefcase.

As I walked into the main terminal building, I still felt a little shaky from the flight.

The bustle of the airport was dizzying, and made me feel the larger bustle of this great Western metropolis. Jumbo jets whined down onto the crisscrossing runways, or took off with an earthshaking rumble, trailing black exhaust. People ran this way and that, hugged, kissed, and looked for lost luggage, argued about expensive flight insurance, sipped coffee, bought trashy souvenirs and paperbacks in the shops. For years I hadn't been anywhere outside of western Montana, and I felt confused.

I found a shiny new public telephone with clear plastic fittings that was almost a work of art. Putting a dime into it with shaking fingers, I got ready to dial the fatal number. Then I put the phone back on the hook without dialing, and waited for the dime to come tinkling back.

Chicken, I told myself. *Some martyr you would have made.*

I was starved, so I sat at one of the lunch counters, and had a cheeseburger and two cups of strong black coffee. People whizzed around me, talking about their relatives and their jobs and their operations. No one knew that the blond young man with the black turtleneck sweater and black jacket, carrying a small suitcase, was a guilt-ridden priest who was about to flout 3,000 years of Western religious discipline by dialing a phone number. Flight departures and arrivals were announced as if I didn't exist. The security people searched baggage, and found pairs of scissors and ounces of marijuana instead of guns.

When I'd eaten, I felt better. I paid and went back to the beautiful telephone.

This time, when the dime tinkled down into the guts of the work of art, I dialed the number with a shaky finger.

After two rings, the phone at the other end was picked up. A man's deep voice said, "Hello, Father Doric speaking."

It didn't sound like the voice I remembered at all. Maybe this was another Doric Wilton.

"Uh, hello," I said in a smothered voice. For a minute I couldn't go on. "Hello, I'm the priest that wrote Dignity from Cottonwood, Montana. They said they would tell you about me."

"You wrote under the name Stump, didn't you?"

"I just landed at Stapleton," I said. "What do I do next?"

"What arrangements did you make for a place to stay?"

"I didn't make any," I said. "I was kind of, uh, confused. And anyway my pastor couldn't give me much money for the trip."

"Okay," he said. "We can put you up. Hop in a taxi and go to 1568 East Martin Avenue. It's not far off the Denver U. Campus. I'll meet you there."

The address was a stucco private house with an arcaded porch. The big blue spruces around it made it look sheltered and safe. A Camaro was parked in front. I paid the taxi driver and walked shakily up the concrete walk to the door. Before I could ring, the door opened.

A tall dark slender young man stood there, wearing slacks and a red shirt. It was Doric, all right.

"Doric," I said. I thought I was going to collapse at his feet.

His eyes searched my face.

He hadn't changed much—I would have recognized him on the street anywhere. But a lot of the electric young quality was gone now, leaving a sternness that had been hidden before. Some landslide in his life had cut away the whole green mountainside of him, baring the layers of granite and chilled lava. Doric had always had something of the Jesuit in him, though I doubt that the Jesuits would have tolerated his independence of thought.

"Tom, for God's sake," he said. "Is it really you?"

Inside, I was introduced to the man who owned the house. He was Professor Joseph Hurlihe, a middle-aged professor who was just leaving to teach a summer-school class at Denver University. They sat me down on the couch and gave me a glass of whiskey. They seemed to be used to shattered priests arriving, as if they were conducting an underground railroad for escaped slaves or prisoners of war.

Then Doric and I were alone.

I sat numbly, the warmth of the whiskey spreading from my stomach to my arms and legs, but not having much effect. Doric sat leaning forward in an armchair, his elbows on his knees, his fingers twisted together in an odd way.

To break the silence, I asked, "Who's Professor Hurlihe?"

"He teaches social sciences here at Denver U.," said Doric. "He's a deacon at a church in my diocese. He's straight, but he's involved with Dignity because he believes in it."

We fell silent again. His eyes were still searching me.

"How did you know about Dignity?" he asked.

"I read about it in the *Advocate*. There was a list of the chapters, so I finagled my way down here to the conference . . ."

My voice kept fading out, like a mayday from a light plane lost over the mountains.

"So you read the *Advocate*," said Doric, smiling. "How do you manage that?"

"My lover has a subscription," I said, managing to look him in the eye.

Doric nodded slowly, and made his knuckles crack. I kept studying his face, remembering all our earnest conversations in the seminary, our long walks together, praying together—the whole rapt and precious closeness that Father Matt had shattered, saying it was dangerous.

He was the same age as me, as Vidal, but he looked far older than either of us. His close-cut black hair actually sported a few silver hairs at the temples. He had always had an ascetic look, but now you got the feeling he had recently finished a long fast and was trying unsuccessfully to put on a few pounds. He had that distinguished bookish look of a priest who might have studied at the North American college in Rome, might have been chosen as a papal diplomat. Instead, here he was in Denver counseling faggots.

"How did you get involved with Dignity?" I asked.

He shrugged a little, as if trying to shake off the weight of memory too.

"Oh, I was doing some on-campus counseling," he said, "and a couple of the gay student activists who are Catholics came to me for help. That was how I found out about Dignity. I helped organize the chapter here."

"You do it *openly?*"

"My bishop knows I'm doing some gay counseling," he said. "Homosexuals give him the willies, so he thinks I'm doing the Lord's work. He doesn't know I organized the chapter, and I hope to God he doesn't know I'm gay."

I sat there flabbergasted to hear him say it out loud.

"We've come a long way, baby," said Doric softly, and took a swallow of his Four Roses.

"Do you, uh, do you . . ." I couldn't hold the question back.

"Yes, I have a lover," he said quietly.

We stared at each other.

Doric smiled a little wryly. "Don't get the idea that all Dignity chaplains have lovers. Some of us are straight. Some of us are gay, but feel called to celibacy anyway. To each his own . . ."

"Mine is on his way down here. Would it be okay if he stayed with me here? We've never been able to stay together."

"Yeah, it's all right, I'm sure."

"Well, he's going to call your number, so you can tell him where to come. What's the plan?"

Doric shrugged again.

"Whatever you want it to be," he said. "We don't put on any pressure. You can talk to everybody in the chapter if you want. You can come to a meeting and join in a rap session. You can talk only to me, or to another gay priest if

194

you'd rather. We're having a special affair tonight—you can come if you want. How much do you know about Dignity, anyway?"

"Not much. I was afraid to put myself on the mailing list. About all I know is what was in Vidal's newspapers. That you guys think you're children of God, same as everybody else, and that you are trying to dialogue with the Church."

"That just about says it," said Doric drily. "As long as the Church stands pat on abortion and a few other things, it's a cinch She won't change on homosexuals either. But we can try to soften the attitudes, for now, and make some kind of place for ourselves at the edge. It's going to take a long time. The churches will probably be the last places left in America where we're persecuted, if legislatures go on passing gay rights laws like they are . . ."

Doric drained the last of his whiskey and stood up.

"You look awful tired," he said. "Why don't you fall over for a little while? I'll go back to the office and do a few things and wait for your friend to call. Then I'll come back here."

The guest room was such a placid sunny little room that it seemed unreal. The furniture was blond modern, and the double bed was covered with a red satin quilted spread. Doric pulled the spread off while I wearily opened my bag. This is funny, I thought to myself, Doric tucking me into bed after all these years.

"How about something to make you sleep?" said Doric. "I don't use them anymore, but I keep the prescription going for other people."

He held out a prescription bottle of the small blue Valiums. I took one and swallowed it.

Doric clapped me on the shoulder. "Try to relax. See you later."

I took off everything but my underwear, slid into the clean fresh bed and lay there staring at the ceiling. For the

195

first time I was among people who were working to defend the things I felt and suffered through—but I felt more alone than ever.

Doric had changed so much since the seminary years. He had always been quiet, but it had been the quiet of a deep glacier lake. Now it was more like the charged silence of a functioning nuclear reactor. He had always been more of the intellect than I was—his mind would go off on daring tangents while I would sit openmouthed and listen to him talk. Considering the sharp theological precision he loved, he must have suffered a lot at finding himself gay.

Maybe even more than I had.

The dull golden haze of the Valium crept over me.

Someone shook me awake. I shoved myself up on my elbow, shaking my head dopily.

Vidal was sitting on the edge of the bed, still wearing his dusty leather jacket. His face was sunburned, except where his goggles had been, and he smelled of gasoline and wind.

He bent down and kissed me. I held him hard, and we shared a moment so warm that it was hard to remember we'd had so many fights.

"Doric sent you a cup of coffee," he said. "I'm going to jump in the shower. Do you want to go to the Mass? Doric says you don't have to talk to anybody if you don't want to, just watch."

"Mass?" I said blankly.

"It's some kind of special mass," he said. "They do dancing with it."

I had heard a lot about masses with liturgical dance, mostly from Father Vance, who thought they were a scandal. But I'd never seen one.

196

"Okay," I said.

Vidal shut the bedroom door, stripped off his dusty clothes and went in the bathroom.

The cup of coffee sat steaming gently on the bedside table. Feeling like a convalescent, I sat up in bed and drank it. Outside the window, the evening sunlight slanted gently through the blue spruces. The suburban neighborhood was quiet, and I could hear an occasional car purr by. Some children were screaming with laughter up the street. A woman was calling, "Here, kitty, kitty, kitty!" All that peace and order around me only raised the noise level inside my own head.

Vidal and I both put on clean jeans and T-shirts. He wore his motorcycle jacket, and I pulled on a brown goathide jacket my parents had given me years ago. I wanted to look unpriestlike, just an ordinary leather-jacket kind of gay man. It was strange to think that no one would threaten us in that room, and that we could actually opt to stay there instead of going out.

≡

Ironically, the hall where the dance mass was being celebrated belonged to the St. James Episcopal Church. No Catholic church in the city would lend its facilities for this shocking affair, so it found a home with the Episcopalians, whose current attitude toward gay people was a little more relaxed.

Still dulled by the Valium, I found myself jerking with a kind of slow-motion nervousness. There was no butterfly mask on my face here. People could see me, maybe recognize me later, somewhere else.

The large hall was empty of furniture except for the altar. It stood halfway down—just a long table draped in white. Panels of red and black cloth hung from ceiling to floor, and there were cathedral-size white wooden candelabra along them, already flaming. The setting had an almost medieval splendor.

A crowd of people was milling quietly in the back of the hall, talking in whispers. They were mostly young, both sexes. Through a doorway, in a little side room, I could see a priest putting on his vestments.

We drifted gently into the crowd. A couple of young women in their late twenties came up to Doric, and he chatted with them for a few minutes. When they left, he said to me:

"Those girls are two of the charter members of the Denver chapter. They were Benedictine sisters and in the same community. Now they're lovers."

The dancers were standing in a group, relaxed but silent. They were six men and six women, all wearing white leotards. For a minute I was a little shocked at the idea of these muscular young bodies being part of the Mass.

One of the male dancers stood out. He was a little taller, and his straight silver-blond hair hung to his shoulder blades. His face had the beauty of an angel, lit from inside by some softly flickering light. An insensitive person might have called him "effeminate," though there was surely nothing female about his hard-muscled body.

Even in my dulled state, I could react to his attractiveness. The reaction told me all over again that I was gay as a goose.

"Look at that blond number," said Vidal softly.

Doric laughed. "You stay away from him," he said.

Vidal laughed too—now we both knew that the blond was Doric's lover.

Suddenly an electrifying sound ripped through the hall. It was a wooden clapper, being shaken by a kid standing near the doorway. The sound was harsh, rattling, like the dance of death. The whispering crowd fell silent.

"There's no music to this Mass," Doric whispered in my ear.

The priest came out of the side room, carrying the sacred vessels, his vestments flaring. Behind him was his acolyte. He went to the altar and set his things down. With a hushed shuffling of feet, everyone crowded up behind him and kneeled on the bare wooden floor. The idea, I thought, was to get the congregation as close to the priest as possible. On the other side of the altar, half the hall was left bare for the dancers.

Pressed between Doric and Vidal, I craned my neck to watch, so curious and nervous that I didn't have the proper prayerful attitude.

The clapper kept rattling now with a martial beat. The dancers came striding, two by two, in heterosexual pairs. They moved stiffly like wind-up soldiers. While the priest prepared the altar, they circled all around us. Finally they lined up on the other side of the altar, still in wooden straight pairs.

The clapper stopped rattling.

In the silence, the priest spoke the first words of the Mass.

The line of dancers shifted softly to form six gay pairs —women together, men together. I felt a ripple of feeling go through the congregation. Probably many of them, like me, were seeing it for the first time.

The pairs faced each other, placed hands gently on each other's shoulders, and exchanged such prim and gentle kisses of peace that they might have been cardinals electing a new pope in the Sistine Chapel. Yet the bodies were there under the tight virginal leotards—young, bursting and sticky with strength and youth, like the red oozing buds of the cottonwood trees in the Rockies spring.

As the priest and the congregation murmured their way through the opening section of the Mass, the clapper stayed silent. The dancers moved and twined through stately patterns—now in pairs, now in a group. They seemed to be celebrating their paired-off state as lovers.

But as the priest started into the heart of the Mass, the Consecration, the clapper shattered the air again. Everyone else's nerves shivered the way mine did. Abruptly the dancers shifted back into man-woman couples—all but one pair, the blond and his dark-haired partner.

The straight couples marched again, almost goosestepping. You could almost hear the clank of weapons down the centuries—armored knights, tanks. It was the march of a society armed against a way of feeling that it feared. They circled the lone pair of men, who held each other and turned slowly, as if trapped. Suddenly, in slow motion, they tore the pair apart. Five of the soldiers held the partner back, while the other five marched the blond away. He didn't fight them, but went quietly.

Suddenly, as the priest approached the Consecration, the blond man was thrust out alone and stiff, as if tied. Then it dawned on me that we were watching not just the passion of the gay lover but the Passion of Christ, superbly recreated as one event by some mad genius of a choreographer.

The clapper beat with a frenzy.

While the dark-haired partner watched in anguish, the marchers strutted past the tied prisoner. As each one passed him, she or he uncoiled in a whiplash motion, arms slashing against him like living cat-o'-nine tails. Suddenly we began to be very aware of the blond youth's body, but not in a sexual way. All his muscles jerked, all his tendons strained. The sweat started to stain his leotard. His body language was so real that we could hear the crack of the whip, and see the skin and flesh tear, and the blood start to trickle down his arms and legs. He was being destroyed before our eyes. He was being executed. He was dying for our sins.

I wanted to yell, "Stop! Don't do that!"

The clapper stopped. The priest was bending over the wafer of bread on the paten.

"This is my body," he said.

With a rush, the soldier couples surrounded the blond youth. They seized him by the legs and raised him high on the writhing mountain of their own bodies. They formed a living Golgotha.

As he was lifted toward the ceiling, he spread out his arms stiffly. His head was bent back, his hair streaming, his body tensed in agony, as if stretched on the rack.

Nothing I had ever seen, in the movies, or in great religious paintings, or in my own imagination, stunned me with the reality of the Crucifixion as that gay kid raised by his partners. So often, during Lent, when I made stabs at meditation, I had tried to visualize how they killed Our Lord, so that hopefully I would appreciate Him more. But I had never succeeded, until now. I could feel the nails hammered through my own hands, feel the splintery wood against my back, and the heat of the Roman sun.

All around me, the congregation were reacting in the same way. We watched wide-eyed, in a collective state of shock.

The hall was dead silent. You could hear cars passing on the street outside. Slowly the priest raised the consecrated wafer high above his head, toward the lifted body. Then he lowered it back onto the paten.

Then he bent over the chalice of wine. "This is my blood."

As he said the words, the stiffened dying body seemed to change before our eyes. The dancers still held it up by the legs, but the life went out of it—you could almost see it draining out, through that invisible wound in his side. His head fell forward, and he slumped slowly down. They caught him, their arms reaching up like a forest. They lowered him gently from that invisible cross.

As the priest raised the chalice of consecrated wine, the dead body of the blond youth was handed down to the ground. The Golgotha of soldiers softened into the gay pairs again.

Now they were the mourners, the grieving Apostles, the weeping women.

The dark-haired lover was kneeling alone on the floor, sitting back on his haunches, his head thrown back with grief. They carried the body toward him. It was so heavy they could hardly lift it. They laid the body across his knees.

The blond Christ lay across the thighs of his lover, arched backward, his hair, arms and legs trailing on the bare board floor. The lover bent forward over him, hiding his face against the body's side, in a mind-shocking Pietà.

Something cracked inside of me. The weight of all those months of guilt and overwork cracked the beams of my mind at last. The lump that had been in my throat for such a long time now tore its way out, and I started to cry.

I covered my face with my hands, because I didn't want my sobs bouncing around that big hall. Curiously enough, some other people around me were crying loudly—they didn't care who heard them. Vidal pulled my head against his leather collar and held me hard. Someone else squeezed my hand. Maybe this was Doric.

The sound of the clapper shattered my head again.

"Alleluia!" shouted the dancers. It was the first word they'd said since the Mass began.

The congregation reacted like they were at a gospel meeting.

"Alleluia," a few of them sang out. Then more of them. "Alleluia!"

I raised my head and looked blurrily through the tears.

The body was coming to life. With a slow joyous wrench, it rolled off the lover's knees onto the floor. It sat up, stretched, lay down to roll again as if in a meadow of

202

mountain flowers. The priest was back at the missal, reading the closing passages. The dancers were stooping and shuffling in a joyous circle. As they slowly straightened up, shuffling faster and faster, the blond came to his feet with them. He was transfigured. He made you see the blinding light from within that nobody is supposed to see.

As the priest finished the Mass, all the dancers closed into a tight little group. Now there were no couples, only singles. They were reaching, waving, high-stepping joyously, like a beating of angelic wings around the Godhead. Even the blond was no longer prominent, as if he was now part of each of the others.

The dance mass finished in this explosion of light and joy.

===

The four of us sat in a restaurant, and I picked at my food. I was still in shock.

The place was a combination—bar and disco downstairs, restaurant upstairs, called Touch and Go. It was one of the several places of its kind in Denver, where young gay couples of both sexes could make a complete evening of it: eat, get drunk and dance. Doric said there were also the usual bars that tended to have customers of one sex only, including a couple of classic leather bars.

Vidal sat beside me, busy cleaning up his cheap steak. Across from us sat Doric and his lover. It was disconcerting to see the blond Christ now wearing torn Levi's, a cowboy shirt and huaraches, and to find out that his name was Andy Jorgenson. From downstairs, we could hear the beat and wail of hustle music from the disco.

". . . It still blows our minds to see the effect the thing has on people," Andy was saying softly.

"Where did you get the idea?" I asked him.

"Oh, it just evolved naturally," said Andy. He spoke

and thought as gently as he looked. "There was this little group of us at Aspen, and most of us were into dance and music and religion. We heard about the Dignity group here, and we came over, and things sort of interacted. . . ."

"Word is getting around," said Doric, grinning. "People in California want to see it. So, come fall, the bunch is going on the road. Maybe even back East." He punched Andy gently on the arm. "New York. Broadway. Jesus Christ Superstud."

Andy blushed beet-red. Vidal burst out laughing.

I abandoned my steak—the cheeseburger from the airport seemed to be still in my stomach—and sat looking nervously around. Here I was in a gay place again, with a lot of other gays. Admittedly no one was paying much attention to me. The tourist stage of my identity crisis was over.

Doric called the waiter over so we could order dessert. Everybody ordered the homemade apple pie except me —all I wanted was black coffee.

The four of us were interacting in curious ways. Andy seemed to sense the intellectual tension between Doric and me—I wondered if Doric had told him about our sublimated affair long ago. Doric and Vidal kept looking at each other with a combination of muted respect and hostility. Doric was amused at Vidal, and Vidal was amused at Andy, and had now told me that he wasn't his type.

When we'd finished, we went downstairs. It was past eleven, but not many people were in the disco because it was Sunday night. The turning globe lights flashed on the glass mosaic walls, and the shrieks of the soul singers split the air. But the dance floor was half empty—just a few male couples, and one lonely pair of lesbians.

Vidal was looking so hungrily at the dancers that it was obvious he wanted to get out there and dance. I knew he was now safely out of the dope-and-drinking stage, but he was building up toward a spree. Too much church, too much priestly lover, too much talk about the natural law and moral teachings.

But Vidal pulled himself away from the bright lights.

We went out to Doric's car. It was raining, and the neon lights flared on the wet street. I felt like I was dreaming with my eyes open.

Vidal brushed his arm against mine. "Tonight you and I get to spend the whole night in the same bed," he said in a low voice.

"Imagine that," I said numbly.

═══

But back at the professor's house, when Vidal tried to make love to me, I just couldn't get in the mood.

Vidal was mad.

"Not *again,*" he said.

I sat numbly.

"Every time we get a whole night together, you pull this trick on me," he said. "Maybe you want me to get lost, huh?"

I took another Valium.

If it had been Vidal's own house, he would have slept on the sofa. But he couldn't, so he went to sleep on the very edge of the other side of the bed, with his back to me.

As I drifted into that golden haze, it occurred to me that I had still been in Cottonwood at nine o'clock that morning. This day had been the longest day of my life.

The decision was there in front of me. I would probably have to leave the ministry.

13

The next morning was Monday.

Doric dropped me at Regis College. I registered for the conference in a daze. Vidal had still been sleeping when I left the professor's house, and I had a feeling he wouldn't be there when I came back that evening.

All morning long, there was the auditorium full of clergy and lay people, and the podium with the little lamp on it, and the speakers, and the discussions of how Catholics would regroup to fight the abortion law, but I sat slumped in my seat not paying much attention. The depression of the fight weighed on me, and the vision of that living crucifix still blotted out everything else.

At noon, Doric met me on the steps. In the clattering college cafeteria, we took our trays of mashed potatoes and spun-vegetable-protein meatloaf, and sat in a corner by one of the big windows, away from everyone else.

"You look pretty grim," said Doric.

"I think I'm going to leave the priesthood," I blurted.

Doric's logical mind ground into action.

"You can't leave the priesthood," he said. "You can leave off practicing your ministry. But the priesthood you take to the grave with you."

It was like old times back in the seminary. Arguing with Doric was hard.

"I know that," I said. "But I can't go on trying to have my cake and eat it too."

Doric chuckled.

"What's so funny?" I asked.

"You just made an awful pun. You always used to do that."

"Doric, how did you get . . . where you are? I mean, you seem to be in a fairly peaceful state of conscience."

Doric was attacking his fake potatoes and meat as if he was still determined to put on twenty pounds.

"I knew I was gay when I was thirteen years old," he said. "I'd never heard the word, but I knew what I was."

"Everybody I've talked to so far has known it that early," I said. "Except me."

"You knew," said Doric. "You just stuck your head in the sand. With me, it was one of my conscious intelligent cold-blooded decisions. I deliberately decided that I was going to ignore my feelings. I already wanted to be a priest, so I told myself: Doric, you're going to lead a pure life, so the fact that you like other guys won't matter at all." He smiled. "I was sure that God would understand, as long as I controlled it."

I made an effort to eat the meat, but it was awful—even worse than the hamburger-stretched-with-bread-crumbs that Father Vance and I ate.

"And then," said Doric, "the fatal moment comes. We meet the person who makes all our prayers and our decisions seem like a sick joke."

"Where did you meet Andy?"

"He came to a dance clinic at Denver U. last summer. I was doing some summer counseling, and taking a couple of courses here at Regis. The sight of him drove me insane. My indecision just about drove him insane."

I summoned up enough courage to take a dig at Doric. "He doesn't really look your type. How old is he, anyway?"

Doric's brown eyes flashed up at me with a hard kind of amusement. "If you call me a chicken hawk, I'll deny you absolution." He took another mouthful of meatloaf. "Andy's twenty."

"He looks like an angel."

"He isn't, really. Just naïve and shy, with a kind of vision that goes beyond conscience." Doric's eyes were still digging back at me. "Vidal is exactly what I would have predicted for you."

"Oh?" I said.

"Let's face it—you've led a pretty sheltered life. Suddenly you show up with this biker, this half-blood leather man who looks like something straight out of *Colt* magazine. I have a theory, Tom. The first lover is always the closest we come to fantasy."

"I guess you're right. My feelings were so foreign to me that I picked a foreign kind of guy. I mean he *is* kind of exotic . . ."

My eyes were making one of those paranoid sweeps around the dining room to make sure that nobody was listening. About two hundred priests, religious and laymen were decorously eating their meatloaf and discussing abortion or whatever. I wondered if anyone else was talking about the same subject as we were.

"You don't like Vidal," I said.

"I know where his head is at, and he knows I know," said Doric. "He knows a lot, and there's a lot to him, and he's taken you a long way. But he's a honky-tonk queen."

I was ready to get mad at Doric for this remark, but remembered just in time that butch gay men seemed to like insulting each other by using the feminine.

"Gays are always arguing about which is better, monogamous or polygamous," said Doric. "Vidal is the polygamous type. Be ready for it, Tom. Because you're the monogamous type."

"Is this the way you counsel?" I said. "It's pretty brutal."

"I'm not counseling now," said Doric. "I'm talking to a good friend. I was watching him last night. Eyes everywhere, on me, on Andy, on you too, of course."

"Well, we're not married, for chrissake," I said.

"Take your head out of the sand, Tom. Be ready when he moves on."

"He's not like that. He loves me."

"Has he told you so?"

I was silent.

"It's so easy to get hurt the first time," said Doric.

The cafeteria was at its peak noise level, trays clattering, people scuffling, the cash register ringing, the cooks yelling in the kitchen.

"Did you?" I asked.

"Yes, I did," said Doric.

"Andy?" I said.

"Yes."

"He seems so gentle."

"Gentle people are the most dangerous kind. They don't ever mean any harm."

We finished eating, shoved our trays onto the conveyor belt, and left the dining room.

Outside, we walked across the campus, scuffing along the sidewalks. The trees were already showing the first yellowed leaves. Fall comes early in the high country. The Cottonwood ranchers always said there were two seasons: winter and July. And July was over.

"Think a lot more about this decision to leave the Church," said Doric.

"What else can I do? What good am I?"

"Don't make a soap opera out of it. You're a priest, that's what good you are. Being gay shouldn't prevent you from functioning. And like I said earlier, you'll take the priesthood with you wherever you go."

"The funny thing is," I said hollowly, "the whole thing has made a better priest out of me. I was getting too action-oriented there, too proud of my balanced budget. This whole thing set me back on my heels, made me take a second look at myself and other people. But . . . how can I function in a state of mortal sin?"

"Did it ever occur to you that it's not a mortal sin?"

My mind floundered at this.

"Vidal and I have talked about that. He even tried to show me how the Church is misinterpreting Scripture."

"It's all tied up with the other sex issues. Women not being allowed to be priests or deacons. Why not? Celibacy. How in hell does celibacy qualify you to deal with souls? And you think of all the other sex issues, and you come back to the gay question. In New York City, the Catholic Church helped to defeat the gay rights bill. Even if being gay *were* a sin—does the Catholic Church deny jobs and housing to people who commit adultery? The logic is crazy."

"The way the Church sees it," I said slowly, "gay people are called to celibacy. The way we see it, all that matters is whether love is real."

"That's it, exactly," said Doric.

"But that's all Jesus cared about," I said. "Real love."

"Isn't that what a priest is supposed to be?" Doric asked. "Someone who helps other people learn how to love?" He walked on, scuffing at the yellowed leaves. "That's why I decided to stay a priest. So when someone like you finally cracks up and cries, there'll be someone there who has already done the crying."

He stopped scuffing, and stood looking at me with a strange defiance.

It was funny how the old mesmeric appeal that Doric had had for me could still grab at me, a little. Even after all these years, and with the possibility of a relationship between us now past and over with.

———

When I got back to the professor's house that afternoon, Vidal had gone out. I had no idea where he'd gone or what he'd been doing, but he'd left his shaving stuff in the bathroom, so he was sure to come back.

I knew what he was doing. He was out catting around. That day, at the ripe old age of twenty-eight, I discovered the pains of jealousy.

There was a Dignity/Denver rap session that night, but I was too upset to go there and try to verbalize and relate to people with Vidal's absence gnawing at my guts. So Doric left me with a packet of articles on homosexuality gathered from magazines all over the country, written from the liberal Catholic point of view. There was also a pre-publication "underground" copy of a study on homosexuality by some American theologians, in which they were beginning to say out loud some of the things about the Bible and the Church's teachings that gay Catholics had been saying among themselves.

The professor went off with Doric, and I was left alone in the house.

In the cozy little guest room, I lay on the bed and tried hard to read. But not even that earthshaking report could get my attention. I kneeled by the bed and tried to pray. I even went in the living room and tried to watch TV.

Shortly after eleven, the front door opened. I thought it was Doric and the professor coming back. But it was Vidal.

He smelled of beer, and he was a little high, but not

drunk. He sat down on the edge of the bed and stared at the wall.

"I'm sorry about last night," he said.

"So am I," I said.

"I'm just so goddam impatient anymore," he said.

"Me and my hangups drive you straight across the creek, huh?"

"I don't know what it is," he said.

Suddenly he threw himself down across me and tried to get his arms around me. With a rush of relief, I hugged him.

The good lovemakings, the ones that haunt you later on when it's too late, don't come at the beginning of a relationship, I found. They come toward the end. Something in that conversation with Doric earlier in the day had loosened me up a little, and I made love to Vidal in a way that I'd never quite had the courage to do before. Something, too, had been stirred by the fact that he'd left his prowling around the bars and come back to find me.

For once he was not urging me on. For once I was abandoned. We had turned out the light, but I could see him clearly in the dark, writhing slowly on his back, his spine arched, his head straining back into the pillows, or tossing from side to side. His outflung hands were clenched in the sheet. Suddenly he gave a short sharp cry, almost as if he'd been hurt, and one of his hands, straining blindly, tore the sheet.

It gave slowly, majestically, with a shuddering rip, as the temple veil must have done when Our Lord died.

———

In Denver, that night, I started to have the dreams.

The mere fact that I was having crazy dreams didn't scare me. I'd studied enough primer psychology to realize that the shocks of coming out were finally getting down to my subconscious. My mind was turning over, the way lakes do in the late summer when the cold murky bottom waters come roiling to the top.

Shortly after falling asleep that night, I dreamed that I was walking through this huge Victorian house.

It might have been my parents' house, but it wasn't. And yet the big rooms seemed to be disquietingly familiar and dear to me. I walked and walked, and beyond every doorway, there was another room. I went up wide stairways and there were acres more of rooms. Fires burned in the marble fireplaces, clocks struck softly on the mantels, motes settled gently in the sunlight streaming through the lace curtains. The rooms were dusted and neat, as if the housekeeper had just been through them. But no one was there. It was almost as if I wasn't there either—like the clocks were striking with no one to hear them.

Then I was walking up a winding rickety attic stairway. It led up into some kind of tower room. I had a happy feeling that I was going to find an old rocking horse up there.

The attic tower was empty except for a couple of old steamer trunks with greenish brass fittings. There was no rocking horse, of course. A ray of sunlight came through a single dormer window. On the bare board floor, Andy was lying stretched out, naked.

He was not only dead, but he looked as if he had been dead for several days. His battered body and his blond hair were caked and crusted with dried blood and sweat. The gaping holes in his hands and feet had the ends of severed tendons sticking out of them like dried-up spaghetti. He had the kind of grotesque swollen erection that executed men are sometimes said to get.

A feeling of horrified anxiety swept over me.

Doric stood looking down at the body. He was dressed in an immaculate black broadcloth suit. The creases in

214

the black pants were sharp, and the white Roman collar was freshly laundered and starched. I wanted to turn and go back down the stairs, but I couldn't.

Slowly Doric unbuttoned his pants, took them off and threw them over one of the steamer trunks. His wrinkled shirttail hung below his jacket, around his thin white hairy thighs. He kneeled down by the body and tenderly caressed those broken legs.

I wanted to scream, but you can never scream in dreams.

Doric lay down on the board floor and took the body in his arms. It moved limply, with that heavy nerveless cold limpness of the dead whose rigor mortis is already gone. Doric fondled the stiff dirty hair and kissed the dried-up mouth.

Suddenly the limp hands twitched, as if an electric current had shot through them. Then they flexed. The mouth sucked in a harsh, whistling breath. Even the legs were moving, though the lower part of the legs trailed brokenly.

Still trying to scream, I ran. I went slowly and dream-like down the attic stairs, almost like falling down a cliff. With great insane bounds I went back through those pleasant sunny rooms. The clocks were striking softly. The velvet cushions looked as if the housekeeper had just plumped them.

I woke up gasping and drenched with sweat.

═══

The next morning, when Doric was dropping me off at Regis College, I said, "I've got to talk to you today. I feel like I'm losing my mind."

"I'm not free this noon," he said. "Some people are here from Dignity/Portland. Why don't you meet me at the Botanic Gardens this afternoon around five?"

"Why the Botanic Gardens?"

"It's a favorite place of mine," he said. "I'll wait for you in front of the Boettcher Conservatory. It's like a big greenhouse."

When I walked into the conference auditorium, another ugly surprise was waiting for me. As I was going down the carpeted aisle toward the row where I usually sat alone, an unpleasantly familiar voice said:

"Why, it's Father Tom."

Mr. and Mrs. Shoup were coming down the aisle behind me, also with briefcases and pads to take notes on.

Never had my abilities as an amateur actor been so taxed. I had to look absolutely blah and mildly pleased to see them, when in fact my stomach was lifting off some infernal runway with a sickening roar, like a jumbo jet.

"Why, hello," I said. "Father Vance didn't tell me you folks would be here."

"Oh, we decided at the last minute that it would be a good idea to attend. After all, the abortion issue is important too, you know," said Mrs. Shoup. "We're staying at the Brown Palace. How about having dinner with us tonight?"

"Well," I said, "that'd be nice, but I've already got plans for tonight. Could I interest you in lunch at that awful cafeteria?"

When everybody had sat down and the Shoups had gone, I sat shaking like a leaf, not hearing a word of the first talk.

What on earth had made Mrs. Shoup decide that abortion was so important? As far as I knew, the only thing Mrs. Shoup felt strongly about was dirty books, and Mr. Shoup didn't feel strongly about anything. Vidal would probably tell me I was paranoid—but could they have followed us down there to spy on us? It didn't make sense.

At lunch with the Shoups, I was calm and blah, and

knew for the first time that my acting abilities were approaching their limits.

When the conference adjourned around four-thirty, I grabbed a taxi to York Street, where the Botanic Garden was. Doric was waiting in front of the conservatory.

As we walked through the hot humid place inside, the closeness of all the rare palms and ferns and orchids started to choke me. I told Doric about the Shoups.

"What'll I do?"

Doric was silent for a minute. "That's one of the beauties of being out," he said. "You look back on those fears of being exposed like it was a bad dream."

"Speaking of bad dreams—" I said.

Doric listened in silence as I told him about the dream. We walked slowly, brushing past the plants, hardly looking at them. Great staghorn ferns dripped down from the ceiling, where light poured through the glass. We finally stopped by a rock cliff overplanted with all kinds of creeping ferns and mosses. A tiny waterfall trickled down it, into a pool edged with baby's tears. I kept my voice down, because there were other people wandering through the conservatory.

"So now you know," said Doric softly.

"I want to go to confession," I said. "I don't really know what I want to confess, but I feel so sick . . . so vile."

"Now you know. The Bible," he said softly, looking at the tiny waterfall as it dripped down through the maidenhair ferns, "is only an excuse."

I searched his face. "For what?"

"So they can have something easy and simple to slap us with," he said. "So they don't have to talk about the hidden collective fear that you've finally confronted in that dream."

"My mind must be incredibly dirty," I said. "No wonder Mrs. Shoup is after me."

"Is that what you want to confess? That you had the

dream? You're really convinced that you committed a grave sin?"

"I don't know. I just feel confused and filthy."

"The dream is nothing more than the fact that you've finally lanced the boil and the poison is coming out."

"You're going to *rationalize* it?" I said.

"But isn't it the core fear at the heart of Christian spirituality? Isn't that what happened when the simple gospel of love that Jesus preached came up against the flesh-hate of man that became part of Christianity? The fear that we might slip and love Jesus as a man?"

The horror of the dream was coming over me again. I wanted to float away screaming through that steaming glass grotto.

"Isn't that why they've made theological criminals of us?" Doric persisted. "Don't you see it now?"

"But that's a monstrous idea," I choked.

"No, it's not," he said. "Don't get so excited. Let me finish. Doesn't the Church use the language of heterosexual love to describe the relationship between the Church and Christ, and the soul and Christ?"

"You mean the Mystical Bridegroom?"

"Is there—could there be—any sexual intention on the part of the soul?"

My mind was floundering around in terror. As usual, Doric's thinking was way ahead of me, and I was panting and running to try to catch up.

"Maybe," I said. "God knows we're carnal creatures. We can't help that. But by giving us grace, He changes that carnal thing into something pure. Isn't that what the love of the mystic for God is? It's love where even the passion has been raised to a higher plane."

"Exactly," said Doric.

He turned and looked at me with a curious unseeing intensity, as if his mind was lit by such a strong light that it blanked out his eyes from behind.

218

"Then," he said, "if the straight people dare to talk about Christ the Divine Bridegroom, maybe we gay people can dare to talk about Christ the Divine Lover."

This idea sounded so shocking that I almost felt faint.

"Let's get out of here," I said. "The air's too close."

We went out into the bright sunshine, and walked through the famous rose garden.

All around us, wide beds of tea roses were in their last flush of bloom. Petals littered the rich soil under the plants. The thought of Clare Faux and Missy Oldenberg came to my mind.

"I don't mean anything much different by the Lover idea than the traditional theologians do," said Doric. "There's nothing shocking about it at all. It's just a different way of saying the same thing. But it frees us from that awful complex. I don't know what to call the complex. It ought to have a helluva name, like the Oedipus complex, or something. Part of your mind was trying to tell you the truth with that dream. The other part masked the truth with fear, so that you experienced it as a nightmare."

We sat on a stone bench, with the perfume of the doomed roses floating around us. It was a splendid day, and the usual inversion layer of blue haze had lifted from the Denver flats, so that you could clearly see the blue mountains all around.

Doric kept talking. Years of thinking must have gone into the ideas that he now dumped in my lap.

"If there was sex between man and woman before the fall, then there must have been sex between man and man, and woman and woman," he said. "For us to argue the validity of our love, we have to go all the way and say that it is rooted in original innocence, like heterosexual love is. Isn't that innocence what we're really trying to recapture in our relationships?"

I shook my head. "You make me dizzy," I said. "Now I

don't know what to confess. It's been months since I confessed, and I've been dying of guilt. But . . ."

"Think a few more days," he said. "Then if you want to confess before you leave, I'll be glad to hear your confession."

That night I went back to the professor's house in the usual state of mental shock. Vidal had gone out again, without leaving a message.

The professor and I ate a little supper and talked about Dignity, and then I took a Valium and went to bed.

About midnight, Vidal came in. I could barely open my eyes, all woozy in that golden haze. But when I saw that Vidal was badly beaten up, I woke up a little.

"What happened to you?" I asked.

"Was hanging around in a leather bar, a place called the Golden Spike," Vidal said bluntly. His lower lip was split and swollen, and it was hard for him to talk. "I went home with these two guys. I thought they were just into games. Turned out they were into heavy stuff. They tried to tie me up. They were going to beat the living shit out of me. I just about wrecked their place on the way out."

He was climbing stiffly, sorely out of his clothes.

"First time you've been in a fight since I met you," I said.

"Felt pretty good too," he said. "I missed it."

"Going to backslide, huh? Throw away all the progress you've made."

Vidal sat down creakily on the edge of the bed, naked. He had bruises everywhere.

"Can't you really see what's the matter with me?" he said.

"You're bored with me," I said.

"Not exactly," he said. "Maybe I'd better tell you what's on my mind."

"All right, let's get it over with," I said hollowly, out of the yellow haze.

220

"All summer, you've made me feel guilty and inferior," he said. "And everybody else here makes me feel guilty and inferior."

"That's the last thing I want you to feel."

"You don't understand what I mean. I've accepted being gay, but where does that leave me? There I am creeping around Cottonwood with my fake wife. I'd like to be free and open like some of these people I've met here."

"All right, you want to come out. What else is new?"

"You make me feel inferior, because you're doing something with your life and I'm not. Even if you *are* a mess, you're committed to something. In a way, your ministry is your lover. I can always feel it between us. And here I am just wasting my life around cars and bars. I've got to get going."

We were silent for a moment.

"So you want to leave me," I said.

"What I really want is to go back to Missoula this fall and finish college," he said. "I've saved a little money, enough for the first semester. There's a new state scholarship for ex-cons, maybe I can get it. Winter said he'd give me a recommend. And he said he thought Father Vance would give me one too."

I would be left alone in Cottonwood with an aborted pastoral mission and a frightening new identity.

"And Missoula's kind of a liberal town," he said. "I'm going to come out there, and anybody who doesn't like it is gonna need false teeth."

Valium being a depressant, I was very depressed.

"You're mad at me," said Vidal.

"No. All summer I've been praying for you to talk about college."

"It doesn't mean we won't see each other. We'll get together a lot."

"Sure, sure," I said, knowing I was being childish.

"Look, gay people talk an awful lot about how hard it is to find a good relationship. You say to some guy, 'This is forever,' and a month later you can't stand the sight of him. But I've always felt that isn't the real problem. Look at the divorce rate for straights. My God, even married people in their sixties are splitting up. Straight people don't have such an easy time finding a good lover either. Maybe I'm biased, because I'm such a loner anyway. But I feel we're going into an age where it's important to know how to be alone. If you get too dependent on a good relationship, it goes bad. You have to have a good relationship with yourself first. People don't know how to be emotionally self-sufficient anymore. I think that's the real sickness of our time."

"Vidal," I whispered, "you've just barely given me a bite of the apple, and now you're taking it away."

"You've gotten too dependent on me," he insisted. "You're working it out with these religious guilts of yours, and you're going to need every ounce of strength you've got. You can't be dependent on someone in the state you're in. And let's face it, I've gotten too dependent on you."

"You—on me?"

"It's gotten so it bothers me a lot."

"You wouldn't even say you loved me," I said bitterly.

"Do you really need to have it spelled out?" Vidal was very cross. "You believe God loves you, but did God ever tell you so? I mean, in person?"

I was silent, overwhelmed.

Finally I said, "What about Patti Ann and the baby?"

"They'll go with me," he said. "Who else is gonna look after them? I just won't use them anymore."

"Common-law marriage is recognized in Montana. If you live with her for two years, she really will be your wife."

He shrugged. "Who gives a damn?" he said.

222

He crawled painfully under the covers. "I'm in no shape to get it up tonight, okay?" he said.

"Neither am I," I said.

———

The conference week passed.

Every day I smiled at the Shoups. I had lunch with them a couple more times. When I left Regis in the afternoons, I found myself looking back to see if we were being followed.

The Shoups' presence in Denver made Vidal a little nervous, but not much. He didn't have as much to lose as I did. He had already written to the registrar's office at Missoula and had the necessary forms mailed to Cottonwood.

Pains were starting to knot my stomach, and every night the only thing that could knock me out was the Valium. Sometimes it took two instead of one. Next it'll be phenobarbitals, I told myself. My scalp was so tight with tension that an iron band seemed to be tightening around my head. Sometimes my skin burned as with some fiery disease, but it looked perfectly healthy.

"You better watch it," said Vidal. "You look like a wreck."

I finally went to a couple of Dignity meetings.

Those people were so enviable with their peace of mind and their involvement in their crusade. I wanted to be involved too—the retreats, the publications, the sit-ins, the workshops on homosexuality that were starting at a few of the big Catholic universities. But I hung back.

On Friday, the day the conference closed, I finally had a formal confession to Doric, at his office.

It was a general confession. I went back over my whole life, being as honest as I could. It took about an hour. For my penance Doric charged me to make a special effort at understanding the next thorny case of a gay person that came into my life.

But curiously, the absolution brought little peace of mind.

While I was close to believing that my feelings were not sinful, the fear of exposure now overwhelmed everything else. Every time I saw the Shoups, a terrific shock wave flashed through my system.

It would have been nice to linger in Denver over the weekend. But I called Bill Flavey, and he said, "Better be at the airport at eleven Saturday. I've gotta fly back up that day."

≡

Doric drove me out to Stapleton Airport.

It was a rainy day and the great terminals and the maze of runways glittered in the rain. The fog lights were on along the runways. A chill in the air hinted at fall. Vidal was already on the highway north, and he must be chilled to the bone.

Doric and I had a last cup of coffee together, and then we walked out to the smaller hangars where the little planes were parked. Flavey was waiting, talking to a couple other pilots.

Of course Doric didn't kiss me good-bye. He shook my hand, but he also smiled warmly.

"I'm so glad that God brought us together again," he said. "We'll keep in touch."

"We sure will," I said.

He held my hand a fraction of a second longer. "Stay a priest, Tom," he said.

"I still have to think about it," I said.

"This is Able four-six-eight-three-nine requesting permission for take-off . . ."

In a few minutes, we were lifting off, out of the ground mist.

Denver lay below us, immense, smoky, sparkling with lights. Cars poured along its avenues and highways. I could make out the Regis campus, and the Denver U. campus, and the Botanic Gardens.

I couldn't cry in front of Flavey, so I just gulped and took a Dramamine. He had warned me that it might be a rough flight.

Rain spattered on the Cessna's windshield as the plane banked away to the north.

14

Back in Cottonwood, in the week I was away, life had gone on its measured course.

At St. Mary's Hospital, three babies had been born. Two people had died. A fire had burned out a little family grocery story that had done business on Placer Street for nearly thirty years. On Main Street, the pennants and bunting had been strung up for the rodeo and Bicentennial activities. City crews were just finishing the planting of the young cottonwood trees. The saplings stood straight as soldiers in their wire stays. The singles bar had opened.

Other than that, you would have thought that nothing had changed.

Yet the town was eerily different. I was looking at it from a new fixed point in the map of my conscience. Driven by a new tenderness, and by a closing-in of loneliness now that the break with Vidal and my possible departure from the ministry were so near, I checked up on the local brothers and sisters.

Jamie Ogilvie was getting ready to go to college. His family were disappointed that he wasn't going to the seminary, and had given him no help with applying. But his own excitement had carried him through all the letter-writing and clothes-shopping. He had been accepted at Rutgers.

"I really wanted to go to M.I.T.," he said. "They're supposed to be terrific in biochemistry. But Rutgers is okay."

I felt a little sad. Jamie would go away to a brilliant career in the East and probably not come back.

"I'll miss you, Father," Jamie said. Then he grinned and added, "Don't misunderstand that."

I laughed.

"Father, I'm worried about you, though," said Jamie.

"Oh?" I said.

"Father Vance said you went to Denver for some vacation, but you don't look like you got much. You work too hard, Father."

One of my first house calls was to Clare Faux's place.

To my astonishment, I found a crew of strange young people bustling around the old dairy farm. A few of the boys were painting the house, sanding the weathered old clapboards and making them a warm yellow. A sign was up on the road that said COTTONWOOD CRAFTS. A couple of young women were unpacking suitcases and strange bundles of stuff out of a Volkswagen bus, and carrying it up on the front porch.

But the busiest scene was around the old milking barn. The young men had ripped out the stanchions, mangers and other cow-barn fittings, and a truck was loading them for the trip to the town dump. The cobwebby windows had been washed clean, the vast concrete floor scoured down with hoses and brooms. A couple of electricians were busy installing bright lights and electric heating. Some of the girls were already carrying in some big looms and setting them up, arguing about where was the best place to put them.

I met Clare marching slowly from the house to the barn.

She was wearing a black and white checked summer dress. Her old-fashioned black stockings, which she must have kept going since 1930, bagged around her reedy ankles. She was holding the eternal black silk umbrella over her head.

"What's going on here?" I asked, grinning. "It looks like the Seven Dwarfs have moved in."

Her eyes twinkled. "You told me to make plans, Father."

"You didn't fool around, did you?"

"I knew some young artists around the state who do the kind of thing Missy and I did, only sometimes more modern. But they didn't have facilities to live cheap and do it all together."

"Are you telling me this is a commune?"

"Oh, something like that. We'll work and market as a group. The girls are going to live in the house with me. The boys are fixing up a dormitory out in one end of the big building. Have to keep them separate, you know. Of course, I know there's going to be a *little* hanky-panky." She winked at me. "But I wouldn't want to be run out of town, after all the fuss people made about those co-ed dormitories at Missoula."

I grinned. "Mrs. Faux, be careful, or Mrs. Shoup will come down on you like a bomb."

Her eyes glinted combatively. "There's nothing for that nasty woman to do around here. You can burn books, but there's not much point in burning embroidery."

Proudly she took me in the house and showed me

examples of her new associates' work. Patchwork pillows with herbs in them, wall hangings, crewel work and batiks were thrown all over the living room.

"I'm learning so many new things," she said. "Batiking is something new that Missy and I never tried. And then some of them have the cleverest new ideas about things Missy and I have done all our lives. One of the boys crochets better than me. He takes lace crochet patterns and does them in big wool instead, and he uses the most amazing color combinations." She spread out a rich and striking-looking afghan done in red, salmon, purple, pink and blue. "Now look at that. Why didn't we ever think of that?"

I thought to myself that people in town would wonder no end about a boy who crocheted.

We finally made it into the kitchen and sat down.

"The coffee pot goes day and night now," she said.

We sat drinking our coffee, and Clare made me eat a couple of freshly baked brownies.

"This must be costing you a lot of money," I said.

"Some," she admitted. "But Missy and I do have some savings, and she left me hers in her will. And we're doing a lot of things ourselves." She started to laugh. "Oh, the kids have a lot of grandiose notions. They even want to have cows and chickens and a great big garden. Most of them don't know a blessed thing about cows. They want to do everything all at the same time, yesterday."

"They must wear you ragged," I said. "You take care of yourself."

"Speaking of taking care of yourself," she said sternly, "you look pretty peaked, Father."

"Working too hard," I said.

She peered at me shrewdly. She knew I was in trouble of some kind. But I had declined to invade her past, and perhaps that was why she didn't now invade my present.

230

One afternoon, Father Matt called me up from Helena. He said bluntly, "It's been two months now since you've been to see me."

"I know, Father," I said, my insides shrinking into the familiar ball of nervousness.

"You missed that time that your car supposedly broke down, and now you've missed again."

"I know," I said. "Things have been pretty frantic here, with the Bicentennial thing coming up, and then I was at the Denver conference for a week."

"Don't make petty excuses, Tom," he said sharply. "The last time you were here, I suspected that you were hiding something. Now I'm convinced you are. All this time, you have been lying to me. I'm very afraid for you."

"But, Father, there's no need to be," I said.

"Tom, please come and see me, and tell me what is happening to you. Your immortal soul is in serious danger."

"I'm the judge of that," I said, "and I don't think so."

"Your problem is of a sexual nature, isn't it?"

A shock wave of fright went through me. "What on earth makes you say that?"

"Knowing you as I do," said Father Matt, "it's the first thing that comes to mind."

He had to suspect something. After all, he had brusquely separated Doric and me. At the time, he had questioned me sharply about our friendship, though he hadn't asked questions that were specific on sex. I had been in a panic for all the reasons that I refused to understand, and I was confused and terrified by his questions. I insisted that there was nothing wrong with my friendship with Doric. But afterward I had avoided Doric, and he had avoided me too. Father Matt remembered all that for sure, and now he suspected it again.

"Father, how can you say that? I'm the most unsexy thing around," I said hollowly, thinking of Vidal's dissatisfactions.

"No one is unsexy," said Father Matt in his best Jesuit tone of voice. "Have you considered that you are in grave contradiction of the Church's teachings on sexuality? That you have violated your promise of celibacy in an unspeakable way?"

My feeling of panic turned to anger.

"Father, I don't know what you're talking about," I said coldly. "The fact is, I don't think you're the right spiritual director for me anymore. I've been coming to you for nearly six years, maybe it's time for a change."

"You really insist on deceiving yourself, don't you?"

"No. I'm finally working my way out of the self-deceptions. But I won't be over to see you any longer."

"You're lost, Tom."

"No, Father. I'm finally finding myself, and my real relationship with God. I have another spiritual director now."

"May God have pity on you," he said.

We both hung up.

═══

The next time I was up the valley on a sick call, I took the opportunity to tear over to Drummond and visit Larry and Will.

It felt a little strange to go there alone, without Vidal. But the thought of those two happy men had haunted me ever since I'd met them, and I wanted to know how they were getting along.

When I got to the ranch, Will wasn't there. He had

gone to Missoula to buy a load of feed. But Larry was there, and seemed very glad to see me.

We sat on the terrace with a beer, and Larry talked compulsively.

They were concerned with the shakiness of the cattle market. It was the eternal decision: sell now, or hold the cattle till spring and hope that the market would go up fifteen or twenty cents a pound. On the other hand the roan stud was all ready for the big endurance race.

"Do you think he has a good chance to win?" I asked.

"We sure hope so," said Larry. "A win by a Spanish mustang is good publicity for the breed. But there's going to be some stiff competition. There's an Arabian coming up from Wyoming that's one of the toughest horses around." Larry sat scratching the ears of Lady, the little blue dog. "Vidal tells us he's going back to school."

"Yeah," I said.

"Pretty lonely for you," said Larry.

I shrugged. "It's the best thing for him."

"You feel pretty hurt, don't you?" said Larry. "You even feel a little bit used."

"Sometimes I wake up in the middle of the night and think he was just looking for a local trick."

Larry shook his head.

"You haven't got any idea of the effect you had on him. When he first met you, he used to drive down here and talk to us for hours. And in a way it's the things he likes in you that are driving him away. He can't live with them or compete with them as long as he doesn't make something out of himself."

I nodded dumbly.

"And if he stays where he is," said Larry, "then what is he? An ex-con, a garage mechanic, a leather man, a bike queen? A fancy dancer? With all those brains boiling around in his head?"

I was silent.

"Be smart, Tom," said Larry, finishing his beer. "Let him go with your blessing. He's stayed longer with you than he ever did with anybody else. A lot longer than he did with me."

"You?"

"Sure. I knew Vidal way back, when we were both at Montana U., before he went to jail and I dropped out of school to rodeo. We had it together for a little while, but . . . We were both pretty fiddle-footed then. And then I met Will."

"Will knows?"

"Sure. He also knows we're just good friends now, so it doesn't trouble him at all."

I laughed. "Broadminded of both of you. I'm afraid I'd be the jealous type. Or I'd eat my heart out, anyway."

"I suppose you've thought about quitting the priesthood."

"A million times. I'd like to live with somebody, have a life like you guys do, but I could never do that the way I am now, without a lot of sneaking around."

I stood up. "Speaking of sneaking around, Father Vance will put out an APB on me if I don't get back."

We walked across the lawn to my car.

"You gonna be at the finish line next Sunday when we come across?"

"Darn right," I said. "Father Vance has stuck me with being the chaplain at the fair. Any jockey or bronc rider that gets his neck broke, I'll be right there to kick his ass on up to St. Peter."

═══

When I got back to the rectory that day, Father Vance yelled at me out of his office door.

"Father Meeker! Will you come in here?"

As I went in, my mind got busy inventing a cover story for the hour spent at Drummond.

Father Vance was sitting at his desk, opening his mail. Just the way he was using the letter opener told me he was boiling mad. He shoved it under the flap and ripped the envelope open in one neat swoop like a vengeful sheepman disemboweling a coyote.

My legs got a little shaky. Now the price would be paid in full for the talk with Larry.

But that wasn't what Father Vance wanted to see me about.

"Shut the door," he snapped.

I obeyed. Through his open window, and through the thick screen of lilac leaves outside it, we could hear the yell of boys playing baseball on the academy playground across the street.

"I don't want Mrs. Bircher to hear," said Father Vance. "She's as free with her tongue as she is with butter when she bakes cookies. Sit down, Father."

A scorching feeling was spreading across my chest, back and shoulders, under the cassock. It made me feel cold, and I shivered.

"You and I," said Father Vance, "are going to have a plenary session right now about what to do with that Shoup woman. This time she's gone too far."

"What did she do?"

"She was in here to see me this morning," fumed Father Vance. "She tried to tell me some kind of trumped-up story about you."

All the blood was falling out of my head, as if someone had poured it out of a bucket from a small plane flying at fifteen thousand feet, and it was falling in dizzy drops toward the earth nearly three miles below.

"It's all these women's lib ideas," Father Vance was fuming. "First they want to leave their Christian homes to be senators and phone-company linemen. Then they

235

want to be deacons and priests. Next thing you know, some bra-less old biddy is going to want to be the Pope. And in the meantime—" his voice was rising, "—this two-bit inquisitor comes in here and is telling me how to run my parish, and what to think about my own curate. Well, boy howdy, I told her if she didn't cut it out, she wouldn't get any absolution from me the next time she comes around on Saturday. I told her she was committing a mortal sin of gross slander."

"What did she say about me?" I asked, trying desperately hard to look only halfway concerned.

Father Vance ripped open the last envelope as if it was the belly of a sheep-eating wolf. "She was insinuating that there is something unnatural in your friendship with Vidal."

Those drops of blood were spaced out now, and falling with the speed of light. The trees and mountainsides were rushing up toward them.

"Unnatural?" I said, as if I didn't know what the word meant. There had to be Academy Awards for acting jobs like mine.

"She and her husband went down to the Denver conference. She says they saw a lot of you down there."

"Well, not a lot," I said. "We had lunch three or four times at the cafeteria. They're not my most favorite people in the world, so . . ."

"She said Vidal was down there too. You didn't tell me that he was going down."

I shrugged casually. "It didn't seem to matter. He went down on his own. He had some vacation coming, so he took it. There's a sister of his living in Denver. He spent some time with her and some time with me. I didn't see too much of him because I was tied up with the conference."

So far, so good. Nothing that was really a lie.

"Oh, I didn't know about the sister," said Father Vance.

"She's married and has two little kids in school. Her husband is a Blackfeet too. He's a carpenter. Vidal took me over there one evening and we had dinner."

Father Vance was beginning to relax a little.

"Now, let me tell you, young man, the Shoups did a little bit of private-eye stuff down there. I'm not saying that what they did was right. But they followed you around a little. She told me that you and Vidal stayed together."

I shook my head as if wonders never cease.

"There's a priest in Denver who was in my class at the seminary," I said. "To save some money, he put me up at the house of a friend of his, a Catholic who teaches at Denver U. The professor had plenty of room, so he put Vidal up too. I don't see what's so strange about that. Vidal can't afford a room at the Brown Palace. That's where the Shoups stayed, the Brown Palace."

The point about the Shoups' affluence was not lost on penny-scraping Father Vance. "Why didn't Vidal stay at his sister's place?"

"You should see it. A room and a half. One of the kids sleeps on the sofa."

There was a suspicion of a fiendish grin coming at the corners of Father Vance's mouth. I was telling him exactly what he wanted to hear. In his wrath against the meddling Mrs. Shoup, he would probably believe anything I told him, and not double-check it.

"Now, this priest friend of yours," said Father Vance, reaching for his rolling papers and tobacco. "Mrs. Shoup did a little sleuthing on him too, because she saw you and him together a lot. She says that your friend consorts openly with . . ." Father Vance hesitated, then spoke the horrible word. ". . . with homosexuals in Denver."

I kept shaking my head and grinning. That grin seemed fixed on my face like the grin of death on a skull.

"Mrs. Shoup gets things all mixed up," I said. "Doric is doing some homosexual counseling on the campus. He's doing it with the knowledge and blessing of his Bishop. It's no big deal, really. Denver just passed a homosexual-rights law, so there are a lot of homosexual students coming out on the campus there. The diocese there is concerned about it, as you can imagine."

Father Vance had rolled his cigarette and was smiling happily. He was probably rehearsing mentally the things he would say to Mrs. Shoup the next time he saw her.

"If Mrs. Shoup was Henry Kissinger," he said, "I sure as hell wouldn't send *her* to see the Chinese commies."

I started to relax just a little. Long ago, in the matter of Meeker vs. Shoup, my pastor had made up his mind that he was on my side. After all, I belonged to the brotherhood of Melchisedech, and she didn't. By attacking me, she was attacking something close to Father Vance's heart. Once having made this commitment to defend me, he could hardly back down now, or he would lose credibility with his parishioners.

"How come you flew down, anyway?" he growled. "I didn't think you'd be caught dead away from that fancy car of yours."

"I was too tired to drive down."

"Well," said Father Vance, "what do we do about St. Mary's female Torquemada? I'm asking you, Father, because it's your hide she's after."

"Well, I don't know. I'd have to give it a good think."

My mind was racing. If Mrs. Shoup had been frustrated in getting Father Vance to listen to her story, she wouldn't stop at telling other people in town.

Father Vance must have picked up my thought.

"I told her," he said savagely, "if she spread this vicious gossip around town, I would deny her the sacraments until she made a public retraction. And I've got half a notion to kick her off the parish council."

The burning sensation had spread all over my head and torso. It felt as if somebody had doused me with gasoline and set me on fire.

238

"If we do that," I said, "it'll make her feel very self-righteous. More than she does now."

Father Vance rubbed his bristly chin in his hands. "You're probably right. Better not make her a martyr. But how are you going to feel, having her there at the meetings every week?"

"Hell, I'm not afraid of her," I said.

That was the first barefaced lie since walking into the office.

"Well, maybe the warning will keep her in line," said Father Vance. "It'd better. Why, she even said she would take the matter to Bishop Carney if I didn't act."

"Oh?" I said.

Somebody dumped my blood out of the airplane all over again.

"I told her," he growled, "if she went to the Bishop, I would make a personal trip to Helena to call her a liar. And I haven't been to Helena for fifteen years."

═══

Just before nine that evening, I drove downtown on the excuse I needed something from the drugstore. I wanted to talk to Vidal, but I didn't dare go see him. I didn't even dare call him from my office phone. If Mrs. Shoup was willing to drive all the way to Denver to see what kind of things I did away from home, then she might be willing to have my phone tapped.

There was a pay phone in the drugstore. I dialed Vidal's number. No one answered. Maybe he was eating supper at Trina's.

"Oh yes, el hermoso biker, he is here," said Trina. "Jus' a minute, I call him."

In another minute, Vidal's voice said hello. In the background, the jukebox was playing some woeful country music.

"It's me," I said. "Listen, we're in trouble. Mrs. Shoup

239

did follow us around in Denver. She's got the goods on us. She told Father Vance about it. Father didn't believe her, but she says she's going to the Bishop, and she'll probably tell everybody in town."

"Holy Jesus," said Vidal.

He was silent for a minute. Then he said: "Well, we might as well get it over with."

"It's easy for you to talk," I said. "You're leaving town in a week. I'm not."

"You should have thought about that before you—"

He broke off, because he was in Trina's. But I knew the next words would have been, "went to bed with me."

"You should have thought about it," I snapped, "before you went cruising after a priest."

"Look," he said, "I'm in no mood for your bullshit tonight."

He hung up on me.

Desolate and shaken, I went to the counter and bought some toothpaste I didn't need. Then I drove back to St. Mary's.

In the dark church, only the red flickering sanctuary lamp and a couple of votive candles in front of Mary gave any light. The last dull glow of mountain sunset gave some color to the stained-glass windows. The church was empty.

I walked slowly up the stairs to the organ loft. It had been a long time since I was up there. The last time I'd played the organ had been that Saturday in June just before Vidal cornered me in the confessional. Without turning on the light, I sat down on the organ bench.

Above the console, the mirror stared back into the murk of the nave, reflecting the rows of empty pews. In that mirror I had first seen his face. Now, in the horrid light of circumstance, I saw that his beauty was death to all my hopes.

Mrs. Shoup, sexual bloodhound that she was, wouldn't

stop till she had bayed and bugled me out of the Church. My ministry in Cottonwood would be a joke. "There goes the queer priest." Parents would point me out on the street, keep their children away from me. The Bishop would suspend me from my pastoral duties.

In view of all this, there seemed to be just one thing to do. Pack my things and leave Cottonwood quietly, now. Leave the state. Go to Denver or somewhere in the West where I could see other gay people. Get a job, go back to college, get a regular degree. Fall in love with somebody I could get along with, and move in with him. Forget about caring about other people, and just care about my own sanity.

I flicked on the organ switch, and the organ drew its deep breath of life. Pulling out the proper stops for a favorite Bach fugue, I put my fingers to the keys.

The first few notes cut the dark of the church like a fiery knife. But then my hands slid from the keys, almost by themselves. I shut the organ off again.

That night, three Valiums weren't enough. The stage was coming for stronger pills. I'd been a fine one to preach to Vidal about dope and booze.

The "Late Late Show" that night was *Captain Horatio Hornblower* with Gregory Peck and Virginia Mayo.

15

Decisions made in the dark night of insomnia usually look a little strange in the daylight. I decided I'd hang tough for a few more days and see if there were any noises from Bishop Carney.

On Monday, I saw Mrs. Shoup at the regular meeting of the parish committee. She didn't say anything during the meeting, though it wouldn't have surprised me if she'd announced to the members that Father Meeker was a fruit.

We all discussed the rather secular issue of St. Mary's musical participation in the Bicentennial parade. The Knights of Columbus would play, of course. But some of the St. Mary's kids now in the high school also played instruments, and we wondered if we could scrape together enough of them for a second band to escort our wonderful cardboard float. We still had the old red-and-gold St. Mary's band uniforms stored away in mothballs.

But a few days later, just a week before the fair started,

the mail brought me a crisp white bond letter from the Bishop.

> It is urgent that you present yourself in the Bishop's office on Friday, at 11 A.M. in regard to a highly important matter.
>
> Yours in Christ,
> Rev. John MacFee
> Secretary

A few false hopes fluttered around in my mind. Maybe this summons had nothing to do with Mrs. Shoup. Maybe it was regarding my possible appointment as the Bishop's secretary. Of course, if this controversy kept raging around me, even that appointment would now be blighted.

When Father Vance saw the letter, he flew into a rage.

"If that woman goes on defying my authority," he roared, "I don't know what I'll do."

"Do you think that's what it's about?" I asked.

"I'll bet my bottom dollar it is."

"Do I have your permission to go to Helena? The sooner this is straightened out, the better."

"Sure, sure." Father Vance waved me out. "Go to it, my boy."

By Friday morning, the insomnia had affected me so much that I felt as if I was losing my mind. My vision was blurred by rainbow showers of hallucination. Dizziness washed over me now and then. Sometimes I heard voices and ghostly telephones ringing in my head. Joan of Arc must have been an insomniac too.

It was a hairy drive to Helena. Up on the pass, as I went by the Holiday Inn, I had a strong temptation to drive the car off the Magan Wall.

A thousand feet below, the thick treetops of the timber waited for me. In the deep shade beneath them, I would find a shattered but total peace. The Rockies rolled out

244

before me, and for the first time, their beauty was that of death, not life.

But I argued with myself like a crazy man, keeping the car near the white line in the center of the road. I talked out loud, as if I were one of my own parishioners in counseling.

"Don't be a dope, Father Tom. There's no peace down there. The devil is showing you all that, as he showed Our Lord the cities of the world from that other mountaintop. That's the real unforgivable sin. It's unforgivable because you make it that way. God can't undo that one act of your will to destroy yourself."

Sermonizing to myself like that, I made it over the pass.

As I drove past the Broadwater Hotel, it seemed like a thousand years ago and in another life that I had gone to a drag ball there, with a butterfly painted on my face.

═══

At exactly eleven A.M., Father MacFee showed me into the presence of Bishop William Carney.

The study was crafted in the same painfully correct Victorian Gothic style as the cathedral. The dark walnut walls were covered with their carved flamboyant tracery. Five or six curious tapestries hung from ceiling to floor. They were Art Nouveau ink washes on cloth, showing scenes of various Jesuits being martyred by Indians. Through the heavy green-draped windows, I could see the green lawns of Carroll College, and thought of Father Matt.

The Bishop was sitting at the huge Gothic desk, flipping through some diocesan reports. By calling me to his study, I knew, he intended to have an informal-type meeting with me.

"Ah, hello, Father Meeker," he said, getting up and

coming toward me. He wore the plain cassock of a working priest, and nothing gave away his rank except the pectoral cross. As I kneeled and kissed his ring, I thought sorrowfully of my fantasies about being a bishop.

We sat down in two massive Gothic armchairs upholstered with cushions of old red velvet, and I looked at him. That burning sensation was at work over my shoulders and back again.

Bishop Carney was known throughout the state for a mild manner that hid a granite forcefulness. In that grandiose study, he looked a little like the Wizard of Oz in his throne room—he had a round cherubic face, round spectacles and blue-gray eyes as mild as a kitten's. The curls of iron-gray hair around his temples gave him the look of an altar boy aged overnight. He was a small man, five foot nine or thereabouts, and didn't have any of the bearing traditionally associated with princes of the Church.

But in the ten years he'd been bishop, Montanans had learned that he was not a man who retreated into sanctimonious abstractions. He was conservative, but open-minded and realistic, in that tradition of grass-roots populism that seemed to characterize Montanans. He had made a singlehanded turnaround in the economic decay of the Church in the state, though lately inflation was putting the thumbscrews on his accomplishments.

Usually Bishop Carney didn't waste any time getting to the point. But today he took a different angle.

"Two years ago," he said musingly, "we gave you a tough assignment. One that might have broken some young priests."

I sat there listening with a sheen of hallucination in front of my eyes. The Bishop was really on a television screen, an apparition of yellow, green and purple dots.

"We sent you to one of the most difficult parishes in the diocese, and one of our most admired but difficult pastors.

And you responded very well." As he kept talking, it was plain that he'd kept close track of St. Mary's parish business.

"More than that," he said, fixing his kitten-soft gray eyes on mine, "you seem to have won the admiration of most of the town."

He was silent for a moment, sitting very still. Every priest in the diocese knew that Bishop Carney liked to use his physical stillness to test the poise of an interviewee. Anything you did, even normal things like breathing, seemed fidgety by comparison.

"Which brings me to one of the few exceptions," he said. "Your famous Mrs. Shoup has been to see me."

My heart sank. There was no point pretending that I had a chance at the secretary's job, now or ever.

"So I presume you know what this is about," he said.

It took every ounce of strength to sit there straight and quiet, and not fall apart in front of the Bishop's eyes.

"Yes, I do," I said. "Father Vance told me."

The Bishop's keen eyes took in what must have been my strained look, the dark smudges and lines under my eyes.

"I had a long talk on the telephone yesterday with Father Vance," he said. "Of course he's very indignant at this woman's accusation. But I wanted to talk to you too. Because it is, as you realize, a very serious accusation. And also because we've had our eye on you for some time."

He sat there very still, thinking again, his hands making a steeple in front of his chin, his elbows resting on the beginnings of a stomach under the cassock.

Suddenly he took another unexpected tack.

"Last year," he said musingly, "I attended the National Conference of Catholic Bishops in Washington. For the first time in the Church's long history, we saw a nationwide organization of Catholic homosexuals attempting to make official contact with us. As many priests and reli-

247

gious belong to it as laymen. Needless to say, it was quite a shock."

I knew without his telling me that this was Dignity.

"However, they were so—shall we say—well-behaved that we consented to meet with them. Frankly, we were curious to see what they had to say for themselves. They weren't permitted to address the general assembly. But our committee did meet with them and examine their . . . ah . . . basic philosophy and their demands. I was on that committee."

He paused, musing again, looking out the window at the Helena flats and the mountain slopes beyond. The phone on his desk seemed to be ringing, and I wondered why he didn't answer it.

The Bishop changed tack a third time, and shot a question at me.

"What is *your* opinion of the homosexual issue, Father?"

Knocked a little off balance by this question, I pulled myself together. There was no harm in an honest general answer.

"I think it's a serious issue," I said. "A handful of well-written pastoral letters are not going to make it go away."

"I agree," said the Bishop. "All through the history of the civil rights movement, the Church has been in the forefront, for the black people, for Indians and Chicanos, for women. Now states and cities all over the country are starting to pass what they call gay rights laws, and the Church is opposing them. I am very troubled by this. It's one thing to oppose the murder of an unborn child . . . but it's another to oppose civil rights laws for a minority, however repugnant the Church may find that minority."

I sat there in hallucinating silence, as physically still as the Bishop.

"Father Meeker," said Bishop Carney, "the truthfulness with which you answer the next few questions will

248

determine how we handle your case. Do you understand that?"

"Yes," I said.

"These charges of Mrs. Shoup's—are they true?"

Maybe it was my sleepless state, in which the contents of my subconscious lay naked to the big sky. Maybe it was my weariness with the endless lies and word games. Maybe it was the realization that now I had nothing more to lose. Maybe it was God who gave me strength, the way He did to those Jesuit martyrs in the tapestries. For the first time in my life, I discovered that when your back is to the wall, the only way you can go is forward.

"Yes, they're true," I said.

The Bishop's gray eyes were boring into mine. The kitten was getting ready to pounce on a fluttering moth. "But you told Father Vance they were not true."

"No, I didn't," I said. "He never even asked me if they were true. He was so mad at Mrs. Shoup for meddling that he seemed to assume they weren't true."

The hint of a smile played around the Bishop's mouth. He knew Father Vance's mossback ways even better than I did.

"*Would* you have lied to him?" he asked.

"I've been lying for years," I said. "First to myself. Then, when I tried to be honest with myself, I had to lie to other people. Yes, I might have lied to him. Last week I still thought I could protect my secret. Now I know I can't. So there's no point in lying anymore."

"Did you discuss this matter with your confessor?"

"No."

"Why?"

"At first I was afraid to. I knew he'd tell me to stop seeing the person in question, and I couldn't. Later on, I reached the point where I didn't think it was a sin."

"Oh, you didn't," he said, with the first hint of episcopal sarcasm. "Why not?"

"If the Dignity people stated their theological grounds to you in Washington, then you know my grounds."

"Then this relationship that Mrs. Shoup alleges—it is a fact?"

"It's the first overt relationship I've had. So far the only one. But the feelings go back for fifteen years or more. I tried to bury those feelings with discipline and prayer, but . . ."

"Do you intend to continue the relationship?"

"He's going back to school, and we're both backing off a little, so I doubt I'll see him much now."

"But there may be another. Others."

"Maybe. Probably not till I sort myself out a bit more."

"Have you considered leaving the priesthood?"

"It was the first thing that entered my mind. Not so much because I love him, but because I wasn't sure I'd be a good priest any longer."

"Since your ordination, have you ever had temptations toward women?"

"I've *never* had any temptations toward women," I said. "There was the moment when I thought my vocation was invalid. I thought I'd become a priest just to run away from the pressures to respond to women that society puts on you."

"Did you change your mind about your vocation?"

"Yes. Now I'm sure that I also wanted to serve God."

"Mrs. Shoup said she saw you in the company of known homosexuals in Denver. Was this the Dignity chapter there?"

"Yes."

"You are a member?"

"Not yet."

"By that, I take it that you might join."

"Maybe."

The Bishop broke his statue stance and got up out of the big Gothic chair. He strolled thoughtfully around the room. I noticed a small patch on the seat of his cassock. Even the Bishop's office was tightening its belt these days. I kept my frozen immobility in the chair.

It was all over now. I had spilled my guts, given myself away, borne witness—and to my own Bishop, of all people. I wasn't sure whether I felt good or bad about it. I had no feelings at all. Nothing was left but that rainbow haze of insomnia.

"You've been honest with me," said the Bishop, "so I'll be honest with you. You have been one of the young priests in my diocese that everyone looks at and says, 'He'll go a long way. A biretta, maybe.' Obviously, this revelation puts your future in a different light. Have you considered that?"

"Your Excellency, I've considered everything."

"You have an impressive folder on file here. Your school and seminary records, your social justice activities, your impressive record in the past two years. Even Father Vance thinks highly of you, though he'd rather be boiled in oil than say so."

I shrugged wearily. My shoulders felt charred, about to fall off.

"I know what I am throwing away," I said.

"You would be sorry to leave the priesthood?"

"Very sorry."

The Bishop was still strolling around. Behind him, on the tapestries, the Jesuits agonized and died.

"I would be less than honest," he said, "if I didn't admit that your affliction is a common one in the priesthood. Maybe commoner than temptations to the fair sex. Naturally we don't have any statistics. All I know is what I've seen, and sensed, and heard through the confessional. And by no means is it limited to the rank and file. Once in a great while, some impressive man far up the ladder is overwhelmed by the kind of feeling you describe. I could tell you the sad story of a European cardinal, but . . . Two courses of action are open to him. He can give in to his feelings, and lead the kind of hidden life you've been leading. Or he can kill the feelings by mortification and prayer . . ."

My head seemed to be clearing. I had a weird feeling of coming out of the haze, and I stared at him steadily. My intuition told me that he was not talking about himself. He was just a realist about other men that he knew.

"Or," I said, "he can live openly as a gay priest."

"Would you do that?"

"I've tried your first two alternatives. Either way, you do violence to yourself. And, well, it's hard to stay hidden. There's always a Mrs. Shoup who sniffs you out."

The Bishop sat down in his Gothic chair again. He seemed to be coming to a decision.

"You're young," he said. "You're just becoming aware of your—ah—tendency. It may be permanent. It may be only a temporary phase. In any case, I don't want to be the one who throws you away. You know that line in Shakespeare, Father, about the base Indian who throws away the pearl. That line should have come from the Bible—"

I could hardly believe what I was hearing.

"I had thought of you as a possible secretary," he said. "But there is a post that would better use your activist talents. I am creating a diocesan council on the order of the one you started in Cottonwood. It will examine and report to me on contemporary problems as they affect my diocese. Both economic problems and moral problems such as the one you are so familiar with. Will you serve, Father?"

I was open-mouthed.

"Among your duties, you would maintain a liaison with these Dignity people. I want to stay informed of what they're doing, because I don't doubt that a chapter will be popping up in my own diocese one of these days.

252

But I'll insist that you conduct yourself with dignity, small *d.* No public scandal of any kind, is that clear?"

I shook my head dazedly.

"I don't know what to say."

The Bishop smiled a little. Like most bishops, he enjoyed surprises, and he was relishing the rather fiendish one he'd sprung on me.

"You were sure I would order you away on a long retreat to recant your sexual heresy," he said. "Well, as a matter of fact, by the look of you, I'd say that a good retreat, and some rest and food, might not be a bad idea before you report for duty."

I sat thinking. Bishop Carney was kidding himself. He was sure my state was "transitional," and that I would grow out of it. By plunging me into the kind of intensely humanistic activity that I loved, he hoped to help the process along. If I agreed to serve, wouldn't I be deceiving him?

On the other hand, Doric had talked so much about how it was better to dialogue with the Church from the inside than make noises at Her from the outside. Doric would tell me that I was being offered a magnificent chance. But something inside of me shrank back from this very chance.

"What about Father Vance?" I asked. "How can I leave him?"

"I have just the young curate for him," growled the Bishop. "Father Vance will have him in shape in no time."

"What about Mrs. Shoup?" I asked.

"I have told her that she is not to interfere anymore in disciplinary matters regarding my priests. So . . . do you accept, Father?"

———

My father was at the bank, but my mother was home. She was out in the side yard, cutting the last of her roses before the first frost hit.

"Tom," she cried. "What a surprise. Why didn't you tell us you were coming?"

We went in the house. She arranged the roses in a cut glass bowl and put them on the dining-room table. Then she and I sat at the table with cups of coffee. The peacefulness of the early afternoon light streaming through the windows, and the gentle curls of steam going up from the cups, seemed to have no relationship whatever to my torn-up insides. I felt like I had a fever of 102°.

"You'll want to say good-bye to Rosie," Mother said. "She's leaving at the end of the month."

"What're you and Father going to do?"

"Oh, we're buying a nice little house down on the flats," she said. "Not far from St. Peter's Hospital and the governor's house. Then we're going to convert this house into apartments, one upstairs and one downstairs, and rent them." She looked around. "That'll be less sad than selling the house."

"But won't it be sad to think of strangers living here?"

"Oh, no," she said. "There are happy feelings in the walls. Anybody who lives here after us can feel them."

I was sitting there burning alive, playing with my cup.

"Do you think we've been a happy family, Mom?"

"By and large, I think so. The only big disappointment your father and I had was that you didn't get married. Of course we're proud of your accomplishments as a priest, but . . ."

The moment had come to tell her, too. I realized one doesn't come out all at once. The Bishop was only the first of many bits and pieces.

"Mom, even if I hadn't become a priest, I wouldn't have gotten married. Or maybe I would have gotten married, and then got divorced in a few years."

She was silent for a moment. Then, to my surprise, she said in a low voice, "I know."

"What do you mean, you know?" The TV-colored rainbow of hallucination was parting again.

"Your father and I have always known," she said simply.

"How long, for God's sake?"

"When you were a teen-ager, and you didn't show any interest in girls. Your father and I braced ourselves for all the usual problems. We know what young people are like these days. But ... the problems just didn't come. We wanted to think it was because you were such a good boy, but we couldn't. We both knew you were just ... indifferent, just going through the motions to please us."

I had my hand over my eyes.

"You seemed so normal in every other way. Sports, school activities ... I mean, if you'd had a lisp or a clubfoot, or something, or if you were frail, we could have thought it was just shyness." My mother was struggling with the stereotypes. "But we couldn't find any of those things to blame, so it was the first thing that crossed our minds, that you might be ... that way."

"You should have told me," I said.

"Oh, no," said my mother, horrified. "You had to find out for yourself. We always wondered when you did, and if you did. And when we saw your young man friend, well ..."

In the warm house, I seemed to be shaking with cold. My head was on fire. When I ran my fingers through my hair try to ease the burning on the scalp, a lot of blond hairs came out on my fingers. I stared at them, stupefied. My hair was falling out.

"Of course, he doesn't seem quite your type," my mother was saying. "He seems a bit ... wild, isn't he? But if you admire him, then he must have some fine qualities we don't know about ... Tom, are you all right?"

"Well, to tell you the truth, I haven't felt so good lately," I said. "I think it's just tension and overwork."

She felt my forehead. "Why, you're burning up."

She went straight into the living room and called Dr. Lasance, the family doctor. He told her it sounded like a problem for a dermatologist, and recommended a Dr. Nugent. My mother called Nugent and made an appointment. An hour later, as if I were a little kid, she hustled me into her car and drove me downtown.

I sat shivering in the examining room while Dr. Nugent looked at my scalp and my skin.

"You have a type of eczema that usually results from extreme tension. The skin looks normal, but the nerve endings have become irritated and that produces the burning sensation you feel. The tension also cuts off the circulation in your scalp, and some of the hair follicles are dying. That's why you're losing some hair."

I wasn't supposed to be worldly enough to care about my hair, but I asked mournfully, "Will it all fall out?"

"No, I don't think so. It may be thinner. We'll just have to see how your skin responds to treatment. Have you been using any drugs for tension?"

"Valium," I said. "But it's gotten so even three or four don't knock me out."

"Oh, my, even Valium is dangerous," said Dr. Nugent. "Let's try something else that's less addicting and maybe more effective."

He told me to massage my scalp all over for fifteen minutes morning and night, and showed me how to do it. Then he wrote out two prescriptions. One was for drops containing cortisone, to rub into the scalp twice a day. The other was for a muscle relaxant called Atarax, to take four times a day including bedtime.

Finally he said, "Wash your hair with a shampoo called Sebutone, every day if you feel the need. It's a special coal-tar shampoo that soothes the scalp. You can get it without a prescription."

On the way home, my mother marched me straight into her drugstore and we got everything. I downed a muscle relaxant and washed my hair right away with the icky green-gray Sebutone. A delicious cooling sensation took hold of my head. After a while I felt very mellow, and lay down on the sofa for a nap.

When my father came home at around five-thirty, we sat in the parlor with glasses of sherry and talked about it. I should have felt more eased at telling my parents, but I didn't.

"You are accepting the Bishop's offer, aren't you?" my father asked.

"Well, I told him yes, but ... The whole thing scares me. I've been through so much already. It'd mean more pressure of a different kind. I don't know if I can hack it."

My father had a businessman's disdain for shillyshallying about promotions.

"You'd be a fool if you didn't take the job," he said brusquely. "Any man who turns down an offer like that is out of his mind. Especially a man in your position."

"If you did leave the Church now," said my mother hesitantly, "would you, uh ... would you ... well, I read in the papers that homosexuals try to get married now. There was that famous case of the county clerk in Utah—wasn't it?—who started giving marriage licenses to them, until the DA stopped her ..."

I laughed drily.

"Don't worry. Vidal isn't the marrying kind. But I might live with somebody. Would that shock you?"

"Well," said my father, "I guess not. We'd hope that you were as happy living with ... that person as your mother and I have been. We always felt that if you could have been straight, you would have ..."

They both looked at me from where they sat together on the sofa—a tenderer kind of American Gothic. I was awed, and thanked God for their understanding.

They listened with interest to my account of the trip to

Denver, and asked intelligent questions about gay life-styles. I tried to make them see and feel that other world as Vidal had done for me. When I told them about Doric, my father said, "We always thought there was something between you two. When you were in the seminary, all you talked about was Doric and God—in that order."

I blushed.

After dinner, I called Cottonwood.

"Everything is straightened out," I said. "You'll be hearing from the Bishop."

"I already have," barked Father Vance. "He called me this afternoon. What I want to know is, why do they always pick me to break in these pilgrim kids?"

The drive back to Cottonwood was less scary than the drive that morning. I stopped at Vidal's house for a few minutes and told him the news. He was still sorry he'd hung up on me the other night, and he hugged me.

"It wasn't as bad as you thought, huh?" he said.

"I still haven't decided," I said.

═══

That night, an early frost hit. When morning came, I saw that the lilac leaves outside my cubbyhole window had turned a purple-bronzy color. The seed sprays were dried up and spent.

The ninety-five-day Rocky Mountain growing season was over. Fall had come.

16

Bishop Carney had told me I could postpone the move until after the Labor Day rodeo weekend, since I was involved in a number of the Bicentennial things. I had already made arrangements for a week in a quiet retreat house on Flathead Lake. But my mind had shut off, postponing the real decision of whether or not I would join the diocesan commission.

Between the muscle relaxants and the shampoo, my condition was better, though sometimes my head burned so much that I got up in the middle of night to wash it.

Meanwhile, in those last days before the fair, Vidal and I made one last trip together. He wanted to show me his own home town and introduce me to his parents.

"I really miss my dad," he said. "We didn't fight when he found out I was gay. He laughed at me. That was even worse."

"What do you think he'll do if you go back?"

"Laugh some more," said Vidal.

It's a 250-mile drive from Cottonwood north to

Browning. We made it in four hours, both of us at the wheel. Most of the drive is through the dry-land wheat country that lies just east of the mountains. We could look across the great stripes of wheat and fallow, things that man hath wrought, and check out the far-off peaks, already dusted with early snow. The wheat harvest was on, and the great combines went spinning slowly along the fields.

It is Browning's fate to be the gateway to Glacier Park. The town is garish with motels and Indian curio shops.

You are also made forcibly aware that it is a reservation town. There were Indians everywhere, going in and out of stores, driving along the street in old cars and trucks, or just standing around talking on the street corners. Nearly everyone, even the women and children, seemed to be wearing sun-faded jeans and denim jackets.

As we stopped at stop lights, the flash of black eyes and the occasional babble of the Blackfeet language that we heard from older passersby gave me a sudden feeling of getting off an airplane in a foreign country and going through customs. It suddenly surprised me that my lover was from this town. His Indianness had never been very real for me, maybe because it wasn't very real for him either.

"I hope my folks are home," Vidal muttered as he turned off Main Street by a supermarket.

"You mean you didn't tell them you were coming?"

"Didn't have the nerve," said Vidal.

We came to a small but painfully contemporary ranch house on a corner lot, and Vidal said, "They're here."

The house sat exactly in the middle of a square of sunburned lawn. Except for a few juniper bushes at the corners, there was no shade. It looked as if the Stumps were too busy to putter in the garden. In front of the walk, a battered brown Chevy was parked, with a red squad-car light on the top.

Vidal grinned, though I could see he was uneasy.

"People's habits don't change," he said. "I knew if he wasn't out on a case, he'd be here for supper at six-thirty on the dot. Don't let people tell you that punctuality came over on the *Mayflower*. It was invented by the Indians, mainly my dad."

When we knocked on the door, it was opened by a rotund little middle-aged man with short coal-black hair and a gray policeman's uniform. He wasn't built soft and round, but hard and round, like a grizzly bear. You had the feeling he could roll a redwood tree over looking for ants to eat. This was Carl Stump.

A small smile cracked his moon-round face.

"Well, well," he said. "The prodigal son returns. Come on in, kid."

We went in. I sensed that Vidal felt as self-conscious as I did.

At first, in the living room, I looked in vain for anything "Indian." The furniture was vintage trading-stamp modern, with decorative copperware hanging on the wall-papered walls. The sofa and armchairs were overstuffed brown velvet. But then I noticed several amateurish but arresting landscape paintings on the walls, signed by one John Wolf Necklace. Around the fireplace there were half a dozen stuffed heads of deer and elk—Vidal had said his father liked to hunt in the reservation foothills.

Vidal's mother came in, wiping her hands on her flowered apron. She was tall and spare, six inches taller than her husband. Weathered and grayed as she was, her face with its good boning and hazel eyes was strikingly handsome. Looking at her, you knew where Vidal had gotten his Black Irish good looks.

"Vidal!" She hesitated a second, then said, "Well, I'll set two more places at the table."

Both Mr. and Mrs. Stump studiously ignored me. She herded us all into the kitchen. It was a suffocatingly bright and cheery little room. The picture window looked out into a sunscorched back yard with a clothesline and a white picket fence. The tile floor was flowered, the walls were yellow, and the gas range was new. It burned Indian gas—the federal government had sold oil and gas leases all over the Blackfeet reservation.

Vidal looked around as we sat down at the yellow formica table.

"You've done the kitchen over. The tribal council must have given Dad a raise."

Carl Stump snorted. "They did. But your mother has a job now."

As Mrs. Stump passed us the dishes, the atmosphere was very stiff. Unbelievably, we were eating the same brand of frozen tamales that I had eaten that first night at Vidal's house.

"Tamales!" said Vidal. "What happened to fry bread?"

"Fry bread has too much cholesterol," said Mrs. Stump crisply. She was a dietician at a clinic on the reservation.

"Our relatives in Mexico did pretty good on tamales for a couple thousand years," said Carl Stump.

"Look what it got them, though," said Vidal. "Spanish names and the Catholic religion."

"Vidal, you haven't changed a bit," said his mother.

"Since when are you such an Indian nationalist?" said Carl Stump.

"Who says I'm a nationalist?" said Vidal. "I just stated a fact."

"I can see you haven't changed in one other respect," said Carl Stump. "You haven't outgrown all that kid stuff." He glanced at me.

Vidal met his father's wry little smile with one of his own.

"The sooner you realize that I'm going to the grave with this kid stuff, the happier you're going to be."

His father was still smiling. But the smile had gone a

little wistful, the eyes vacant, as if he were looking out over some expanse of time.

"Look, kid," he said. "I'm not going to do the big white middle-class number with you." He clapped his hands to his head with mock horror and mimicked, "Great jumpin' jehosaphat, my kid's a queer, hand me the bread knife so I can commit hairy-keery."

His voice went back to normal. "If you want to live that way, that's your business. But kindly allow me the privilege of having my own point of view. I've seen everything in the world in this reservation, the good and the bad and everthing in between, and I've learned to smile at it, because otherwise I'd cry and then I wouldn't be a good cop. So kindly allow me to smile at you as part of the great human show, kid. The way I smile at everything else, including me and my other kids and my wife."

The table was silent.

"All right, smile away," said Vidal. "Just don't laugh."

"I never laugh," said Carl Stump softly. "Not any more."

"Vidal," said his mother, "you look real good. Have you stopped drinking?"

"Yes, ma'am, and if you check out my eyes, you'll notice neither of them is black. You can thank him for that."

He looked at me.

Mr. and Mrs. Stump looked at me.

"You can have me straight and boozed," said Vidal, "or gay and sober. Take your pick."

"Look," said his father, "I've put a few drunks in the tribal jail, so you know the answer to that one."

"Are you spending the night?" Mrs. Stump looked at me uneasily, probably wondering if I would consent to sleep on the brown velvet sofa.

"Not this time," said Vidal. "But I'll be coming back to visit. I'm going back to school in a week."

Both his parents beamed with genuine pleasure.

Maybe Carl Stump didn't laugh, but he could get off a large grin.

"Well," said Carl Stump, "if gay and sober means you finish college, then you can be the biggest queer in the world for all I care. But I don't know how the schools around here are going to accept your way of doing things."

"We'll cross that bridge when we come to it," said Vidal. "Maybe by that time, Montana will have a gay rights law anyway."

Carl Stump was looking hard and direct into my eyes.

"Tell us about yourself, young man," he said.

"Tom won't brag about himself," Vidal said. "He nearly went to Harvard, but he joined Vista instead. He finished school here in Montana. Now he's a Bible salesman."

Of all the barefaced lies that summer, that one was the most arrogant, and the funniest.

"Bibles," said Mrs. Stump wonderingly. "I always wondered who left those Gideon things in hotel rooms."

"Well," said Carl Stump to Vidal, "at least you're running around with a better class of people than that Joey Fool Hen. Even if he *is* an Indian."

"Joey Fool Hen," said Vidal, "is the biggest queen south of Calgary."

This remark put an end to the conversation for a few minutes, and we emptied the serving dish of the last few steaming tamales.

Suddenly Carl Stump burst out laughing. He put his fork down on his plate, and laughed and laughed till the tears burst out of his eyes and rolled down his round dark lined cheeks.

"Carl!" said his wife.

Carl Stump hauled a handkerchief out of his uniform pocket and wiped his eyes.

"You know all those Indian jokes about Custer?" he

264

said. "Custer died wearing the latest fashion, he was wearing an Arrow shirt?"

"Campy Indian humor," said Vidal.

"Well, we've got a new joke now," said Carl. "Custer doesn't get killed after all. He and Rain-in-the-Face give each other a big kiss and ride off into the sunset together."

———

After supper, Vidal prowled around the house.

He found things changed, but it didn't seem to upset him. He wanted to show me the room where he and his brothers and sisters had lived when they were little, but his mother had made it into a sewing room.

But in the closet, a lot of his old things were carefully piled up, the way parents always keep their children's old junk. Vidal gleefully fished them up out of the boxes. Schoolbooks, photographs, his Browning High annual. His senior class picture showed a cheerful boy with a mop of black hair whom I hardly recognized as the grim beauty I loved. He even found a stained old pair of satin basketball trunks.

Fishing farther in the boxes, Vidal suddenly drew in his breath a little.

"Look," he said to me.

Slowly, with the same reverence that I'd show my chasuble and stole, he drew up out of the box a magnificent feathered dance bustle like the kind the Plains Indians wore. Rows of feathers were sewn around its richly beaded disc.

"It's my old dancing stuff," said Vidal.

His parents leaned in the doorway, watching, with little smiles on their faces.

He was pulling the rest out: the beaded rawhide moccasins, the bells, the loincloth, the beaded vest, the satin shirt (very wrinkled and faded). In the box beneath it, the great eagle-feather war bonnet was packed in lonely splendor, so it wouldn't crush.

Vidal held the things in his hands, his face suddenly gone pinched and painful. The ropes of bells in his hands gave out shivers of silver sound.

"We always talk about how you danced," said his mother.

Carl Stump looked at me. "For an apple Indian, my kid was a helluva dancer."

Vidal looked up at us, and an unfathomable dark shadow had flooded into his eyes. Without a word he scooped the things up, went in the bathroom and locked the door.

When Vidal came out, I hardly recognized him. It was the same shattering image that I had seen in the poster all summer, above the bed where we made love. But now it was real and alive. The costume he'd made for the Silver State Ball had related to something further down in his subconscious—this one was simply the past, present and future. He carried in his mind an image of me, too, but I couldn't know it or see it clearly. Each of us had dared to unlock, for the other, the closed image of the future. For one moment, I had a vision—quick as a flashbulb going off—of our common redemption worked by God through those images.

"Dad, do you have a drum?" Vidal asked.

"I'm not a drummer, I'm a cop."

But Carl Stump went in the kitchen and found a big turkey pan and a wooden spoon. He thumped the spoon on the pan and it made a musical hollow sound.

We went out on the back porch. The last of the mosquitoes whirred like tiny helicopters through the porch light. Carl Stump sat down on the porch steps and started to thump a stately rhythm on the pan. Vidal walked slowly out onto the sunburned lawn. The dew glittered in the porch light, and his footsteps left dark spaces in it. The strings of bells wound around his legs made aimless jangling sounds.

Suddenly he bent, stiffened and stamped his feet a few times. The bells slapped out slashes of sound that tore the evening. Mrs. Stump watched with her arms crossed over her stomach, rapt.

Carl Stump started to sing in a high cracked voice. It was a minor-key melody that started on E and kept pretty much between E and the A below. He was singing in Blackfeet, throwing in a "hey-ah" here and there. I was aware that we weren't exactly watching the kind of dance that Father Point had seen and sketched. But still, the hairs on the back of my neck stood up in awe and excitement, and little shivers ran up and down my back.

Vidal was dancing in a slow circle, with a peculiar gliding stamping step that seemed to hang in slow motion a few inches above the ground. He bent lower, then higher, twining his body as he stamped along, as if following some invisible winding vine through the air. His hands were on his hips. The bustle slapped his buttocks and bristled smartly as if he was a ruffed grouse doing a mating dance. His face, under the waving eagle feathers and the beaded brow of the bonnet, was intent, framed by black and white animal tails hanging by his cheeks.

My lover was dancing. No gay bar on earth would ever see him dance like that. In the light from the porch, he danced around and around on the grass, till circles of footprints were stamped in the dew. He straightened, almost skipped joyfully, then suddenly bent again to turn slowly, right on the spot, as he stamped. He was alone now, as I was. I didn't exist for him anymore, except as someone in the past.

17

Far off down the crowded Main Street, we heard the marshal's whistle blow. The band struck up. The great one-and-only Bicentennial parade of the Cottonwood Fair, Rodeo and Horse Races was about to get under way.

"Here they come!" said Father Vance.

I had learned something new about my pastor. The snorty old mossback priest liked parades as much as a little boy.

Father Vance, Vidal, Mrs. Shaw and I were standing on the curb by Mitchell's Drugstore, crushed in the mob. People had driven in from all over the county, and some of the smaller communities out there had even entered floats in the parade.

Main Street was brave with flags and bunting, and bright with the results of the beautification program. The restored buildings in the Landry block gleamed with new paint and new windows. The antique shop had just hung out its sign, and the owner had rushed around chasing garage sales and estates, trying to get together a minimum stock, so as to have something to sell over the holiday weekend. The tearoom had been open a week, and reported a land-office business. A few young people lounged by the door of the singles bar, which had reported moderate business, though not a land rush. The garden center was looking ahead to the long Montana winter, and had filled its windows with exotic house plants.

Mrs. Shaw had a proprietary gleam in her eye as she surveyed what she and the town had wrought.

"I think we've done it," she said to me. "Thank God."

But the spirit of Cottonwood was more humanly expressed in the boisterous parade now coming down the street. When I saw the grit and pride and humor in it, it came over me all over again why I'd wanted to be a priest in a small town. The sadness that one way or the other I'd be leaving it was there in my throat.

Vidal was standing right beside me. In the crush, he dared to fumble for my hand, and hold it. I squeezed his hand back. No one could possibly see this, especially Father Vance, who was in front of us, trying to see past the yellowing leaves of one of the cottonwood saplings.

The parade was rounding the corner by City Hall and coming down the street toward us now.

A dozen horsemen were all carrying the Stars and Stripes. Their horses pranced along and foamed at their bits. When they got closer, we could see that all the flags were different, from the thirteen stars of the Colonies to the fifty-star flag of today. Vern Stuart, the big local quarter horse breeder, was riding his famous Bobcat and carrying the blue flag of Montana with its motto, *Oro y plata*.

After the flags came the Knights of Columbus band, mostly older businessmen, blasting away and looking very smart in their blue uniforms. Then they were passing, and we were drowned in the sounds and sights of the parade—the hot smell of horseflesh, exhaust fumes from the floats, flowers, popcorn, cotton candy. Vidal was playing sexily with my fingers, and with the emotion in me, I kept trying to hold his fingers hard. It was the only time we touched each other in public in Cottonwood.

"Don't you think the K. of C. band is a little weak on

clarinets?" Father Vance asked. He was craning his neck. I was tempted to buy him a little flag to wave.

The floats were rumbling past now.

The town's official float was a mountain peak of red and blue with silver snow, crowded by young men and women wearing what Vidal would have called cowboy drag. They were grinning and throwing confetti and paper streamers at the crowd. On top of the mountain sat the rodeo queen, Beth Stuart, smiling shyly and waving.

The Cottonwood County Historical Society's float dramatized the Skillet Creek Fight between the U. S. Army and the Nez Percé Indians. Several of the older businesses in town had floats. The big sheep ranch up the valley at Whalen had a float with live sheep in a pen and a sign that read LET US PULL THE WOOL OVER YOUR EYES.

Finally the float came along that our little group had been waiting for. The St. Mary's band preceded it. The kids looked very brave, though some were cheerfully out of step and they were missing a piccolo and a couple of trumpets. If you looked closely, you could see a moth hole here and there. In the last file of musicians, Jamie Ogilvie had his cap set at a rakish angle and he was whanging away at the glockenspiel.

Our float was mounted on a big flatbed truck loaned to us by Fulton's Nursery. The cardboard brick church had nearly come to grief when the boys hoisted it up there that morning. But now it looked fine. The stained-glass windows were very recognizable, and the lilacs. The white and Métis hod carriers were at work around it with a few real trowels and real bricks.

I watched it pass, thinking that in a curious way, Vidal's and my love had closed the circle begun by the building of the church a hundred years ago. The white man started by trying to exterminate the Indian, then to Christianize him, and wound up in bed with him. We had healed the last wound of the West.

Father Vance turned around to me, and I quickly let go Vidal's hand.

"The float looks pretty good, Father," he said. "Considering it only cost sixty-eight dollars."

"Yeah," I said, "the kids' construction costs ran a little over the estimate."

Now a long line of horses and riders was clopping past. The street began to be littered with road apples. The Cottonwood County Posse, a real civilian posse who assisted the local police, swept by on their matched Morgans. Some riders were local—ranch families riding their working horses, wearing their Sunday best. Others were the professionals who'd hit town to complete in the rodeo—the barrel racers in their flared pants and brocades, the bronc riders in their fancy chaps.

My eyes had already fixed on another float coming up. I jogged Father Vance's elbow.

"Hey, Father, look at that. Clare Faux and her crew have got a float."

"Bless her heart," said Mrs. Shaw, "she's the bravest lady I know. To do what she did at her age really takes guts."

Clare's kids had set up their biggest loom on another borrowed flatbed truck, and were actually weaving something. The truck was draped with beautiful new patchwork quilts, and a sign on the side said COTTONWOOD CRAFTS. Amid all the kids in jeans, Clare Faux was sitting beside the loom like a queen, on an old kitchen chair, with her umbrella over her head to keep off the sun. Like the kids, she was smiling and waving at the crowd. She was too nearsighted to see me there, or she might have thrown me a special wave. The crowd gave her loud cheers as she went along.

Suddenly a curious feeling came over me. Everywhere in that crowd, that parade, I saw faces whose inner secrets I knew. Those people had reached out to me some time that summer, in confession or in counseling, or just in five minutes' talk on the street. They had reached out to Christ in me, and I had tried to make myself His instrument of their healing. Wounded and confused as I was, I still served. The proof was there in front of me.

The parade ended, leaving the street littered with confetti and horse manure. The crowd started to break up.

"The endurance race started at eleven, didn't it?" I asked Vidal.

"Yeah," he said. "I wonder how Will and the stud are doing."

"What's this?" said Father Vance.

"The endurance race," I said. "We know one of the outfits in it."

"Larry borrowed my bike," said Vidal, "so he can wait for the horse at all the places where the trail comes up near the highway. He wanted to see how they're doing."

"Well," said Father Vance, "I'm a wee bit tired. You two run along to the rodeo, and I'm going back to the rectory."

———

At the fairgrounds, we lost ourselves in the sights and sounds of the rodeo and the fair. But that spooky feeling stayed with me of knowing the secrets of people we ran into.

For the farm and ranch people who supported the town, it was getting to be the end of the year. The hay was up, the grain was coming in, the feeder cattle would go to market in another month or two. Their paranoia about the weather was over. Their main worry now was money —what they'd get per ton for their hay, per pound for their steers. They flooded into the fairgrounds to be town folks for a day. They wanted to have a good time and forget economics.

For the town folks, it was a chance to put on Levi's and

a straw hat, and catch the smell of horses and cattle that they didn't get all the rest of the year in their stores and offices.

Vidal and I wandered around the fairground, drunk on the tenderness, keeping our distance from each other. The announcer knew I was there—all he had to do was yell my name into the mike if I was needed.

We looked in on the fat cattle show, where the local breeders led their prize exotics, Herefords, Angus and Simmenthals around the straw-covered ring. I was pleased to see a red ribbon on the halter of a Simmenthal bull from the Clem Malley Ranch. The young widow and her kids told me that, so far, they were keeping things together pretty well.

We wandered through the carnival and spent a quarter each at a rifle booth, shooting tin ducks. The sound of rock 'n' roll floated in the air.

In the big exhibits building, so many families had entered their canned fruit, vegetables and baked goods in the competitions that the fair board hadn't known where to put everybody. One of the booths was Clare Faux's, and we stopped a few minutes to chat with her and the kids. It made me smile to think that even Vidal didn't know she was probably a sister. The booth was decked with blue ribbons for their handcrafts, and the crocheting boy's afghan had gotten a grand championship.

Clare took my hand and patted it. She looked a little flushed and tired from all the excitement.

"Thank you, Father, for my new life," she said.

"Thank God, Mrs. Faux," I said. "He's the great quiltmaker. He takes the bits and pieces of our lives and stitches them together for His design."

"Hm, that gives me an idea for a new quilt," said Clare.

Vidal and I hung around the rodeo and the races, and watched. At any minute, a contestant or a jockey might be fatally injured, and I'd have to grab the kit of holy oils out of my car parked by the arena. A couple of Protestant clergymen were hanging around too, in case their services were called for instead of mine.

We sat on the arena fence. The dust from the bucking horses and bulls drifted into our noses and nearly choked us. We could hear the explosion of hoofs up close, as calf and rider burst from the chute in the roping event. I thought how many of the rodeo events were just the everyday work done in the old days—those times that had made us all.

Every half hour, the rodeo stopped to make way for a horse race. One of the band trumpeters played "Boots and Saddles," and the skinny thoroughbreds filed out onto the track, just as they'd done for seventy-five years. They jumped from the starting gate, flashed around the half-mile oval, and the crowd screamed as they crossed the finish line in a big cloud of dust. In another two minutes, the rodeo was under way again.

Vidal, still a gambler at heart, put twenty dollars on a horse that he had a hunch about, named Gay Reveler, and lost.

People kept coming up to me. "Father, remember christening my baby in May? See how big he's gotten." "Father, my wife and I are sure glad we came to talk to you. We've getting along a little better these days." "Thanks for coming to see me that time, Father. I was depressed about losing my job, but now I'm working at . . ."

If Doric was right, every person who came up to me wore the face of Christ the Lover.

But I noticed, however, that not everybody was so friendly. A number of people, some of them parishioners, some of them just townspeople, either studiously ignored me or actually gave me an unkind look. It had taken only a few days, but Mrs. Shoup's gossip was already getting around town. I wondered if the people who spoke nicely to me were doing it to demonstrate their sympathy in the most subtle way they could think of.

Now and then, as I picked up these hostile looks, the terror of being unmasked in a place like Cottonwood really got through to me. But mostly I managed to block the feeling out. In a few days, I was going to say good-bye to it all, and leave the state.

Just as the horses in the third race were going to the post, the announcer said: "Ladies and gentlemen, the first endurance horses are just a mile out of town now. And they're coming fast."

Vidal and I looked at each other, and our blood leaped with excitement. The announcer up in his high tower above the arena, in his big hat, was looking out toward the highway and saying, "In just a few minutes here, we're going to have the very exciting finish of the first Helena–Cottonwood Endurance Race."

"Let's get on over to the finish line," said Vidal.

The announcer's voice ricocheted around the fairgrounds. "I can't give you any information at this time about which horses they are. But I can see two in the lead from here, ladies and gentlemen. It's going to be a close finish. You people up there at the top of the grandstand can probably see 'em coming, out there along the old highway . . ."

A rustle went through the grandstand as people craned their necks and half-rose to look north.

Vidal and I pushed through the crowd to the finish line. Larry was already there, looking sunburned and nervous.

"I parked your bike over by our trailer," he said to Vidal. "Hope nobody steals it."

"How's he doing?" I asked.

Larry shook his head. "Last time I checked on them was up by Dog Creek. Will was half a mile behind the goddam Arab. The Arab looks pretty tired. But this is the first time we've raced the stud, so we don't know what kind of a finish he's got. I couldn't stand to watch no more, so I came on in."

The packed grandstands waited, rustling, babbling. A lot of the rodeo contestants had come over to the finish line too. They didn't give a hoot about thoroughbreds, but this was their kind of their horse. Larry's bright blue eyes stayed fixed on the announcer's tower, waiting for the next news.

Then the announcer's voice cracked over the waiting fairground.

"Ladies and gentlemen, the first two finishers in the endurance race are entering the fairgrounds. They're turning off the highway and through the outside gate there. Horse number one is about three lengths ahead of horse number two. It's *very* close, ladies and gentlemen. And the first horse is now . . ."

The entire grandstand had risen to its feet, people straining their eyes, talking, putting down their cups of beer, taking their cigarettes out of their mouths.

Through the drop gate, a single lonely horse and rider came onto the track. They both looked sun-beaten and dusty. The horse was moving along at a curious quick sidewinding gait.

"It's Flint," said Larry. His voice choked up. "It's Will and Flint." Vidal and I traded happy looks.

The grandstand erupted with applause.

Now a second horse came through the drop gate, at a regular trot. This was the Arab, a bay horse. But he was obviously not going to catch the little blue roan stud. With every stride, Flint was putting a yard more between himself and his rival.

Larry and Vidal forgot themselves just a shade and hugged each other. They were both grinning like apes. Me, I had a huge lump in my throat. Of all the tens of thousands of people at the fairgrounds, the four of us were the only souls who knew the special significance of this victory. I dared to thank God for the results of a horse race.

Right down the middle of the homestretch Flint came.

He was pacing lightly and boldly like those legendary mustangs of old, who ran their pursuers into the ground and died free. He had lifted his tired neck a little, and pricked his ears toward the noisy grandstand, which must have been a strange thing to him. Will had his hat pulled far down over his eyes against the afternoon sun, and the eternal little cigar was clenched in his teeth as he sat the pace easily, rooted in the saddle.

". . . And the winner is Flint," yelled the announcer. "A six-year-old stud owned by Will Mills and Larry Deisser of Drummond. Ridden by Will. A local horse, ladies and gentlemen. I think we can say on this proud day that Drummond is local, don't you?"

As Flint paced across the finish line, Will's grin got just a bit wider, and he threw a little wave of his hand at the grandstand.

"Something you ought to know about this horse," said the announcer. "He's a real son-of-a-gun mustang. Foaled right down in the Pryor Mountains. His mammy and pappy were wild. He's the real thing, ladies and gentlemen. Take a good look at him, because you're going to be seeing more of these horses. A few ranchers like Will and Larry are breeding them . . ."

From the look on Larry's face, he was as pleased with this unasked-for advertising as if he'd been given a free ad in *Time* magazine. He and Vidal and I ran out on the track.

Will pulled the horse up gently. The stud saw Larry coming and whickered through his dusty wide-flared nostrils. He was streaked with sweat and dust, and looked as if he had dropped some weight during the hard race. A couple of minutes later, the bay Arab crossed the line too.

Will dismounted, and he and Larry pounded each other on the back.

"Howdy, partner," said Larry.

"Howdy partner yourself, you horny son-of-a-bitch," said Will happily in a low hoarse voice.

The grandstand was still applauding.

The announcer said, "We now have the official time for Flint over the fifty-mile distance. It's three hours, thirty-two minutes and five seconds. That's a real good time—"

The awards committee and photographers came out on the track now. One of the officials was carrying a big silver loving cup, and another was toting a pail of water and a sponge. They formed a little group, and solemnly shook hands with Will and Larry. Flashbulbs went off, and the stud shied a little. Hands reached out to pat the stud's sweaty neck. I patted it myself, feeling less afraid of horses by the minute. I was very happy to be out on that sunlit track with that little group.

The mayor of Cottonwood, Del Fahey, gave the loving cup to Will and Larry.

"Congratulations, boys, we're real proud of you," he said. "And we hope you'll be back next year, and keep them out-of-state horses out of our hair."

Larry and Will took one look at the loving cup and guffawed. It was brimming with ice-cold beer. The pre-race publicity in the local paper had mentioned Flint's fondness for the fruit of the malt.

"Now that's real thoughtful of you," said Will, "and I think I can speak for Flint too."

The stud already smelled the beer and came shouldering up to thrust his muzzle into the cup. He sipped greedily, getting foam in his nostrils. Then Will pulled the cup away. "No more now," he said to the horse. "You're hotter'n a stove. You wanna founder yourself?"

Right there on the track, the two men stripped the saddle and blanket off Flint and sponged him off with water. The horse shook himself like a dog and spattered the awards committee, and the people in the grandstand had a good laugh.

Suddenly the announcer said, in that cozy joking way that announcers have at small rodeos, "Father Meeker, what the hell are you doing out there? We didn't know you were Irish enough to have a weakness for horses. . . ."

I started guiltily and gaped at the announcer's tower. Then right away I realized he was just kidding me. He couldn't possibly know the truth.

To answer him, I did the only thing I could possibly do under the circumstances. I solemnly raised my right hand and made the sign of the cross before the dripping little stallion.

The announcer and the packed grandstand burst into laughter.

And if you mention my name in Cottonwood today, people will say, "Father Meeker? Oh yeah, the queer that blesses horses."

≡

That night I had dinner at Vidal's house for the last time. We all pitched in, and made some creditable hamburgers and fried potatoes. Maybe it was my imagination, but Patti Ann seemed to have improved slightly. She kept her clothes on, and was more aware of things. She even spoke now and then. Maybe Vidal's gentle therapy had had some effect.

After supper, Vidal and I went in the bedroom, as usual, and shut the door. The shades were down, as usual. But cardboard boxes stood around the room, packed with their miserable little bit of stuff. The poster of the fancy dancer had been taken down from the wall and rolled up, leaving a rectangle on the wall where no dust had settled.

For the last time, we were alone together in there, with the mattress and box spring on the floor. And suddenly, without our even discussing it, we both had the same feeling that we didn't want to make love.

"I don't want to make a funeral out of this." I said.

"I feel the same way," said Vidal, looking relieved. "It's no big deal. Let's just lie down and be warm and together."

We got down on the bare mattress, with our heads on

the mashed old pillows, in which the feathers had been ground to dust, and we held each other very close. The shade moved gently at the window, flapping in a stiff fall breeze. We could hear the wind in the willows, and the whisper of the yellow leaves they were already shedding, and the TV from the next house, and the hoot of a diesel truck passing the town far out on the Interstate.

"After all," said Vidal, "it's only eighty miles from Missoula to Helena. We'll get together a lot."

I was silent a minute. "Maybe not," I said.

"Why?" said Vidal.

"I've just about decided to leave the state, go somewhere else, go back to school, maybe, or get a job. As a Bible salesman, for instance," I added bitterly.

Vidal raised himself on his elbow and looked down at me.

"I think you're making a big mistake," he said. "You'll hate yourself for it."

"Don't think I can hack it if I stay," I said.

"You care about it too much to leave it. You'll be miserable the rest of your life, a drifter, a misfit. You'll be like I was after I got out of jail."

My gut told me he was right. The feelings I'd had all day long at the fairgrounds told me he was right.

"I'm going away, and I'm gonna fuck around with this guy and that guy," he said. "But with you, it's different. You're lovers with everybody you deal with. That's the way you are. That's your way of being gay, and that's your way of being a minister too. When you first started counseling me, I thought you were being extra special with me because you were attracted to me. But after a while I realized you were giving me the same treatment you give everybody."

"I can keep that attitude, and not be a priest," I said. "I'll go on being a Catholic, for chrissake."

Vidal shook his head. "It won't be the same, and you know it."

He sat up and leaned back against the wall and the pillows, his long hard legs sprawled with ease in the faded jeans. The Yucatan wedding shirt, much-washed and getting faded now, was open, showing the silky black hair on his chest. He looked every bit as fine as the famous Jim French models I had seen in the gay magazines, but his eyes didn't have that hot come-on look. They studied me with a certain anxiety. On the wall behind him, my memory made the fancy dancer visible.

Uneasy, because I knew he was right, I said:

"Why did you go for me? Do you know? I mean, I'm not your type."

He dropped his eyes and shrugged. "I've always thought about that a lot. I think I had a real resentment against priests because of the way that one guy treated me when I was fourteen, when I tried to talk to him. Maybe my motives weren't exactly nice when I tried to get to know you. Sleeping with you was a way to degrade the Church and get back at him. And the idea of a gorgeous number in a cassock was . . . fun."

He shrugged, and looked back up at me with that disarming grin. "But I wound up getting more emotionally involved than I'd planned."

"That night you first came to confession," I said. "Was that a terrific acting job, all that bull about your sins that you wouldn't tell me about? Or did you really mean it?"

He cocked his head. "Maybe a little of both. I mean, I did need help, didn't I?"

All summer Vidal had been my Virgil, leading me through a part of earth that I'd never seen before. Now he was the Beatrice, tugging me toward a paradise that I was half-afraid to look at.

"Time to go," I said. "Father Vance will be wondering where I am."

I kissed him. "This is for tomorrow," I said.

18

The next morning, Vidal and I had breakfast at Trina's for the last time. Neither of us ate much, and Vidal actually played with his frijoles.

Trina came by and gave him a kiss on the cheek.

"Adios, my bes' customer," she said.

After breakfast, we went back to Vidal's house to get Patti Ann and the baby. It was amazing how little they had—a few cardboard boxes and cheap suitcases, some odd things tied up in a pillow case, and the dogs. The furniture stayed with the house, which was rented furnished. Vidal was shipping the bike to Missoula, where he had rented a basement apartment in an old house near the campus.

Somehow we piled or tied all the stuff onto the bumpers and luggage rack on my sports car, so that it looked like some swinger's version of an Oakie truck in *The Grapes of Wrath*. The three of us, the baby and the dogs squeezed into the car, and we chugged back over the river, to the Rainbow Hotel.

Bus depots in small Western towns have a certain

283

melancholy that must be tied up with the times and the slow death of the railroads and the airlines. It's the longest, cheapest, most uncomfortable way to travel. You leave, and you may never come back. Or you come back because you're fed up with the rest of the world.

The Cottonwood depot was at the desk of the Rainbow Hotel. We walked into the musty little lobby, where the cleaning lady was just cleaning the stand ashtrays. Several ancient leather chairs sat along the lobby windows, along with a couple of the eternal dusty rubber plants. In one of the chairs, a weatherbeaten old man in a cowboy hat and khaki pants sat reading *The Montana Livestock Reporter.*

Vidal walked up to the hotel desk, where the Greyhound sign hung. The bus schedule was posted on the wall. He pushed a ten across the counter.

"Two one-ways to Missoula," he said. "Is the ten-thirty bus on time?"

"Fifteen minutes late," said the desk clerk, pushing the tickets and the change back.

The bus was half an hour late. There was just a little feeling of anticlimax, as we sat in the hotel coffee shop and had a last cup of coffee to pass the time. I would be going back to the rectory shortly to pack my own things, which were as few and as worthless as Vidal's and Patti Ann's. We didn't talk much, and Patti Ann jounced the baby on her lap.

Suddenly the desk clerk was bawling through the door, "Passengers for Missoula!"

We wrestled the luggage out through the revolving door of the hotel. The bus stood roaring by the curb, spewing fumes into the clean fall air. In the distance, above the yellowing trees and the dark red roof of the railroad station, the mountains lay in a blue haze—there must be a forest fire somewhere. The mountains had that indigo look they get in fall, when the new growth in the timber has ripened off. A few people were getting off the bus. A young woman waiting on the sidewalk gave a little scream of joy and hugged an old woman. A few people were getting on.

The bus driver opened the luggage compartment in the side of the bus and showed Vidal where to stow their stuff. There was some discussion abut the dogs, but since Vidal had ropes around their necks, the driver said it was okay.

Then Vidal turned to me. Our eyes met. Here it was: the last lie—this public good-bye scene with nothing to say to each other and no hugging allowed.

"Well," he said, "you've got our new phone number. Give me a call from wherever you land." He sounded hoarse.

"I'll do that," I said.

He smiled. "So long." The dogs strained at their rope leashes.

"Go with God," I said. My own voice sounded as if I was coming down with a cold. I kissed Patti Ann on the cheek. "You too, honey."

"Good-bye," said Patti Ann, fixing me with her strange blue eyes.

"Come on, folks," said the driver. "All aboard. We're late enough."

Vidal helped Patti Ann up the steps, then followed her up with the dogs. The last thing I saw was the word ME on the back of his jacket. Through the windows and the heads of passengers, I could see them inside, making their way back to their seats.

The bus door slammed shut. The bus pulled away from the curb, waited at the light where I'd waited that night I saw Vidal fighting in the alley. Then it turned out on Main Street with a lumbering metal dignity, and disappeared around the corner column of the City Hall.

I could hear the roar of its engine dying away along the street. In a few more minutes it would be out on the

Interstate, hurtling along at sixty miles an hour. The scorched pastures and the cutover hayfields would whip past the windows.

I had been sure that I would cry, but I didn't. There was nothing left inside of me but a great emptiness—as empty and windswept as that Cottonwood countryside along the highway.

===

Getting into the Triumph, I drove back to St. Mary's.

Instead of going to the rectory, my feet carried me into the church, almost from force of habit.

The church was empty. Father Vance had said his own low mass, and would now be eating breakfast. Mrs. Bircher had put two new potted ferns on the altar, because the ivies that'd been there all summer had gotten some kind of mite on them. In the bright fall sunshine, the stained-glass windows threw a blaze of color over the empty oak pews. A couple of candles flickered in front of Mary.

I walked slowly down the aisle.

Suddenly, out of nowhere, a sweet peace came pouring into my empty heart. It came so unpredictably and so fully that I knew right away what it was. I'd never been one for big religious experiences, for the great lights and illuminations that spiritual writers wrote of—never thought of myself as seeking after them. These were more for people like Doric. And yet now, at this unlikely moment of my life, I found myself in the grip of one.

That breath of divine love came gently and coolly to my fevered flesh and soul. It blew away the emptiness and the aloneness like the white fluff from a last dandelion on some Cottonwood lawn. Loving presences crowded around me, holding me, speaking to me—thousands of them. Not only Our Lord and His blessed Mother, but the saints and the souls of the departed, and the souls of those still living and those still unborn. They jostled me, whispering: Father, will you serve?

I sank on my knees at the altar rail. I felt an unutterable sense of oneness with that godly love, that Lover, all those celestial lovers, who accepted me as I was and raised all my senses to a higher order, purifying them and turning them to His purposes. All the shocks and anxieties of that long summer in a small town had finally emptied out all my fears, stupidities, hesitations. And, as the spiritual writers never tire of telling you, divine love can fill only an empty place.

My Beatrice in a fancy dancer's costume had led me to the very beginning that Father Matt had always scolded me about. For the rest of my life, I would pray that his Beatrice—the blond stud in the cassock—would lead him to his own beginning.

After a while the rapture died, just the way a breeze dies. I came back to reality.

But my soul was saying with words: Yes, I will serve.

Today I would clear my cubbyhole room in the St. Mary's rectory and say good-bye to Father Vance—but not to flee Montana for another life. I would sign in at the retreat house up on the Flathead this afternoon, and report to my Bishop next week. And I would have to call Doric and tell him the good news. God would give me the light and strength to live through whatever followed.

Instead of going out through the sacristy, I climbed up to the organ loft. It had been a long time since I'd played.

I switched the organ on, pulled out a few stops and sat there for half an hour. Anybody who came in the church would have found it empty—except for some young priest up in the loft, playing all the Bach fugues he could remember.

COMING OF AGE

☐ **THE SALT POINT by Paul Russell.** This compelling novel captures the restless heart of an ephemeral generation that has abandoned the future and all of its diminished promises. "Powerful, moving, stunning!"—*The Advocate* (265924—$8.95)

☐ **PEOPLE IN TROUBLE by Sarah Schulman.** Molly and her married lover Kate are playing out their passions in a city-scape of human suffering. "Funny, street sharp, gentle, graphic, sad and angry . . . probably the first novel to focus on aids activists."—*Newsday* (265681—$8.95)

☐ **THE BOYS ON THE ROCK, by John Fox.** Sixteen-year-old Billy Connors feels lost—he's handsome, popular, and a star member of the swim team, but his secret fantasies about men have him confused and worried—until he meets Al, a twenty-year-old aspiring politician who initiates him into a new world of love and passion. Combining uncanny precision and wild humor, this is a rare and powerful first novel. (262798—$8.95)

Buy them at your local bookstore or use this convenient coupon for ordering.

NEW AMERICAN LIBRARY
P.O. Box 999, Bergenfield, New Jersey 07621

Please send me the PLUME BOOKS I have checked above. I am enclosing $_____
(please add $1.50 to this order to cover postage and handling). Send check or money order—no cash or C.O.D.'s. Prices and numbers are subject to change without notice.

Name _____

Address _____

City _____ State _____ Zip Code _____

Allow 4-6 weeks for delivery.
This offer is subject to withdrawal without notice.